What people are saying about …

A BEAUTIFUL

"A beautiful story of romance, healing, and redemption … a reminder that God so often uses the people in our lives to show us what really matters and to demonstrate His steady love that forever pursues us."
—MEREDITH ANDREWS, SINGER,
SONGWRITER, AND WORSHIP LEADER

"For the born romantic in all of us, a sweet tale of the simple life rediscovered."
—GINGER GARRETT, AUTHOR OF *IN THE SHADOW OF LIONS*

"In A Beautiful Fall, *Chris Coppernoll shows himself once again to be a master at bringing characters so close you can touch their hearts. If you dare get this close, don't be surprised to meet yourself somewhere in the pages."*
—J. SAM SIMMONS, PhD, COFOUNDER
OF ROCKBRIDGE SEMINARY

"You'll find yourself longing for more of this book as it draws to a close. You won't be ready to put it down. And in the end, you will discover that love is all that matters after all."
—MARLENE A. RAUCH, MALL OF GA
BOOK ENDS BOOK CLUB

"In A Beautiful Fall, *Coppernoll made going home again an interesting and intriguing prospect."*
—TISHA CLEVELAND, MALL OF GA BOOK ENDS BOOK CLUB

What readers are saying about ...

PROVIDENCE

"I purchased your book on Sunday and literally could not put it down once I opened the first page. The story you have told is truly amazing and it defies my ability to find the right adjectives to describe it."
—SKIP KROEGER, NASHVILLE, TENNESSEE

"Just finished Providence. *What a great story! Your writing is very similar to that of Nicholas Sparks, who is my favorite author. Now I have two favorites!"*
—SHIRLEY DOTSON, CLEVELAND, OHIO

"I just finished Providence. *It was absolutely gripping and powerful. Not wanting to be done with the book, I read everything in the back as though I could prolong the experience! I keep track of the authors and books I really like. Yours will be in there with the best."*
—GEANNINE MILLER, GREENVILLE, OHIO

"I read your book and thought it was awesome! This book proves God still has miracles behind every situation."
—LANA BROCK, KANSAS CITY, MISSOURI

"Providence *was an amazing book. I can't remember the last time I enjoyed a book so much. It is most definitely going to be our next book-club selection!"*
—BETH ROGERS, FAYETTEVILLE, ARKANSAS

"I finished reading your book today and there are no words to describe how profoundly it has affected my life."
—JONATHAN HARVEY, WEST PALM BEACH, FLORIDA

"I just wanted to drop you a note to tell you how much I loved Providence. *It's probably one of the sweetest books I've ever read—it really dropped into my heart. A couple of months ago, I re-read your book and though I rarely read a book a second time, I loved it even more the second time around."*
—DAWN BURNS, CHARLESTON, SOUTH CAROLINA

"I will be recommending your book to my Christian Bible-study/book-club group right away as well as my family and other friends. You have written something very special, and I will be sharing it with many others—those who have chosen to take up their crosses and follow Christ and those who have not yet found Him."
—PRISCILLA LINSKY, MANHASSET, NEW YORK

"I just finished reading Providence, *and I wanted to take a moment to tell you that it is by far one of the best novels I have ever read. I really felt inspired by your words, and the characters in the novel really spoke to my heart."*
—CAROL REIMER, WINNIPEG, MANITOBA, CANADA

"I want to thank you for allowing God to lead you into writing this book, and I can't wait for your next book."
—DEBBIE JOHNSON, OKLAHOMA CITY, OKLAHOMA

A
BEAUTIFUL FALL

a novel

Chris Coppernoll

David C Cook
transforming lives together

To my mom, Lois Coppernoll,
for her love of reading and everything she does for others

A BEAUTIFUL FALL
Published by David C. Cook
4050 Lee Vance View
Colorado Springs, CO 80918 U.S.A.

David C. Cook Distribution Canada
55 Woodslee Avenue, Paris, Ontario, Canada N3L 3E5

David C. Cook U.K., Kingsway Communications
Eastbourne, East Sussex BN23 6NT, England

David C. Cook and the graphic circle C logo
are registered trademarks of Cook Communications Ministries.

This story is a work of fiction. All characters and events are the product of the
author's imagination. Any resemblance to any person, living or dead, is coincidental.

LCCN 2008933682
ISBN 978-1-4347-6852-0

© 2008 Chris Coppernoll
The author is represented by MacGregor Literary.

The Team: Andrea Christian, Stephen Parolini, Amy Kiechlin,
Jack Campbell, and Susan Vannaman
Cover Design: David Uttley, The DesignWorks Group
Cover Photos: Getty Images (woman in swing);
Steve Gardner, PixelWorks Studios (cowboy)

Printed in the United States of America
First Edition 2008

1 2 3 4 5 6 7 8 9 10

073008

ACKNOWLEDGMENTS

In all the excitement of releasing my novel *Providence*, I didn't stop to mention some very important people who made its publication, and this book's, possible. A very special thanks to my agent, Chip MacGregor of MacGregor Literary, for his professional representation, astute counsel, and personal career guidance.

An extraspecial thanks to Don Pape, Andrea Christian, and everyone at David C. Cook for creating an atmosphere where writers can produce their best work. May God richly bless you for your books that inspire readers the world over.

A big thanks to my editor, Stephen Parolini, who also edited *Providence*, for his skill and creativity evident on every page, and for bringing it all together.

Thanks forever to my daughter, Gray, for the creative person that she is. I love you.

Lastly, I want to express my gratitude to the Lord Jesus Christ who makes all things new and all things possible.

CC
April 22, 2008

~ ONE ~

Pretty woman—
You look lovely as can be
Are you lonely just like me?

—ROY ORBISON
"Pretty Woman"

At 5'8", Emma Madison would have described herself as too tall. That's why she rarely dressed in high heels. She wore her dark auburn hair past her shoulders, something she'd done since childhood, thinking the length gave balance to the rest of her body. Emma looked beautiful that morning in the downtown Boston courtroom although she would never describe herself that way. She stood near the mahogany plaintiff's table, beyond the waist-high wooden railing lawyers call "the bar" separating the area for official court proceedings from the spectators' galley. Even though she hadn't left the city since June, her face retained a trace of a summer tan, and her skin looked so clear and soft she could have passed as a model for skin cream. Emma's eyes were her most striking feature— two brown orbs that somehow made her seem vulnerable and strong all at the same time. Their color appeared so dark it overshadowed her pupils, making the windows of her soul a deep pool to look, or fall, into.

To jurors, the thirty-four-year-old attorney for the plaintiff had been captivating to watch over the long August trial, but not for mere beauty alone. Emma expressed an intense passion for her client's case that had in turn induced strong emotions in the jury. They'd been swept up in the drama of her client's sympathetic story and felt themselves standing in Anna Kelly's shoes, wondering how they'd feel in her circumstances, and knowing somehow they'd feel good about Emma as their attorney.

Her body language conveyed an easy openness when she cross-examined a witness. On good days, the jury grinned along with her good-natured humor. On difficult days, Emma displayed courtesy and grit; confident and comfortable in her own skin. She was clear and honest when she spoke, articulate in matters concerning the law, and always upbeat in spirit.

Emma's client was a young, fair-skinned woman named Anna Kelley. Anna had approached the law firm of Adler, McCormick & Madison months earlier when her Northeast health-care provider, Interscope Insurance, dropped Anna from coverage without explanation during a difficult battle with breast cancer. Eventually it was revealed that Interscope had instituted a controversial new profit-making policy called "Retroactive Review." Even though Anna had been approved for coverage and had been paying premiums with her employer for over two years, Interscope cut her coverage, claiming there were "inconsistencies" on Anna's application after the hospital began submitting bills. As it turned out, there were inconsistencies on *lots* of customer's applications—inconsistencies discovered by Interscope only after one of their clients got sick.

On the final day of the trial, twelve earnest jurors watched from the jury box, listening to closing arguments from defense attorney Kenneth Blackman. In the end, the jury trusted Emma, agreed with the evidence she'd presented in her case, and returned from deliberation with a favorable verdict, and ultimately, a seven-million-dollar award.

"I didn't know where to turn," Anna confided to her after the trial. "I felt so hopeless and didn't think there was anything I could do. I felt so small, you know? Like these were the big guys. They could do whatever they wanted."

The courtroom bustled. Dismissed jurors headed back to the jury room, Judge Brown stood and collected papers from his bench, and Kenneth Blackman briskly exited the courtroom. Emma reached across the table to touch Anna's sleeve.

"But you *did* do something, Anna. You stood up to those big guys, and you won."

Anna smiled with the realization that all they'd set out to do had been accomplished. She leaned over and gave Emma a hug.

"Thank you."

"I'm proud of you," Emma said. "You could have run away, but you didn't. That's what most of us do when we have to face a giant."

In the hallway, her colleague Colin Douglas congratulated Emma with a cordial embrace. Colin represented the new breed of smart, young, and hip Northeastern lawyers: the man in the Kensington suit with a racquetball-thin and money-clip-thick physique.

"You were incredible," he said to her in a near whisper, letting Emma slip back out of his arms, the space between them returning to a more professional distance. "This calls for a celebration. What would you say to dinner tonight at 33's? You've earned yourself a night of extravagance."

"Frankly, I'd welcome any diversion from the endless stacks of depositions I've been reading."

She smiled at Colin. "How come you always make me feel so special?"

"Because you are," he said.

Emma tried to read his expression, but wasn't quite sure where the smooth lawyer ended and the intriguing friend began. Colin was a man who drove too fast in his BMW and thrived in the accelerated pace of a seventy-hour workweek. She imagined him guarding his Sundays for tennis at a private country club or three-day weekends at Martha's Vineyard.

They were both up-and-comers in Boston city law. His star shone a little brighter, though Emma suspected her Interscope victory might raise her own status a notch or two. Did he picture the two of them together? Could she?

"Then it's a date," he said. "I'll make a reservation for seven thirty."

"It makes me nervous when you use the word *date*. You know I think of us as just friends, don't you?"

Colin reeled back on the heel of his Allen-Edmonds dress shoe.

"Emma, can I help it if only one of us has seen the light?"

"Maybe we should put dinner on hold until one of us changes his light switch."

"Congratulations, counselor." Robert Adler stepped into their circle and patted Emma on her shoulder. "I can't tell you how much I enjoyed seeing Kenneth Blackman crushed this morning."

The seventy-five-year-old senior partner of Adler, McCormick & Madison crowed at the taste of sweet victory.

"He had a tough case to argue," Emma said. "Interscope shouldn't be dropping clients just because they become ill."

"Blackman's the one who's going to be ill when he sees the repercussions of losing this case," Adler smirked. "I expect news of your victory to reverberate through courtrooms and cocktail parties all over Boston and New York."

"Robert's right, Emma. This morning you slew Goliath," Colin said. "To the victor goes the spoils. All Blackman can expect to walk away with is a headache."

"Before long," Adler continued, "we can expect some of those clients who've been hiring Blackman & Lowe to come knocking at our door."

Robert Adler pressed his right eye shut in a slow, wrinkled wink. He turned to walk back down the courthouse's cold marble hallway, leaving Emma and Colin alone again outside the courtroom doors.

"Well, my boss seems happy, and Anna's gotten a verdict she was hoping for. Today has all the markings of a great day."

"I couldn't agree with you more," Colin said, now walking beside her down the corridor. "Now that Anna has what she wants, and the firm's getting what it wants, what about you, Emma? What do you want?"

Emma stopped and pursed her lips as she thought about the question. Colin watched Emma's face intently.

"Oh, I don't know, a vacation. Time to just slow down, relax, and dream awhile." She sighed. "It's the scourge of the age I guess. Too much stress and not enough time to dream."

The thought of a stress-free getaway pleased Emma. Colin picked up on it right away.

"Listen, I have a friend who owns a beach house in Costa Rica," said Colin. "Why don't we fly down there this weekend—just as friends, of course—and get away for a while."

"Now look at who's dreaming," Emma quipped. "And by the way, how *did* you manage to play hooky and be in court this morning?"

"Officially, I'm not. I was scheduled to be in court downstairs. One delay from Judge Stalling later, and I was on my way up to see you spike the ball. And for the record, Emma, I'm no dreamer. The plans I make are very practical. When I see two things that go together—like your elevated stress levels and a private beach chair in Costa Rica for example—I move in to close the deal."

Colin's cell phone buzzed. He glanced down at the number on the screen.

"Sorry, Em. Gotta take this."

Colin stepped away from Emma, placing his cell phone against his left ear and covering the right with the palm of his hand.

Emma understood. She watched him as he walked away, knowing all too well the practice of law and its demands on attorneys to create billable hours.

Colin's call reminded Emma it had been more than an hour since she'd checked her own messages. She reached in her attaché and retrieved a sleek, charcoal-colored cell phone. Emma powered it up with the push of a button, and stared at the blue backlit screen. Two missed calls. Two messages. The first number she recognized from the firm. The other was unfamiliar except for the area code.

803.

The call was from a place as far away from Boston as you can get. Or as Emma once thought of Boston, a place as far away from Juneberry, South Carolina, as one can go. But who had called her?

She tucked the thin cell phone under her chin the way she sometimes did when deep in thought, trying to solve a riddle her skillful mind could sort out given enough facts and time. She pushed the message button.

"Hi, Emma? It's your cousin Samantha. I have news about your dad. Please call me back right away."

Emma wandered around a large, marble pillar while she listened to the message, then stood in the rainy daylight of a paned-glass window overlooking a landscaped city park.

Emma felt a cruel lump of fear choking out her breath. Her hands shook as she flipped up the lid on her phone, scrolled down to the mystery number, Samantha's number, and pushed Send.

Pick up, pick up.

The phone rang once, twice. Then she heard a woman's soft Southern accent on the other end of the line.

"Hello?"

"Hello, this is Emma. Samantha, what's going on?"

She meant for her voice to sound calm and controlled, but it had cracked as she'd said the word *on*.

"Emma, I know we haven't talked in a while, but I had to get in touch with you. I have some bad news."

Emma suddenly felt as cold as the marble columns in the alcove.

"It's your father. He's had a heart attack."

Emma froze.

"How … how is he?"

"We don't know, honey. An ambulance came to the house this morning and took him to Wellman Medical. The doctors have him in surgery right now."

"Oh my gosh."

"I'm so sorry, hon."

Emma turned and looked for Colin. She found him on the other side of the crowded corridor near the banister overlooking the first floor. He was standing with his back to her, still talking on his cell. In a room filled with people, she'd never felt so alone.

"Are you able to come down here?" Samantha asked.

"I'd have to move some things in my schedule," she said. "I'll call the airport right away."

"Emma, he's in surgery right now. There's a chance he won't make it. Please, please hurry."

"I'll reserve a seat on the next flight out," she promised. Going back home to Juneberry wouldn't be easy, but what choice did she have?

"Let us know when you think you'll be arriving, Emma. We'll send someone to meet you at the airport."

It was a short conversation, their first in forever. The cousins said their good-byes and Emma dropped her cell phone back into her bag. She accepted the disturbing news with an unnerving mixture of calm resolve and blind panic. Her world had been knocked off its axis.

She stirred from her daze to find Colin standing directly in front of her struggling to interpret the troubled look on Emma's ashen face.

"What's going on?" he asked.

"My father's had a heart attack. I need to get home right away," she said. Her voice sounded lifeless, and her body felt numb. Colin's reaction was decisive. He placed his hands on her shoulders.

"What can I do to help?" he asked.

"I don't know. I need to book a plane ticket. I'll need to call my office."

"Listen, you call your office. Tell them what's happened. I'll contact the airlines and see how quickly we can get you out of the city. At least let me do that much."

Emma nodded and Colin escorted her from the courthouse to the parking garage. As they walked in silence, she whispered a prayer, something she hadn't done in half a lifetime.

"God, please let him live."

The next hour was a blur. She managed to drive her car out of the parking garage and to her Back Bay townhouse without crying or getting stuck in midday traffic. She'd considered making a brief stop at the office to let her partners know she was going out of town for a couple of days, but instead decided to forgo everything else and get home as quickly as possible to pack.

Colin called her at home from his car to say he'd booked Emma a flight on United Airlines. He told her he would arrive in thirty minutes to take her to Logan.

Her father's heart attack had cracked Emma's world like the edge of a knife striking the hard shell of an egg. Her mind raced with fears of returning to Juneberry only to find she'd missed her chance to say good-bye, her chance to say how much she loved him.

Emma wheeled her large black travel bag out the front door of the three-story redbrick townhouse. Colin's silver BMW pulled up out front, double-parked, and Emma began pulling her bulky suitcase down the dozen front steps. As she reached the sidewalk, Emma's cell phone rang. She tilted the phone to glance at the name. CHRISTINA HERRY. The name toggled back and forth on the screen. Emma pushed the Call button.

"Hello?"

"Hi, Emma—it's Christina. I'm *so* sorry. I don't mean to intrude. Samantha just told me about your dad and that you're flying out. I just felt like I needed to reach out and contact you."

"No, no, it's fine, Christina. I … it's nice hearing your voice again. I just don't know where to begin today …"

"I know, I know. You don't have to say anything, but I just wanted to call and say if there's *anything* we can do, please let us know."

"Thank you," Emma said, comforted by another voice from another world she'd allowed time and busyness to erase. "I really do appreciate it. I'm just in a whirlwind at the moment."

"I know, and I'm praying for you and your dad. That's all I wanted to say."

"Thank you," Emma said, then both women said good-bye.

Colin sprung open the small trunk to load Emma's carry-on bag. The larger luggage he stashed in the space behind the seats.

"Any news?" Colin asked.

"No, that was a friend, an old friend from back home just calling to check in on me."

Colin nodded his approval.

"Nice to know you've got friends when you need them."

Colin didn't say anything else. He roared the BMW to life, accelerating into busy midday traffic on route to the airport. Emma leaned her head back into the leather headrest, closed her worried eyes, and prayed a second prayer.

God, please let him live. Please let me talk to him again.

In record time Colin pulled curbside at Logan and helped Emma with her bags. The temperature had fallen, and the sky looked like it was about to rain.

"Thank you, Colin, for being here for me today," she said. "Sorry, I don't know what else to say. I just feel numb." A uniformed police officer blew his whistle, commanding Colin to move his car. Colin opened his mouth to say something in the rushed moment, words of consolation perhaps, but all he could think to say was "Call me." He climbed back in and gave Emma one last wave through the passenger window, then disappeared back into the river flow of airport traffic.

A cold blast of wind hit Emma as she wheeled her suitcase to the outside check-in. She walked through the automatic sliding doors, patiently stepped through the paces of airport security, and finally made her way down the concourse, dragging her black carry-on bag to the gate. Somewhere on her long walk through the concourse, between the bright lights of the Hudson News & Books and warm aroma of the Pizza Hut, the irony of her trip finally dawned on her. She was rushing back to Juneberry, a place she hadn't wanted to set foot in for the past twelve years.

~ TWO ~

That's the way it's done
when you come from, way down south.

—JOSH TURNER
"Way Down South"

"Please return your seat backs and tray tables to the upright and locked position. We want to thank you for flying with us today, and welcome to Columbia."

Emma peered through the plane's oval window as the aircraft descended to eight thousand feet. Beneath the jet, the rural landscape resembled a miniature patchwork world of tiny full-leafed trees bursting with autumn colors. Tangerine, sunburst yellows, crimson reds—each popped with such vibrancy you could almost taste them.

It was unusual for Emma to fall asleep on a plane, but sleeping had done for her what worrying about her father could not. All her scattered thoughts and worries bouncing around inside her troubled mind had settled down. She took some degree of comfort in how smoothly things had come together to travel this far.

Robert Adler had called Emma as she stood in line to board the plane.

"Emma, I just heard the news about your father. I'm so sorry. Is there anything we can do?"

Emma exhaled some of the tension she felt.

"I don't think so, Robert. I'm just trying to get down there and see what's going on. I don't even know how he's doing right now."

"Had I known sooner, I could have hired you a private charter. You wouldn't have had to fool around with all that mess at the airport."

Emma smiled at the care Robert showed. He'd always been there for her, opening career doors, pointing out the pitfalls along the way.

"That's very generous of you, Robert. Fortunately, my plane's scheduled to depart on time and I'll be there shortly."

She heard Adler's grunt, his low-key way of imparting approval. His gruff, unshaven voice could intimate a kind of overbearing authority, even when showing charity.

"Emma, I just want you to know that you've got the firm's approval on this, even though you're leaving on such short notice. McCormick and I have already discussed it and concluded it's a family medical emergency."

Perhaps it was the daze Emma was in, but she couldn't make out the tone in Robert Adler's voice.

"Take a few days, even the rest of the week if you must. Go down to South Carolina and take care of your pa. We'll all pitch in around here and cover your bases while you're gone."

"Thank you, Robert," Emma said, taking his words, whether approval or permission, in their best light. Standing now at the front of the line, she handed the United Airlines agent her boarding pass. He scanned it under a red laser light and set it in a pile.

"Thank you, enjoy your flight."

Emma smiled and nodded at the agent, still listening to Adler as she starting down the boarding ramp.

"Emma, I know this isn't the best time to bring up work, but the sooner you can get things squared away and return to Boston, the better. I don't want to rush you, but this situation with your father couldn't have come at a worse time for the firm."

In a small, cramped space outside the air-conditioned comfort of the airport terminal, Emma couldn't believe what she was hearing. Her mind was a million miles away from the office. Her heart was fixed on one man in a small town no one in Boston had ever heard of.

"I wanted to wait until the close of the Interscope trial, but I need to bring you in on meetings I've been having with Northeast Federal. You know all about them: nine hundred million in earnings last year. Most of it in health care. I've been courting NF for a very long time, but it suddenly looks like we'll get a shot at representing them in part of their corporate litigation. Once they got wind of your victory this morning, they requested a face-to-face this Friday. My gut is they'll want to close the deal. Emma, it's imperative that you be present at that meeting on Friday."

The plane continued its descent into Columbia Metropolitan Airport. Emma watched out the window, feeling the sensation of being pulled into all that color below. The conversation with Robert Adler played over again in her mind. She regretted having said she'd *try* to return by Friday, feeling coerced by pressure from work, but that was one of the sacrifices she'd made to play at the "A level."

Emma had seen the firm ask its associates to put business ahead of family before. As a single woman and a partner in the firm, she'd even been in favor of the practice. The demand seemed reasonable for any ambitious law firm, but suddenly the rule seemed harsh and distasteful. Not least of all because she'd been placing her own career before family for most of the last twelve years. The regret stung.

Emma thought about Samantha and Christina, too. They would want to know why she hadn't seen or spoken to them in the past twelve years. Both women deserved better friendship from her. Neither had a clue why it had been *impossible* for Emma to stay in Juneberry.

Once the plane landed, Emma checked for new messages from the hospital. Her cell-phone screen blinked with one new message from Dena Johnson, an ICU nurse. She'd called during the flight, asking Emma to please contact her as soon as she landed.

"Hello, this is Emma Madison. Do you have—how's my dad doing?"

"Miss Madison, I thought you'd like to know your dad is in ICU now. He's awake and in stable condition."

Emma stopped for a moment in the waiting area, covering one ear to hear her over the noise.

"Oh, thank you," she said, closing her eyes where she stood, grateful for the news.

"Yes, he's had quite a morning, but we're continuing to monitor him, and he's doing all the things we want to see. He's been talking and he's had some fluids. Are you in South Carolina yet?"

"Yes, my plane's just landed."

"Well, when you get to the hospital, just come up to the fourth floor, that's where ICU is, and ask for Dena."

"I will, thank you. Oh, and, Dena?"

"Yes?"

"Would you give my dad a message for me, please?

"Certainly."

"Would you please tell my dad that I'm on my way?"

"I'll make sure he gets the message. He'll be happy to hear you're coming. He asked if you were."

"He did?"

"Uh-huh. He asked me if you knew about his condition. That's when I told him you'd called. I think he was just wondering if you were *able* to come down."

Emma appreciated the sweetness in Dena's voice. She recognized the Southern strength. Dena probably could work a ten-hour shift on her feet at the hospital, dealing with life and death issues, then go home to dinner, husband, family, and laundry all without losing her marbles. She could have made Emma feel guilty, but she didn't.

They said good-bye, and Emma slipped the phone back into her purse, breathing a sigh of relief. She grabbed the pull handle from her carry-on and continued her walk down the concourse toward the baggage claim. She whispered a barely audible prayer, *"Thank You."*

Emma stepped onto the airport escalator. Halfway down, she saw him. He was someone Emma thought she might have known anyway even were it not for the plain brown cardboard sign he carried, bearing her name in black Sharpie. The last time she'd seen him, he'd been all of ten years old, playing a pickup football game in the backyard with his friends. Now, Samantha's oldest appeared at the end of the escalator in full bloom: a lean, muscular, twenty-two-year-old college-football champion.

"Miss Madison?" Noel asked.

"Hi, Noel. Do you remember me?"

"Sure I do. Mom asked me to come pick you up."

The fresh-faced grad had been leaning against one of the airport's support pillars. He wore a pair of faded blue jeans that seemed long even with boots. The fall weather felt warm enough to wear his orange Clemson T-shirt, and his muscular arms were tanned below the sleeve. On his head he wore a straw cowboy hat that seemed to signify a youthful, free-spirited confidence.

"Sorry if this is a burden on you," Emma said. "I'm sure you have plenty of other things you could be doing today."

"Other things, sure, but nothing better," Noel said as the two made their way toward the baggage carousel. "You're probably eager to see your dad, Miss Madison. As soon as we see your luggage, I'll get us on our way."

"Tell you what, Noel, you call me Emma and you've got yourself a deal."

Noel reached for the brim of his straw hat and tipped it slightly as if to say, "My bad." By the smile on his face, Noel appeared to have not a care in the world. From behind them a loud red firehouse bell clanged, and the carousel started running its loop.

Emma pointed to a large black suitcase that matched her carry-on, and Noel reached through the crowd of travelers and snatched it from the moving conveyer belt.

"If you're ready," he said, "my truck's outside."

The airport's hydraulic doors opened as Noel and Emma crossed out of the busy terminal to the open skywalk. Outside, a warm autumn breeze caught Emma's hair and blew it wildly around her. She laughed.

"Guess I should have worn a hat too."

"If you had, you'd be chasing it about now," Noel said.

Emma enjoyed the South's warmer temperature while the two made their way to Noel's truck. Their small talk was blown away by the thunderous sound of a commercial jet taking off behind them.

"I'm sorry, I didn't hear what you were saying," Emma said.

"I said I officially graduated in May," Noel said in a loud voice as the jet rocketed skyward. "I had one more class this summer to finish up my degree, and I've been home for about two weeks now."

They walked across the open blacktop lot in the heat of a midday Carolina sun. It was obvious the yellow parking lines had just been painted.

"How does it feel?" Emma asked. "Coming home after four years away?"

Noel slowed down his pace. He peered over at Emma as if looking through her, and she almost turned away.

"It's always good to come home, Miss Madison, I mean, Emma," he said. Then the carefree look showed itself again like it was the one his face was the most used to. "It's like one season is over, and a new, better one is just beginning."

She smiled at Noel's optimism and felt somehow that whatever season lay ahead for Noel, it would be a good one.

They stopped at the tailgate of an old royal blue Dodge Ram truck. It reminded Emma of the ocean and looked as shiny as a brand-new model just rolling off the assembly line.

"I hope you don't mind trucks," he said, pulling on the tailgate's handle. It popped open with the sound of solid, well-engineered metal and lowered without a squeak. He loaded up Emma's black canvas suitcase and closed up the back of the truck.

"Don't let appearances fool you, Noel. I lived in Juneberry once too, you know, a long time ago."

"I know. I remember." Noel fished out the keys from his front jeans pocket and came around Emma's side to unlock the door. She climbed up into the tall seat in Boston-meets-Juneberry style. Inside, Noel's truck was as well kept as the outside. The interior dash housed a circular speedometer and fuel gauges. Emma noticed the original AM/FM stock radio next to it built into the dashboard.

"You're strictly old school, aren't you?"

Noel climbed in the other side.

"When improvements stop being made, the best things are all found in the past."

He turned the key in the ignition and fired the engine to life. The truck roared with so much power that it startled Emma. She reached for her seat belt and clicked it around her as the truck rolled backward.

"Is this your truck, Noel?" Emma asked.

"Ever since high school. It's been in storage at my mom and dad's the last four years. Sadly neglected. Sorry if it's running kind of rough."

"Sounds mint condition to me."

Thirty minutes later, they exited the new freeway and turned onto SC59, the old highway route to Juneberry. Emma watched out her window as the scenery shifted from noisy eighteen-wheel trucks and SUVs to quiet, wide-open spaces. Every cornfield they passed seemed to harvest its own crop of memories for her. It had been so long.

"Do you mind if I crack open the window? I love the way the pines smell out here."

"Sure. When was the last time you were in Juneberry?" Noel asked her.

"The last time? I'd just graduated from college too," Emma said, sticking her toe in old, forgotten memories for the first time in a long time. "I flew home to celebrate with my dad, thanking him of course, for the money he'd given me, making it possible for me to go to college in the first place."

Emma's voice trailed off, quieted by thoughts that she'd almost lost him, and an uneasy guilt that squeezed her. Her father had always loved her, but Emma had never come back.

"Your dad seems like a pretty great guy."

"He is," Emma said, thinking of how it would be when she saw him again. "He's a great guy, a great father."

Emma waded a little farther into her memory stream. Her mind drifted back to someone she once was.

"It wasn't September when I'd returned the last time; it was spring. Around late May. Got picked up in an old truck that day too," she chuckled. "Old Red. That's the way he liked to get around when he was feeling his roots."

"You mean that old red Chevy? I've seen him drive that classic around."

Emma laughed.

"That's my dad. He never throws anything away."

They raced past the green Juneberry city-limit sign, population 8,000. It had been so long since she'd been back, she felt like the sign was saying, "Welcome home, Emma. Welcome home."

"We're getting close, Emma," Noel said. "My mom asked if you wanted to go to your dad's first, or go straight to the hospital?"

"Hospital," Emma answered, and Noel veered the truck right at the fork, under the railroad tracks where the road was still one lane. The road curved through neighborhoods of houses old and new before bending at the first traffic light. They were in the commercial district on Juneberry's west side, and Emma could see the hospital in the distance.

Within minutes they pulled into the parking lot at Wellman Medical, the small community hospital that had served the community for years. Bantam, especially by Boston standards, the five-story facility housed a first-rate emergency room, an eight-bed ICU ward, two respectable operating rooms, and three floors of inpatient beds. Will Madison could have done a lot worse.

"I know he's in ICU," Emma said, as they left Noel's truck and made their way toward the hospital. "But I don't know exactly where that is."

"I'm sure we can find it. There's usually someone at the information desk in the lobby where we go in," Noel told her, as if he visited the hospital all the time. Just as Noel described, a cheerful seventy-something woman sat at the welcome desk ready to greet them.

"Hello, may I help you?" she asked.

"Yes, my father was admitted this morning. His name is Will Madison, and I believe he's in the Intensive Care Unit."

"Are you Emma?" she asked, looking up. The woman wore a plastic nametag attached to her pretty red sweater. On the top it read, VOLUNTEER, and below was her name, Beverly.

"Yes," Emma answered. Though she lived in Boston, the real location for the fictional bar from the TV show *Cheers*, it had been awhile since she'd been somewhere everybody actually *did* know your name.

"I'm Beverly Williams, a friend of your father's."

The woman stuck out her hand and shook Emma's with a congenial welcome. She tilted the screen in front of her and read it through her bifocals.

"You're right. He's in ICU, but you'll have to check in at the nurses' station on the fourth floor before they'll let you see him. Just a second, I'll write you a visitors pass."

Beverly collected two visitor passes from behind the desk and filled in their names with a blue ink pen. Emma noticed the slight tremble in her hand when the pen wasn't in motion.

"They'll know which room he's in. That information isn't listed on the system's computers."

She handed them both their passes.

"Thank you."

Beverly leaned in over the front counter and pointed down the hallway to her left.

"You'll want to go down this hallway and take the second left. Elevators will be on your right. Go up to the fourth floor, and you'll open up right at the nurses' station."

"Thank you, Beverly."

"Oh, it's my pleasure," Beverly said, giving her a carefree smile, just like Noel's. "Your father is the sweetest man. I was so sorry to hear what happened."

"I'll make sure to tell him hey for you," Emma said.

"You do that," she said.

Noel and Emma turned the corner and walked down a polished marble hallway, listening to the click of their steps, seeing their reflections beneath them as they walked. They entered the elevator, which they found waiting with its doors open, and pushed the button for the fourth floor. Slowly the doors closed and they felt the small, enclosed space creep upward. Emma closed her eyes, feeling emotionally frayed and physically worn. She'd run an East Coast marathon to get there since that morning. Ever since the mystery phone call had jarred her awake, reminding her that Juneberry had been more than just a dream. Only the one thing mattered now. She wanted to see her father.

The elevator doors opened on the fourth floor directly in front of the nurses' station. Emma approached the two women working behind it.

"Hi, my name is Emma Madison, and my dad was admitted here this morning ... Will Madison?"

"Hi, Emma, I'm Dena. Your dad has told me all about you," she said, in a way that conveyed he was doing well. "I know you want to see him. He's right down there in room C."

Noel took a step backward, giving Emma space to see her dad privately.

"I'll just stick around out here," he said.

Dena put aside the folder she'd been charting and led Emma down the hallway. The 5'2" woman gave off an inexplicable feeling of comfort in her powder blue scrub pants, spiffy white tennis shoes, and a basic white smock with teddy bears on it.

Emma followed without speaking. It was like she was passing through the antechamber of a sacred church. Dena walked with light steps. Emma felt weighed down with the mounting anticipation at seeing her father.

Dena stepped through the doorway of room C.

"Will, you've got a visitor."

Emma entered his room slowly, taking in the sight of her father for the first time in forever.

Will Madison lay in a sterile hospital bed with an oxygen feed underneath his nose. An IV line dripped clear fluid down a long, transparent tube into his right thigh. He raised his hand slightly and slowly off the bed to wave.

She stood at the doorway watching him. How much older he looked to her, a mixture of passing years and the survival of a sudden heart attack.

"Hey, Dad," Emma said to him in a tone as soft as fleece. She tiptoed into his room, finding a place by the side of his bed. She reached over the metal safety railing that ran the length of his bed and took hold of his hand.

"You came," he said, in a voice as dry as an old Western movie. A satisfied smile eased up in the corners of his mouth.

"Yes, of course," Emma said, wrapping her other hand around his. "How are you feeling?"

"Better than I was at breakfast," he smiled, trying to settle her nerves with humor. "I'm okay, darlin'. They were able to get in there and fix the problem in no time flat."

Emma leaned in closer, speaking softly to him.

"I got here as quickly as I could."

"I know you did."

Will squeezed her hand.

"Emma," Dena said, checking the IV drip and writing in Will's chart. "I'll be at the nurses' station if you need anything."

"Thank you," Emma called out to Dena over her shoulder.

Emma took a closer look at her dad. His hair was matted, pressed against his chiseled face like salt-and-pepper doll's hair. His cheeks were red, not as a result of his morning heart attack, but from working outdoors around the farm: his favorite summer pastime. She looked into his coast blue eyes. They radiated intelligence and light ... and exhaustion.

This wasn't the time to unravel a complicated past. She squeezed her father's hand again.

"I'm here, Dad. I'll stay with you until you get well."

She smiled and marveled at how the small, simple expression put her dad at ease. She watched him smile too, just before those intelligent eyes turned down for sleep. The South Carolina lawyer, a man the governor called "The Advisor," lay frail and silent beneath a thin, cream-colored hospital blanket. Only the fragile, regular bleep of his heart monitor broke the silence.

Emma returned to the nurses' station.

"Dena, I want to thank you for taking such good care of my dad."

"That's what we try to do around here. That's why they pay us the big bucks."

Emma grinned at the remark, more than a little relieved that her dad was all right.

"Dena, can you tell me anything about the sort of treatment my dad required?"

"I can tell you he was treated in the ER. They were going to do the procedure in the OR, but Dr. Anderson decided that the treatment could be performed on your father there. He's the surgeon who inserted the stint, and he'll be able to answer more of your questions."

"Do you know when Dr. Anderson will be in again?"

"He usually visits patients early in the morning before scheduled surgery. I know he's scheduled tests today to determine the extent of any heart damage, but as far as long-term prescribed medications and that kind of thing, you should probably talk to Dr. Anderson."

Noel approached the nurses' desk.

"Everything okay?" he asked.

"Yeah, I think so. He seems to be doing fine, which is a huge relief."

"Praise God."

"Yes, absolutely," Emma said, knowing that it could have been a much different outcome.

Emma turned her attention to Noel. He'd been so kind all day, but it was time to let him go. Emma wasn't used to depending on others.

"Noel, I think I'm going to stay here awhile. You probably should get on with your day. I'm sure you have a lot to do."

"I can stay," he told her. "I mean, I can just stay in the waiting area. I don't want to get in your way or anything, but you don't have a car. So, if it's all the same to you, I think I'll just stick around." He joked, "Who knows, you might get hungry for a Snickers bar. I'm the only one of the two of us who knows where to find the vending machines."

Emma laughed.

"You're really something, Noel. I once asked a taxi driver in Boston to stay outside an office building while I ran in to pick something up. I was back downstairs in less than two minutes, but when I got outside, the taxi was nowhere to be found, and I was paying him money."

"You forget, this is my vacation. What better way to chill than to hang out here? It's quiet. Besides, I've got a good book out in the truck. I'll just bring it in."

They looked at each other for a moment without speaking. She knew she needed him and that it would be better if he stayed. She also knew the sacrifice he would be making.

"Well, thank you," Emma finally said.

Noel Connor's friendly gesture wasn't merely a small-town custom, although it was in a small town that Noel had learned to practice the art. Noel's kindness sprang up from the marrow of his bones. Character had been fused into his DNA.

"I'm just going to the waiting room to collect my thoughts for a while," Emma said. Noel nodded, the brim of his hat tipping as he watched Emma walk off.

The rest of the day was a slow haze. Emma sat for hours in the wooden chair next to her father's bed. She held hands with the sleeping man, sharing a one-sided conversation with the man who had raised her. Finally, Emma herself had fallen into a deep and dreamless sleep.

In the fourth-floor waiting room, Noel Connor sat, still reading his book, settled into the same chair where Emma had last seen him.

"You've been here all this time?" Emma said, shaking her head in disbelief.

"It's a good book."

"I owe you big-time, Noel, and don't try to talk me out of it."

Noel closed his book.

"How's he doing?"

"He's awake, and seems to be doing a lot better. Says I'm the one who needs to be getting some rest."

"You ready to go to your dad's house?"

"Yes, I'd really like to get settled in."

They left the hospital the way that they came, past Beverly's welcoming center, now dark and vacant for the night. Outside, the orange sun was descending behind the tree line with a faint smoky pink sash trailing behind in the clouds.

"My mom left your dad's house keys with me," said Noel. They seemed to have taken care of everything. Conversation was easy with him. The day's events bonded them into kindred spirits. "She didn't know if you'd have any, so I've got some for you."

"Yes, I'll be needing those," she said, feeling like someone who'd needed assistance at every turn.

"She's the one that found him, you know."

Emma felt like a sleuth picking up details here and there about what had happened that morning. "How frightening for her. I'm just glad she was there checking up on him."

Noel's Dodge hummed down Junction Road as the last ounce of daylight dripped into night. Emma gazed out the window, exhausted and hungry.

Twenty-four hours earlier, she'd been preparing for trial. She left the office late for a steak dinner with Colin at Abe & Louie's before going to bed on the third floor of her townhouse where the muted sound of taxis lulled her to sleep.

Somewhere in her weary mind, a thought rattled again in its little tin cup. Who would be the first to ask her, *"Why didn't you come back?"*

Noel switched on his headlights to drive the rest of the dark country two-lane. Soon, he pulled onto the gravel horseshoe drive and shifted the stick on the steering post to Park.

"Here are the house keys. Do you want me to help you get some lights on?"

"The porch light's on. I think I'll be okay," Emma said.

She swung open the truck door, and Noel got out to unload her luggage. The evening moon gave the farmyard a silvery tint. It reminded Emma of all the nights in high school when she, Christina, and Noel's mom, Samantha, had packed up or unloaded their cars in this drive. Always off on some new adventure, or coming back late from a sunny day at the lake.

"Noel," Emma said, turning around from her route to the front door.

"Yeah?"

"Thanks," she said. "For everything."

He gave her one more nod of the plain straw hat, and Emma dragged her bags up the grassy walkway illuminated by the truck's high beams. At the top of the stairs, she pushed open the heavy oak door and waved Noel on.

Emma walked in and clicked on the entryway lights, peering up the red-carpeted staircase of the hundred-year-old house. It looked weirdly the same as it had when she was in high school. The same family pictures on the walls, younger faces in outdated clothing, looked out through glass and frame. She climbed the long staircase to her old bedroom, toting both suitcases, keeping her mind off the thing she feared most about being alone in the house.

Emma switched on the golden bedside lamp in her old bedroom and sat on the checkered quilt. She barely possessed the strength but managed to shower and change into her pajamas before crawling into a familiar canopy bed. She hadn't eaten much that day, just some pretzels and orange juice on the plane, but Emma felt too exhausted to care.

Emma snuffed out the bedside lamp and lay in the still beam of moonlight stenciled across her comforter. In the murky twilight before sleep, she chased away the absurd feeling that she wasn't alone in the house and thought of the question one last time: Who would be the first to ask, *"Why didn't you come back?"*

~ THREE ~

I'm just a small town girl
And that's all I'll ever be.

—KELLIE PICKER
"Small Town Girl"

Twelve years had passed since Samantha Connor had seen her cousin. More than anything, she wanted to be there for Emma like she'd been there for Will on the morning of his heart attack. She considered her discovery of Will in his kitchen that morning more than just an accident of good fortune.

Emma's and Samantha's mothers had been the closest of sisters, like families often are in small-town America. Emma had been too young to remember anything about her mother's funeral. Samantha, who was five years older, remembered many things, and had many unhappy pictures from that desolate afternoon when her mother broke down crying. She remembered the tears shed behind closed doors, the strangers who came by the house after the service and spoke in low voices. She even remembered the black leggings her mother made her wear to the funeral.

Samantha had always thought her strong maternal instinct had grown out of that day, a flower from dirt, and given her both cause and capacity to watch over Emma. Samantha couldn't imagine a world without her own mother, and seeing Emma grow up orphaned from the love of a mother troubled her. Samantha had filled in missing gaps whenever she could.

She watched over Will, too, when it became clear with the passing years that Emma wouldn't be returning from Boston. That's how she'd happened to find him that morning, sitting at his kitchen table in a white T-shirt and striped pajama bottoms unable to move or speak. Beads of sweat had dotted his forehead on a chilly morning in September. That's what scared her the most. Seeing his right hand clench the front of his T-shirt, his mouth half open but barely able to speak, and the broken coffee mug scattered on the kitchen floor.

Samantha responded quickly, calling 911 from the wall phone mounted in the kitchen. She stayed with him until the ambulance arrived. Two quick-thinking EMTs immediately transported Will to Wellman Medical rather than treat him on his kitchen floor, a decision that may have saved his life.

Samantha called Emma using the phone number she found under E in Will's address book on his work shelf next to the paper-towel rack and her aunt's yellowing Betty Crocker cookbooks that Will refused to throw away. She sent Noel to pick Emma up from the airport because she knew it was the most efficient thing to do. Samantha was just that way and always had been. She cared for everybody, but she cared for Emma most of all.

Samantha would have liked to have picked up Emma or followed the ambulance to the hospital or stayed at the hospital with Will. And she would have, if not for the doctor's warning of keeping away from all excitement until after the baby was born.

At nineteen, Samantha married her high school sweetheart, Jim Connor, and a year later, gave birth to their first child, Noel. As a freshman, Emma often joined the Connor family dinners or helped with babysitting or spent the night when her dad had to travel.

Christina Herry had moved to Juneberry from Phoenix, Arizona, in the sixth grade. She and Emma were locker neighbors and quickly became the best of friends, bonding over their wholehearted agreement that Mrs. Holstead, the science teacher, was psychotic. It was the start of a beautiful friendship that deepened through junior high and high school, and included Samantha as often as not.

After graduation, Christina went on to pursue her four-year undergrad degree at Clemson, a short fifty-mile hop from Juneberry. Emma applied to Boston University, and four busy years later, was accepted to Harvard Law School. Trips to Juneberry became fewer and fewer as her schedule grew more demanding. Inevitably her big-city success pulled Emma away from her small-town past. Like red taillights driving away at night, Emma's presence ebbed in their lives, becoming smaller and smaller as time went by. Even phone calls between the three best friends faded as the years passed, until only Samantha and Christina were left to wonder what had happened. Why had Emma let their friendship slip away?

"Do you think she's changed?" Jim asked, unbuttoning his pale blue shirt.

"Noel said when he picked her up she looked very professional, but that she was friendly. He said they talked a lot."

Jim draped his shirt on a hanger and hung it in the closet. He continued talking to Samantha in his T-shirt and boxers.

"What time are you planning on seeing her tomorrow?"

"Why? Do you think you could join us?" Samantha asked, half hoping Jim would say yes, yet realizing somehow it would probably be better if he didn't.

"I think you need to see Emma by yourself," he said.

Jim pulled on a pair of navy blue sweatpants and a silver Clemson sweatshirt. Samantha watched her husband and smiled an easy, contented smile.

"How is it I never grow tired of your looking after me?"

"I don't know," Jim said. "Guess you'll have to answer that for yourself. I just know you're always the one looking after everyone else. Gotta have somebody watching your back."

Samantha caught her reflection in the bedroom mirror. After two kids and another one on the way, Samantha felt far removed from her high school figure. She drew closer to Jim and laid her arms over his shoulders.

"Do you ever wish you would have married someone else?"

Jim slid his arms around Samantha's waist and pulled her closer, gently closer. As close as a nine-month pregnancy would allow.

"Shhhh. We have to keep all this a secret," Jim flirted with her in a whisper.

"Keep what a secret?"

"That marrying the love of your life at eighteen, having two-and-a-half kids, and living in an old house in a small town is the key to happiness."

Samantha sighed her contentment. Jim lightly rubbed Samantha's back.

"Do you really feel that way?" she asked.

"You always ask me that like you don't believe me."

"Oh, I believe you," she said. "Maybe I just like hearing you say it over and over again."

Samantha closed her eyes and kissed him.

"Mmm, you taste good."

"See, that's just what I mean," Jim said. "You know you've got something special when just the taste of toothpaste is a turn-on."

Samantha laughed, then Jim kissed her again.

"I'm going downstairs to watch TV with Beth and get a snack, but I'll be up in a little while to massage your back. How are you feeling?"

"A little sore," Samantha said, putting her hand on her lower back. "I might take a bath or just relax awhile. It's been a long day."

"Okay. I'll come up in a little bit. Want me to bring you something to eat?"

"Not now, thanks."

Jim jogged down the stairs, and Samantha moved over on to the bed to relax. She didn't mind being pregnant, mostly she enjoyed it. But by the beginning of the ninth month, she was easily tired.

Around eight thirty, the phone rang.

"Hi, it's me. I just had to call and ask if you're feeling as weirdly thrilled as I am that Emma's back in Juneberry."

"I haven't thought about how I'm feeling, Christina," Samantha confessed. "I feel like Emma's coming back is an answer to prayer. One minute she was in Juneberry, and the next she was gone."

Samantha propped an extra pillow against the headboard and lifted her feet up on the bed.

"Maybe this is our chance to find out why," Christina said, always optimistic.

"We can only hope," Samantha laughed. "I keep thinking back to all the things we did and how close we all were. I just can't believe how quickly time flies and how everything changed. It never made any sense."

"I know, and I'm sorry she's coming back under these circumstances, but I'm glad she's back just the same. How's her dad doing?"

"I guess he's doing lots better. I've been worried about him though too. I think it's their estranged relationship that's taken the toll on him."

"They talk sometimes, right?"

"Yes. He's been up there to visit her a couple of times, and they talk on the phone around the holidays, but they've been living with a bubble in between them ever since high school. I think she just decided one day to cut herself off from her past. Speaking of high school, do you think Michael knows she's in town?"

"I doubt it. Bo hasn't mentioned anything to me."

"Hmm, I don't know why," Samantha said, "but he's been on my mind today too. You probably know him better than I do these days, but I've wondered what he'll think of her coming back. He's such a good guy. I've always thought the world of him, wondered why he never married. Maybe it's just my imagination, but ... do you think it might have something to do with Emma?"

"You've really put a lot of thought into this!" Christina laughed.

Samantha got up from the bed, laughing too, and waddled down the hall.

"Well, I knew Michael a lot better when he and I were in school together. I know he had feelings for her back when she was a senior and he was just out of high school. Then they dated that summer before she went back for law school, so it's not all my imagination."

"I don't know if Michael's marital status has anything to do with Emma," Christina said. "I think, like a lot of us, he's just busy."

Samantha turned off the globe ceiling light in the bathroom, snapping on a small night-light next to the mirror. She turned off three lights left on in Beth's room before making the return trip to her bedroom.

"We knew each other as kids, that's the way it is in a small town, you know. I talked with him a lot that summer when they were so in love. I know how special she was to him."

"Do you honestly think he's still carrying a flame for her?"

Both women were silent for a moment.

"That would be very romantic," Christina said.

"There's a lot more to true love than romance, Christina."

Samantha shut off Jim's closet light and closed the doors. She sat down on the bed to rest again.

"Yes, but if he's kept a candle burning just for Emma all these years, that's the kind of thing most women would melt over."

"If he still feels that way, I hope she doesn't hurt him."

"What, like not return his feelings?"

"We're getting *way* ahead of ourselves here, but yeah. None of us has spent any significant time around Emma in twelve years, and after a couple of days in Juneberry, we might not see her again for another twelve."

"By then, we'll all be well into our forties," Christina joked. "Talking about Weight Watchers and wrinkle cream."

"Some of us aren't waiting until then to think about it."

They both laughed again. Samantha picked up her nail file from the nightstand and started smoothing her fingernails.

"So when are you going to see her?

"I thought I'd go by her dad's place tomorrow morning. Noel said the doctors might release Will as early as the afternoon or Wednesday at the latest."

"Close call."

"It was a close call, and absolutely miraculous how they were able to reverse a dire situation when he got to the hospital."

"Are you going to call her first?"

"I don't know yet. I think the first time I talk to her I'd like us to be in the same room."

"That's probably best."

"What are you going to say?" Christina asked.

"I don't know. I feel like she's been on a long cruise and she's coming into port for a few days. I just want to make the most of that time. What about you?"

"I'll pray about it," Christina said. "I want to spend some time with Emma to see how she's doing emotionally ... and spiritually."

"That's the counselor in you."

Christina was quiet on the other end of the phone. Samantha could always tell when she was thinking.

"I don't know what it is, but I've always sensed there's something broken in Emma. Something made her go away. I'd just like to know if she's found peace."

"One thing's for sure, she has some awfully good friends and doesn't know how lucky she is."

"Maybe that should be our prayer," Christina said. "That Emma discovers how loved she is."

The two women said their good nights.

Christina shut off her phone and held it against her chest, lost in thought. Inside her house it was dark except for a delicate string of dewdrop lights tucked beneath the cupboards in the kitchen and the antique Tiffany lamp in the entryway. She had finished writing for the day. The evening promised a long bath and reading a good book in bed. The phone rang in her hand while she was carrying it back to its dock.

"Hey, sorry for calling so late, but remember how you said you wanted me to start calling you more for no reason? Well, I'm calling."

Christina smiled. "Bo, you are getting major points for this. See, and all that time I thought you weren't listening to me, you were taking notes."

Christina turned and walked up the stairway.

"I like working under the radar of your low expectations. That way, whatever happens, you're surprised and happy about it."

"I am surprised and happy by your phone call. I was just thinking about you, and wondering how your night was going."

Christina stepped into her bedroom, a comfortable place lit only by soft yellow light from her bedside lamp. Music drifted in quietly from an alarm clock radio.

"I've decided that Sunday night is a lonely night, Christina."

"Aww, why is that?"

"Well, think about it. Sunday night knows all about the fun Saturday night's had. Saturday night's been bragging about all the date nights, movies, and dinners out. Friday night's been yucking it up too, showing off just because he gets to go out and have fun. But Sunday night, all he gets out of the deal is missing you."

Christina sat on the embroidered quilt she'd just bought, ran her fingers across the fine rouge needlepoint and smoothed the wrinkles atop her bed. The quilt was a reward she promised herself if she reached her professional goal for the summer. Tulsa, the weekend before, was speaking engagement number ten.

"Hmm … sounds like we need to do something for Sunday night. I feel sorry and understand now why he's so lonesome. I think my Sunday night has been saying something like that to me, too."

"Maybe we should let them spend some time together. You know, let my Sunday night go out with your Sunday night? Just see how it goes."

"I miss you, Bo."

Christina laid her head against one of the decorative pillows her mother had bought her for the bed. She loved hearing his words, loved his thoughtful phone calls. More than anything, she loved Bo and lived with the frustration of things hoped for, but not yet seen.

"I think that's what I called to hear."

"No fair. Say you miss me too."

"My phone call should tell you that."

"It does, but I like it when you say it."

In his modest, prefab home by the lake, Bo leaned back into the pocket of his old flannel sofa. He kicked his wool-sock-adorned feet up onto the coffee table in front of him. His black dog, Bear, raised his head at the commotion, then rested it back down to sleep by the fire.

"I wish I was there right now," Bo said. He glanced at his silver wristwatch. He wouldn't need much prompting to put his work boots back on and make the twenty-minute drive out to Christina's.

"I wish you were too. It's probably best if we don't though."

The love between Bo and Christina was obvious; so was the reason they weren't together that night, and every other night.

"Not trying to start a fire, sweetheart. I just called to say I love you."

"Thanks, Stevie Wonder. You're the best."

They laughed. She was certain they'd be together one day. One day the good man she'd fallen in love with would wake up brand new, ready to commit again. And she'd be there for him. Until the end of time.

"No, you're the best," Bo told her. "We both know that. I just want to be the man who gets close to the best. That's enough for an old dog like me."

"That seems a reasonable enough request," Christina whispered to Bo in a voice just for the two of them. "I'll grant it."

~ FOUR ~

I don't know what I want, so don't ask me
'Cause I'm still trying to figure it out.

—TAYLOR SWIFT
"A Place in This World"

Emma woke to a pure and simple sunrise. Normally, it would still be dark when she arose to the sounds of traffic on Boston's busy streets. Her father's house, on the contrary, felt as peaceful and quiet as an early-morning Sunday chapel. The dawning of the new day brought with it the promise of a fresh start. The Interscope trial that had devoured Emma's energy for months was finally over, buried in the past a thousand miles away. Her father would be coming home soon.

After a long shower, Emma propped her suitcase on the bed and snapped open the latches. There had been time to grab only the essentials—a three-day survival kit. She unpacked jeans and tops, two warm sweaters in case of cold weather, a comfortable pair of loafers because they went with everything, and a black turtleneck just in case … she wasn't exactly sure why she'd packed that. She dressed in a pair of jeans and a sleeveless shirt and headed downstairs.

The boards in the old hardwood floors creaked when Emma walked down the hallway to the kitchen. "Old houses," she said aloud, both comforted and cautious by the thought that some things never change. In the sun-kissed kitchen, light overflowed in a room filled with windows. On the tile counter she found a full pot of cold coffee, minus one cup, sitting in the coffeemaker next to the toaster. Emma took the coffee pot out and poured the dark roast down the drain in the sink, frightening evidence of the attack that almost took him.

She's the one that found him, you know.

Will kept his food on a stainless steel pantry rack in the laundry room. Emma found a large blue can of Maxwell House on the center shelf and took stock of the food, hoping to find bagels. Will's pantry wasn't all that different from her own—bare except for a few essentials. Single people only stock what they need. Emma carried the coffee into the kitchen and brewed a fresh pot.

A silver Dodge Caravan pulled onto the horseshoe drive and parked beside the cluster of three weeping willow trees. Samantha opened her car door and stepped out into the cool morning sunlight. She'd already redone her lipstick and makeup inside the van. On the driveway, she tugged the creases from her clothing and walked to the side door that lead into the kitchen. Emma was waiting for her. Their eyes met on either side of the glass and both stood there for a moment until Emma opened the door.

"My gosh, Emma, you've hardly changed at all," Samantha said. The two women hugged.

"It's good to see you, Samantha, and look at you!"

They both stared at Samantha's belly.

"Yep, this makes baby number three."

"Oh my gosh. Well, come in, sit down. Let me get you a chair."

"I brought you something," Samantha said, taking the seat Emma had pulled out from the table. "It's homemade banana nut bread, baked fresh this morning." Samantha handed Emma the shiny aluminum-wrapped loaf.

"Oh, that's so sweet, Samantha. Thank you! Your timing couldn't be better. This will go perfectly with the coffee that's brewing."

"It's just a little welcome-home present."

"It's very thoughtful. Would you like to have some with a cup of coffee?" Emma said, taking a dark blue cup from the cabinet and holding it in the air.

"I would, but mix mine half with water. I can only have one cup a day."

"Would you rather have decaffeinated tea?" Emma asked. "I saw there's some in the pantry."

"Sure, if it's no bother."

"It's no problem. I'll just boil some water."

Emma unhooked a stainless steel pan from the overhead rack and filled it with water from the tap. She lit the gas stove with a stick match and adjusted the flame.

"I have to tell you, Samantha, your son is wonderful. He was such a lifesaver yesterday picking me up at the airport, waiting with me all day at the hospital. He's a pretty mature twenty-two-year-old."

"That's Noel. I always tell people he was our exhale. Sometimes with kids you have to hold your breath, but Noel was born with a heart for serving others. I'd like to think it's something we did right, but he's just been that way all his life. I can't remember a time when he wasn't spiritually grounded. Involved in youth groups at church. He's worked the last three summers at camp mentoring teens and taking them white-water rafting. He's even interned at our church. I really feel like God has His hand on him and Noel will end up in some kind of ministry."

Samantha peeled back the foil, revealing a loaf of banana nut bread that was still warm. Emma served Samantha her tea, poured herself a cup of coffee, and set out serving plates for the bread.

"This bread is like cake. I hope you like it."

"It smells wonderful," she said, joining Samantha at the table. They sat without speaking for a moment.

"It's good to see you again, Samantha," Emma finally said. "Thank you for yesterday. For finding him. I don't want to think about what could have happened if you hadn't been looking after my dad."

Samantha smiled. "How's he doing?"

"Remarkably well. He called this morning and told me to hold off on coming in. He said his doctor told him he'd be released sometime today. I'm just waiting for the next phone call."

"That's wonderful news."

"Yes, I was hoping for some time to get the house ready. I'd like to have a few things cleaned and the kitchen better stocked before I bring him home."

"Emma, I know you've got a lot on your mind, but have you thought about how your dad will live here? I mean, it's a big question, but do you think he'll be able to stay here by himself?"

"I've been thinking about that too, but I don't really know. For now, I just want to get him home and see how he does. Just take it one step at a time."

Samantha took a long look at Emma. She'd always known she would see her again, that she'd feel proud of Emma, and feel complete having her home again.

"Emma, you look so young. I can't get over how successful you've become. You were always focused, but you've done so well for yourself."

Emma laughed and shook her head. "We do the best we can, I guess."

Samantha hesitated over how to ask Emma the question she and Christina wanted an answer to. She hoped a sensitive approach would pop in her head, but it didn't.

"Emma, this probably isn't the best time, but there's something I'd like to ask you …"

The telephone rang, its noisy metal clapper vibrating inside a silver bell. Emma squeezed Samantha's hand and stood to answer it.

"Hello?"

"Hi, Emma? This is Dena at Wellman Medical. You may have already heard the news, but Dr. Anderson saw your dad this morning, and he's decided to go ahead and discharge him this afternoon. Probably after lunch, sometime between one and two. Will someone be able to come and pick him up?"

"Oh sure, I'll be there. I'd planned to catch Dr. Anderson this morning, but I didn't expect him to be there that early!"

"I didn't either. Sorry. I know you hoped to speak with him. Usually, he does his rounds later."

"Dena, do you know if Dr. Anderson called in any prescriptions for him? I'm going to use the rest of the morning to get everything ready for my dad to come home."

"That was my other question. Do you know which pharmacy you'd like us to use to call in his meds?"

"Ah, probably Brown's downtown on Main. I didn't realize there *was* another pharmacy."

"No, that's fine. I can send them there. I'll get everything together and see you at one o'clock."

Emma set the old rotary phone receiver back on its hook.

"They're discharging Dad today at one. I'll have to make a trip into town for a few things before I pick him up."

Emma rejoined Samantha at the table.

"Sorry for the interruption. What was the question you wanted to ask me?"

"It can wait," Samantha said, feeling the moment had passed and that she'd have another opportunity to ask her. "You've got a lot going on this morning, but it's nice to have you home, at least for a while. Do you know when you'll go back?"

"I'm not sure. Probably Friday."

Samantha got up from the table feeling a little wobbly legged. Friday was too soon.

"Well, I'd better let you get on with your morning," she said, not knowing what else to say just then. "But if you or your dad need anything call us, okay?"

"I'll be in touch whether we need anything or not, Samantha. It's been good seeing you."

Emma walked Samantha back to the door, and the two embraced again.

"It's good to have you home again, Emma," Samantha said in the doorway.

Emma thought to say it was good to *be* home again, but that was only half true. She settled for "See you soon" and waved good-bye, closing the door behind her. Emma had seen the question in Samantha's eyes. She had almost asked it. It had balanced precariously on the tip of her tongue: *Why didn't you ever come back, Emma? Why?*

But the telephone had rung. *Saved by the bell,* she thought. Anyway, how does one shatter open their psyche over banana bread and tea? Or remove the lid from the pot, bewildering her cousin with "I was afraid."

After Samantha left, Emma found the keys to her father's truck on the post near the kitchen door, the same green Sinclair dinosaur keychain drawing her eyes to them. The sun perched high in the cloudless blue heavens, and the air was still plenty warm for late September. Emma crossed beneath the cluster of three weeping willow trees on the path to the barn.

The timeworn red barn, raised back when the original owner, John Barry, worked the farm, housed dairy cows on the ground floor and farm equipment on the second floor for its first fifty years. A sliding red door framed in white paint gave access to the top floor. When the Madisons bought the house, Will leased the land to a real farmer to grow corn, and transformed the upper level of the barn into something akin to an oversized garage.

Emma swung open the barn door, pushing its rusty wheels through their narrow track. Old Red, Will's 1971 Dodge truck, looked right at home. The traditional farmer's truck was in many ways just like her dad: strong and reliable. Christina had christened the truck "Old Red" during high school when it was Emma's main mode of transportation around Juneberry.

She climbed up into the cab, peering through the dusty windshield. Emma turned the key in the ignition. She pulled open the choke, and with two quick stomps of the gas pedal, Old Red sprung to life.

"Attaboy."

She wrenched the knobby black shifter into first gear and rolled the truck out from the barn. Emma felt exhilaration and freedom when she cruised down SC59 toward downtown Juneberry. She had the rural highway all to herself so she opened Old Red up, accelerating his speed to nearly 55 miles per hour.

Emma entered Juneberry through the long stretch of North Main Street locals call Canopy Row. Maple and oak trees lined both sides of the street and joined in the middle to form a natural tunnel. With the autumn leaves already committed to their color change, the effect was like driving through a living red and gold swirl. City fathers had planted the trees a hundred years earlier, and Emma had long suspected they'd had this tunnel effect in mind.

At the other end of Canopy Row, Emma steered Old Red through historic downtown.

It was down the sidewalks of Main Street where Emma had ped-aled her bike as a young girl, making trips to the library, where her love of learning blossomed. It was on Juneberry's downtown city streets that Emma and Christina cruised during high school, listening to country radio stations out of Columbia and laughing as they shook off the stress of AP classes. It was on these quaint Southern streets that she and Michael had strolled together that one blissful summer before she left for law school.

Michael Evans.

She could still remember the warmth of their hands together as they walked downtown. She could still remember the feeling of "just perfect" that defined those moments together. But that was a long time ago.

Emma parked Old Red in front of Ace Hardware on Main, across from Brown's Drug Store. The tall neon sign out front bearing its name hadn't changed. She wondered if they still lit it up at night in the summer. People seemed happy then just to eat an ice-cream cone from Baskin-Robbins and stroll up Main Street window shopping.

A gust of wind pinned Emma's collar up and whipped her hair around her face as she crossed the street. She pressed open the glass door at Brown's Drug Store with ease and stepped inside. A bell jingled as the door swung open. She saw a familiar face at work behind the counter.

"Miss Emma Madison. How are you today?"

"Eric Brown? I haven't seen you since high school."

Emma approached the elevated counter where Eric worked as a second-generation pharmacist.

"Been right here. Are you still up in, New York, Boston, some-place like that?"

"Still in Boston. I just came back to see my dad."

"Yeah, sorry to hear what happened. How's he doing?"

"Much better thanks. He's coming home today. In fact, have you gotten a call from Wellman Medical? I'm supposed to pick up some prescriptions."

"Yes, they just called. I can have them ready in about thirty minutes."

"Okay, great. I've got just enough errands in town to fill that time. I'll be back to pick them up."

"They'll be ready."

Emma exited the front door of Brown's and walked to the curb to recross Main Street. Another strong gust of wind blew. She looked up to see storm clouds appearing from out of the west, and the grainy sky meant that rainfall was looming.

As she crossed Main on her way back to Old Red, Emma noticed a white Chevy truck parked behind her. A sign stenciled in black on the driver's-side door advertised a local business:

Michael Evans Construction
Carpentry • Roofing • Repair
803 …

A man wearing a red and black flannel shirt, blue jeans, and brown work boots walked out of the hardware store carrying a roofing bundle. He lowered the shingles from his shoulder letting them fall into the back of his pickup truck. As the roofing shingles fell away from his face, Emma got her first good look at the man.

"Michael?" Emma said, surprised to meet him on the street.

He turned in Emma's direction and stopped dead in his tracks.

"Emma Madison," he said, walking around the side of the truck. "I wondered if it was you driving Old Red."

They shook hands in a cordial greeting, touching them once again on Main Street, but in a way so different than before.

"Yep, it's me."

"Someone mentioned you might be back in town. How's your dad doing?"

"He's good. I was just picking something up from the pharmacy for him. How are you?"

"I'm good," Michael replied, his expression matching his words. Emma motioned to the door sign on Michael's truck.

"Looks like you've got your own company now."

Michael grinned. "It's just me and Bo Wilson. You remember Bo?"

"Yes, of course. I can just picture the two of you building Juneberry houses together."

Michael's face was sun-painted, rugged, and tan. Probably from pounding nails all summer long in the hot South Carolina sun.

"Still up in Boston?" he asked.

"Yes," she said. "Still in Boston. I'm a part of a law firm there."

Michael nodded.

Still in Boston ... part of a law firm there.

That was their story in a nutshell, reviewed in its entirety in just a few precious seconds. The love, the breakup, the move, and a career far away in a big-city law firm.

"Well, you did it," he finally said. "You chased your dreams and you caught 'em. That's something to be real proud of."

The first drops of rain dripped onto their clothes. Emma looked up again to find that the once-blue sky was rapidly changing to a high-altitude landscape of billowing silver.

"And you're building houses," she said, ignoring the rain.

"One at a time," Michael said. "We're working on the old Macintosh place up on the hill right now. Putting up a new roof."

"Oh, I'm sorry. Am I keeping you?" Emma asked.

Just then the skies opened up. A spirited gust of wind struck sideways as thick pellets of rain fell from the heavens. Instinctively, Michael reached out to Emma and pulled her beneath the safety of a nearby shop awning.

"Not anymore. Once the rains come, we have sense enough to climb off the rooftop. How long are you here for?" he asked.

"Probably until Friday. I just wanted to make sure my dad's okay."

Inside, Emma felt a strange sense of urgency. Maybe it was guilt or some feeling of remorse, but she wanted an opportunity with Michael to set things right. She wanted to talk with him again. Maybe this unexpected trip back home would provide just such an opportunity. After all, she wasn't the twenty-two-year-old girl who fled Juneberry twelve years earlier. She was stronger now.

"Michael, I'd like to talk to you sometime when you're free. Do you need to get back to work?" she shouted over the nearly deafening noise of the rainfall. Michael rolled his eyes up at the rain. It was a comedic gesture to point out impracticality of working outside in so much water.

"Not if I don't want to."

"Well, I'm sure not driving anywhere in this."

"Have you had breakfast yet?" he shouted over the sound of the rain hitting the aluminum awning.

"I'd love to have some coffee."

The rain blew sideways in sheets down Main Street. Puddles formed in an instant, rivers poured into gutters and flowed through drains. Car wipers changed from off to heavy, and pedestrians fled for cover.

"We've got that … if we can just make it to the bakery."

Emma watched Michael as he scouted the driest path to Meredith's Bakery, a block away. It startled her when she realized *she knew what he was thinking*. Michael was working out how to protect her from the rain. His protection, it had always been there that summer, maybe even before.

"If we keep on this side of the street," he said, "we'll do all right."

They took off in a bolt. It was like running inside a car wash. At Third Avenue, Michael pressed a guiding hand gently against the center of Emma's back to prevent her from slipping. Back beneath the safety of the canvas awnings, Emma smoothed the rain away from her face, and pulled back her hair. They had managed to stay surprisingly dry.

The last twenty feet to the front door of Meredith's was entirely uncovered. Raindrops the size of gumdrops splashed in on them from all directions. They reached the bakery doors dripping wet.

"Made it," Michael announced.

Emma laughed. "The last time I was this wet, I was underwater."

Meredith's Bakery had already responded to customer requests by turning on the heat early into September. They stood in front of the glass counter where the blower blasted out its dry heat. Soon their clothes were dry and their skin warmed.

"I'll find us a table," Michael said.

Emma watched him walk away, around the corner, and out of sight. Staring through the bakery glass at Meredith's world-famous sticky buns, she wondered if the words would come. Could the star attorney from Adler, McCormick & Madison find the right words to explain how she'd become a missing person in the lives of those she loved? There was a second option, of course. It occurred to her as she stood there in the front of the blower watching Michael come back to her from the other room. She could avoid unearthing the whole mess and leave again just as she had before.

~ FIVE ~

Surprise, your new love has arrived
Out of the blue clear sky.

—GEORGE STRAIT
"Blue Clear Sky"

The inside of Meredith's Bakery brimmed with the smells of sugary cinnamon and fresh-baked, oven-warm breads. The atmosphere was inviting and cozy, a dry homey shelter where patrons could find warmth in more ways than one. The exposed brick interior, hanging wicker baskets, and homespun wooden tables and chairs welcomed them like family. Despite the rains, or maybe because of them, the midmorning crowd was light, and the continuing downpour outside almost guaranteed it would stay that way.

Michael had picked out a table in front of the large window in the main dining room. He rejoined Emma as the woman behind the sales counter was telling her about the day's specials. They ordered coffee and a large sticky bun to share. Michael paid, left a dollar in the tip jar, and carried their food back to the table.

He was the same as she remembered him. If there were any differences, it was in ways that seemed to only improve his looks. Michael's twentysomething physique was now the broad-shouldered look of a fully developed man in his midthirties. He wore a day's stubble on his face, a perk of being his own boss. He was no longer a young man with lots of growing up to do—this Michael was the picture of confidence and strength.

"I wondered if I'd see you," she said finally, when it felt like someone should say something. "On the plane coming down here, I mean. I didn't know if that would be a good idea or not. I just thought, *What if?* I wondered what I'd say."

"You don't have to say anything," he told her. "It was a long time ago, and I don't want you to feel like there's anything that needs to be explained. I assumed you just did what you had to do. End of story."

Emma fidgeted in her chair. The sky outside the window over Michael's shoulder looked bleak and colorless, the rain continued in a steady downpour, and the sidewalks were empty. They heard a crack of thunder.

"It's really not the end of the story, Michael. There's a lot you don't know. I've had this conversation with you in my head so many times, but now that I'm here, it's hard to put everything into words. I'm just sorry, and I want you to know that."

Michael shrugged as if to say her words didn't mean anything, or that it didn't matter anymore. She wondered what he was thinking. Lazy summer days spent underneath a blue sky have a habit of sticking with you. Lying down together on the picnic blanket, holding each other and staring up at the sky in that wide-open country. Surely he remembered that. But how did that make him feel?

"That doesn't tell me much about why, Emma. I thought we were in the middle of great story, and just when it really started to get interesting, I turned a page to find the rest of the book was blank."

"I know," she said, because this was exactly how the conversation always played out in her mind.

"You went to Boston without looking back, and I got myself to work building houses. Without digging through all the minutiae of how I picked myself up, wiped away the tears, and dusted off the heartache, there's really not any more to say."

"I'm sorry," she said, again. "That's not how I would do things today. There were reasons why I left that you don't know about. I really don't want to go into those, but they have nothing to do with you. It's complicated. I'm trying to explain what I can here, but I don't think it's doing much good."

"Do you remember that summer, Emma?" Michael asked, leaning back in his chair. His question brought many memories to mind, but one in particular. The Fourth of July barbecue, the smell of charcoal and lighter fluid, her dad grilling steaks in the backyard, setting up the net for a game of volleyball. The laughter and the water fight, and how good the picnic food tasted with just the three of them eating under the shade of the lonesome willows. The wide-open fields around the house were green and alive with acres of sweet corn. When the moon came out, she and Michael held hands and walked up to the big barn to sit together under the stars in near silence, accompanied by just a whisper of music from Old Red's radio.

"Yes, of course."

"Well, I remember it too. So I'm not going to be angry with you, Emma. Not after twelve years. I loved you too much to spoil your memory with bitterness, and I cherish my life too much now to try and settle up the past with nickel-and-dime words."

Michael got up from the table. The rain outside had slowed.

"It's like that old saying: You open the bird cage door, and the bird flies away. If it comes back, it's yours. If it doesn't, it never was."

"Please, don't say it like that. There was never any cage."

"And there isn't one now."

Michael started to walk out of Meredith's. He took one step toward the door, stopped, then turned back around.

"I don't know if you feel some kind of guilt or remorse about the past; I just haven't figured all this out. But I'll tell you what, Emma, when you burn a bridge, you have to be prepared to live with some ashes. It's just the way it is."

Emma watched Michael walk out the door without looking back. A moment later, she followed, more convinced than ever of the mess she'd made. Samantha had wanted to know why, and Michael didn't. It was a toss-up which one felt more unsettling. It had stopped raining completely. The streets of Juneberry were dotted with puddles, and the air crackled with the scent that comes after a heavy autumn rain.

Emma picked up her father's prescriptions at Brown's Drug Store, climbed back into Old Red, and set the package beside her on the passenger seat. Starting the truck, she switched on the wiper blades to clear off the last remaining drops of rain before making her way home.

Emma hurt for what she'd done to Michael. If only mistakes could be washed away like the rain. But she didn't have a choice then, Emma reminded herself—not a serious one. After all, it wasn't an error in judgment that caused her to leave. No more wrong than leaving a blue underwater world for the life-giving oxygen above.

Emma could clear it all up if she told them the truth—her father, Samantha, Christina, and Michael. She could just dig up the precious jewelry box she'd buried in the cool South Carolina mud and show them all what lay inside.

Her heart raced at the thought. Then she said the words out loud.

"I'm not that child anymore. I won't be afraid any longer."

On route SC59 between downtown Juneberry and home, Emma's cell phone rang. She picked it up off the vinyl seat and answered it.

"Hello?"

"Emma? Hey, it's Colin."

"Colin?"

"Yeah, you sound surprised. How is everything down there?"

"Everything's fine," she said, adjusting to one far-off world intruding into another. "Thanks for checking on me. Are you at the office?"

"No, I'm in my car. I just bought a new cell phone."

"I thought you just bought a new cell phone in July?"

"I did, but I didn't like it. This one's a PDA, but it still feels like a cell phone, plus it plays video, too. So tell me, what's going on with your father?"

"There's good news. He's coming home today."

"That is good news. The sooner he's home and settled in, the sooner you can get back where you belong."

The signal from Colin's phone was remarkably clear. It sounded like he was calling from across the street.

"I'll need to keep an eye on him for a few more days. Sorry to employ such an old cliché, but I'm taking this one day at a time."

"Those old clichés work for a reason. How are you doing with all this?"

"That's a good question. In lots of ways, I prefer the law. Its a lot harder when you have to humble yourself and make things right with people."

"What?"

"Sorry," she said. "I'm not making sense. There's a lot on my mind, I guess."

"Couldn't you bring in a home-care nurse?"

"No, it's not that. I was referring to a much older story."

"Do I detect some history?"

"Maybe."

Emma turned Old Red onto Mills Road, or as Christina always called it, "Madison Avenue." Just a half mile more and she'd be home.

"At least you've got your friends. Someone to talk to about it, right?"

"Right," she said, as if her talks with Samantha and Michael that morning had both gone well. "It'll all work out."

"I want you to know I'm here, Emma. I mean, if you need anything. I'm just now pulling into my building. I know from experience that the signal goes out when I'm underground so I'm going to let you go."

"Thanks for calling, Colin. I appreciate you checking in with me, and I wouldn't mind talking again sometime if you …"

Emma listened for a few seconds until it was obvious the line had gone dead.

~ S I X ~

The elevator doors opened and Emma stepped out onto the fourth floor at Wellman Medical. The hospital didn't feel so foreign anymore after being there most of the day before. Dena Johnson greeted Emma.

"He's all ready to go home."

"You do good work around here," Emma replied. "I had no idea he'd be coming home so soon. It's quite a relief."

Dena made her way around the open end of the crescent-shaped workstation. She was dressed in another cheerful smock, this one a Tweety Bird print.

"He's been chomping at the bit to get out of here, but the process is actually going faster than normal. Usually a patient's moved off ICU before getting released, but it worked out in this case just to release him home."

"Dena, I've been so delighted with the care he's received, both from you and his doctors. I don't know how to say thank you."

"You're welcome. He's been a great patient. Wish they could all be that way." Dena smiled, then paused before continuing. "Do you have a moment?"

"Sure," Emma said. Dena led her away from the nurses' station to a private corner in the hall.

"I don't know why, but I really feel moved to share something with you. I was on duty yesterday when you're dad was admitted to ICU. He was my patient, and I got a chance to talk to him. I just thought you should know that the minute he knew you were coming in from Boston, his condition rapidly improved—not just his demeanor, but his body's response to treatment as well. I know it was a sacrifice for you to drop everything and come down here. I just thought you'd like to know, from a medical standpoint, I think your being here really made a difference."

"Thank you for telling me this. My dad has always been there for me, but I can't say I've always been there for him. This was a wake-up call."

Dena nodded that she understood. She had a father too.

"Well, let's go get him and let you take him home."

Dena moved Will downstairs by wheelchair to the front entrance, brushing off his protests that he could walk, and staying with him until Emma brought the Cadillac around to pick him up. She'd decided to bring the good car since it was easier to climb into than Old Red.

"I can get in by myself," Will protested. "I could drive this car if I had to."

"Oh, that reminds me, Mr. Madison," Dena said. "Remember, no driving for a while. Doctor's orders."

Dena shut the passenger-side door and waved them off before heading back inside the hospital. Emma pushed the button, and Will heard the Cadillac's automatic door locks bolt shut.

"Ugh, what a sound."

"You don't like that?"

"After being cooped up in a hospital bed for a day and a half, no," Will said, a rare agitation entering his voice. "Sorry, hon. I'm just not a sit-around kind of guy. The doctor wants me to change all the foods I eat, and now I can't even drive my own car."

"And ... you have to buckle up your seat belt too. Sorry, Dad."

Will made a sound like he was chewing on aspirin.

"I think once we get you home and settled we'll both feel better."

As smooth as ice, Emma rolled the Cadillac away from the covered loading zone, and minutes later they were on Stoney River Road taking the scenic route around the lake. In ten minutes, Will Madison would be back in his own house where he belonged, but what then? Emma's twelve-year absence from the Madison farmhouse spoke clearly that it wasn't where she thought she belonged. The uncomfortable silence inside the luxury sedan spoke volumes.

"It's good to see you home," he said, breaking the silence. She nodded. It was one thing to treat a heart attack, quite another to treat a wounded heart. Emma glanced down at her father's ringless left hand. She was keenly aware of what it meant to grow up without a mother. The memories she had of her mom were a thin scrapbook with no entries past the age of five. She'd turned those yellowed pages over and over again in her mind. She wondered if he had a scrapbook filled with memories of the wife he'd loved and lost. Did he wish it were not Emma bringing him home but Hannah?

"Don't worry about me," he said.

"What? I'm not worried. I'm happy you're coming home. You'll be more comfortable propped up in your easy chair."

"That's not what I meant."

Emma parked the Cadillac close to the side porch. She walked around the car and helped her father walk into the house. She hooked the car keys next to Old Red's on the key post by the door.

"How long can you stay?" he asked.

"I haven't planned my return flight yet. Probably Friday."

"Trips are always like bookends," he said. "The first one's called 'coming home,' and the other one's called 'going back.' They're always inseparable."

Emma threaded her arm though her father's, helping him to walk into the dining room, and on into the comfortable living room. She'd always loved that room. Recessed white bookshelves filled with everything from history books to novels to framed photographs and souvenirs. The decor hadn't changed in the time she'd been away. A colonial plaid sofa lined one wall, bordered by dark pine coffee and end tables tinted in ebony. Magazines filled the caramel-colored V-shaped rack on the floor next to his reading chair. The house smelled like spiced cinnamon. That was her addition.

"How'd you get the house to smell like this?" he asked.

"I thought it'd be nice to come home to. It's something I picked up in town."

Emma settled Will into his reading chair in front of the television, fishing the remote control from the top drawer of the table next to him and setting it on his arm rest.

"Are you hungry?" she asked him.

"Starved. You wouldn't believe what they had me eating in there."

"I'll make some lunch," she said.

On her trip into town to pick up her father, Emma had noticed the "We're Open" sign in front of the Whitfields' Orchard. She'd purchased a half-dozen Golden Delicious apples. Emma collected them from the Cadillac, emptied them into a stainless steel colander, and set them to rinse in the sink. On the countertop was a wooden cutting board and a set of kitchen knifes sitting upright in a block. Emma clutched the wooden handle of the paring knife with wet hands and pulled the first apple out to slice it in half. She quartered it, removed its dark brown seeds, then sliced each of the quarters once more.

A sharp flash of recognition pierced Emma, a memory so vivid and real she almost cut herself with the edge of the knife. Water continued flowing from the tap, making a staticlike noise as it cascaded over the apples. Emma stood there, frozen. Snapshots of decades-old images of her mother, Hannah Madison, standing at the kitchen sink cutting apples flashed before her eyes.

Her hands trembled as she relived the visual memory, seeing her mother standing at the sink, from the viewpoint of a child's eyes.

Emma laid the knife on its side. She could almost sense her mother's presence in the room. Inexplicably, she spun around suddenly just to confirm she was alone.

Emma shook off the feeling, shut off the water, and picked up the plate of apples, carrying them into the den.

She set the apples on the table next to her father's chair. Will looked at the apples, then up at Emma.

"I wasn't expecting a cheeseburger, but can't we do better than this?"

"The doctor said you'd have to change the way you eat. I thought these might be a step in the right direction."

Will picked out an apple slice and bit into it like he might never see real food again.

"In case you're wondering, I'm also making you a chicken omelet with red and green bell peppers. I'll go to the store later and do some shopping."

Will muted the volume on the TV and turned his attention to Emma.

"I don't mean to give you a hard time, it's been an … eventful couple of days. What is important is that you know how glad I am that you came back home. It's been too long, Emma."

She sat down in the chair across from him.

"You don't have a child yet, but take it as the gospel truth: When you become a parent, there isn't a day, and sometimes not even an hour, when you don't think about them."

"Are you angry with me, Dad? You have every right to be."

"I'm not angry with you, Emma. I don't have anything to be angry about. I'm grateful we've talked on the phone from time to time, more grateful you've come back to help me."

"It's not that I didn't care," she said.

"I know. If you didn't care, you wouldn't be here."

Will bridged the space between the two chairs, the space between the two of them. He placed his left hand on hers.

"I've learned to appreciate what I've got, Emma. I'm not going to waste an ounce of energy on sorting through the past or with worrying about the future. Life's too short for that."

"I love you," she told him, wondering if he'd ever doubted it.

"I love you, too," he said. "In the end it's all that really matters."

Emma saw something new in her father's eyes, a deeper sense of peace, which she explained to herself as probably being a result of the heart attack.

"I'm thinking about starting a fire in the fireplace. Would you like that, Dad?"

"That would be nice, but I feel like I should be doing something."

"You are. You're getting some rest."

After lunch, Will fell asleep in his easy chair, a few golden apple wedges left uneaten on the plate. A fire crackled beside him in the stone fireplace.

The phone rang while Emma cleaned up the kitchen, wiping down the cutting board and setting it in the dish rack next to the sink. She tossed aside the damp towel and picked up the receiver.

"Hello."

"Hi, Emma, it's Christina. I wanted to call you and check up on you and your dad."

"He's resting here in his own home now. I think we both feel better about that."

Emma leaned against the kitchen counter, holding the phone next to her ear and twisting the black cord underneath her arm, just the way she had in high school.

"Wonderful. I want to hear all about how you're doing too, so I was wondering if you'd be interested in coming over for lunch tomorrow? If your dad can be on his own."

"I would love to do that."

"Perfect! Let's make it twelve noon."

"Yeah, twelve noon. I'll see you then."

Emma hung up the phone and walked quietly back into the den to check on her father. Will had slept for over an hour. She was considering whether he'd be more comfortable in his own bed when her presence in the room stirred him.

"Sorry. I didn't mean to wake you."

"You didn't," Will said, clearing his throat. "I just dozed a little, that's all."

Will rubbed his eyes with the heels of his hands, and pulled himself upright in his chair.

"I'm not used to being idle. I'm not used to dropping the ball for my clients either. Tomorrow, I'm going to need you to drive me into Columbia so I can work at my office."

Emma's face tightened.

"Dad, you know you're not supposed to go back to work for six weeks."

"I'm not going to do anything strenuous. It's not like I'm a litigator any longer, but I do have responsibilities. More likely than not, my clients aren't even aware yet of what's happened. I'll need to contact them and make some arrangements.

"Dad, you understand you've had a heart attack, right? That makes you more susceptible to having another." Emma was hesitant to preach to her own father, but it was too early in his recovery to entertain thoughts of cutting corners. Emma sat in the chair next to his.

"I know making changes is hard, but if you overextended ... well, next time you might not be so lucky. Now is the time to revamp a few things, like eating healthier foods, and managing your stress. You can't just go back to your normal life."

Will scratched the back of his neck and cocked his head toward Emma.

"I know there's going to be some changes, but do you honestly think I can sit here watching television and working jigsaw puzzles for the next month?"

"No, I don't expect you to do that, but if you start going to the office one day a week, before you know it, you'll be there Monday, Wednesday, Friday. It's not just the office either, it's the long commute to Columbia, and the pressure from clients that Dr. Anderson's concerned about."

"It's not like I can operate from home," Will said. "If I don't go into work, I'll hardly have contact with the outside world. You're not going to be here forever."

"Of course," Emma said. "That's it!" She sat upright in the wing-back chair. "What if we create a proper working environment here at home so you wouldn't have to commute? We could set up a computer, get you hooked up to the Internet, and you'd have e-mail here at the house. You could work when you wanted to."

Will looked around the den.

"And where do you see this office sprouting up? I don't think there's room, unless you're suggesting we set up a laptop on the dining-room table."

"What about making a few changes to the house?" she said, the excitement of the idea's momentum filling her voice.

"A few changes? You mean tear the house apart? Why didn't I think of that," he said, smiling.

Emma stood and walked from the den to the entryway, surveying the house like a treasure hunter looking for the "X" on a map. Emma spotted the half-open door to the guest bedroom.

"What about turning the downstairs bedroom into a home office?" she said, turning to face her father.

"That's my storage room. I like it just as it is."

Emma charged back into the den animated by a good idea.

"Dad, that would be a great space for a home office."

Emma and Will walked down the hallway and pushed open the bedroom door. It creaked like the door of an old forgotten chamber. They stepped beyond the threshold without speaking.

Inside the ten-by-eight-foot room was a double bed with a brass frame. A dusty rose-colored bedspread neatly made and decorated with pillows covered the mattress. Above the bed hung a pastel water-color print of a bouquet of roses with faded red petals and green leaves. Against the wall stood a tall chest of drawers—an antique Will bought just after his wedding. A delicate lace doily decorated the surface, and in its center was a wedding photograph of Will and Hannah. They both looked at the photo in silence.

"This room hasn't changed at all," Emma said. "Has it gotten any use as a guest room?"

"Not much, but your mother liked the room put together like this. After she passed away, I just decided to leave it this way."

A narrow double window on the long wall let in the room's only light through a sheer curtain, as white as a wedding veil. From the bed the window looked like a frame around a picture of the farm. Emma touched the bedspread with her fingertips. It felt textured and soft like a tightly knitted sweater.

"So it's never been used?" Emma asked, still looking down at the fabric, feeling its pattern against the side of her thumb. Wondering if the sensations would trigger another memory.

"I didn't say that. When your mother got too sick to climb the stairs, this was her room. She liked seeing the farm outside her window, hearing the cowbirds and wrens in the trees."

Emma turned to look at her father. He let out a long exhale and walked over to lean his back against the windowsill.

"That's the chair she liked," he said, pointing to an old Shaker rocking chair in the corner behind the door. "She used to rock you in that chair, praying over you."

"I didn't know any of this," Emma said. "I shouldn't have suggested changing the room. Let's just forget it."

"Maybe that's why we *should* change it, Emma, because it's a room packed with memories. Maybe it keeps me thinking about the last months of her life after she was frail and sick when I should keep focus on all the good times."

"I'm really embarrassed. We can come up with another idea for your office."

Will reached for Emma's hand and gave it a playful bounce.

"Emma, I think you came up with a good idea. We should change this room. It should have been done a long time ago."

"Are you sure?" she asked him.

"Positive. It's a little tight for space, but once we get the bed and everything else out of here, it will look a whole lot bigger."

"Until we bring in office furniture …" Emma said. "Isn't the pantry on the other side of this wall?"

Will focused his gaze on the wall behind the headboard where the painting of a rose hung.

"Yes, I think it is."

"If we knocked out that wall, there would be plenty of room."

Will raised his eyebrows. He knew that was a big job, more than they could handle.

"Michael Evans could probably do it. Right? I mean he has his own construction company …"

It would mean a lot of changes to the house, but Will Madison was ready for change, not only to his home, but also his life. He liked the idea of working on a renovation project with his daughter, even more than the prospect of having a home office.

"Why don't you ask if he could come by? I'm not saying we should start knocking down walls, but I'm open to hearing his ideas."

It was an act of humility and selfless love that brought Emma to the kitchen phone. She paused before lifting the receiver, hearing her dad's hard-soled shoes on the stairs as he went to his room for another nap. Was she really about to call Michael and ask for a favor?

She picked up the receiver and cradled it between her neck and shoulder.

The number stenciled on the side of Michael's work truck had been easy to remember. She pointed her finger inside the rotary dial and spun the numbers.

The phone rang once.

Michael made it clear he didn't like how things had ended after their last rendezvous twelve years before. But she needed his help just the same, even if it meant eating a slice of humble pie. The phone rang a second time.

She sat on one of the kitchen's hard oak chairs, listening to the third ring and realizing she'd probably have to leave a message on his machine when Michael finally answered.

"Hi, Michael. It's Emma."

"Hi," he said.

"I've got a question for you. Do you remember when you asked if my dad needed help with anything?"

"Yeah."

"Well, there may be something you can help us with. I was … we were wondering if you'd come look at the downstairs bedroom here at the house. We're thinking of renovating it. I don't know what your schedule is like, but I figured it couldn't hurt to ask."

"It's been awhile since I was … do you mean the downstairs bedroom off the hallway?"

"Yes. We think that bedroom would be a great space for an office."

"I built a home office for Bonnie Lloyd so she could sell real estate and still be home with her girls. Sure, I could come and take a look. It might a simple renovation."

"There's also a pantry space behind the back wall. We think that might be a way to add some extra room."

"Okay, that's a little more involved but easy to do. I'd have to come out to the farm again and take a look. The only tough part is adding a new project to the schedule. We're committed to working out here on the Macintosh place for another week, unless we get rain. Sounds like your job would be all indoors though."

"I think so," Emma said, feeling a little guilty about requesting something of Michael. He'd always been there when she needed him, but where was the evidence she'd ever returned in kind?

"Last I saw, the weather guy was saying mostly sunny the rest of the week. I'll come by either tomorrow after work or Friday to take a look at it."

"Michael, thank you," Emma said. After a brief, uncomfortable silence, she continued. "I'm sorry for how our conversation went at the bakery. I know that was … awkward. It means a lot that you're willing to help out my dad."

"That's the deal, Emma. It's what I'm here for," Michael's voice was surprisingly sweet and light, his words skipping like stones thrown across a calm pond.

Emma hung up the phone and glanced out the window at the sky. It was more blue than white and that disappointed her. She might not be in Juneberry for the completion of the project, but she wanted to at least be in town when Michael started it. She climbed the stairs, heading to her bedroom for a nap.

As she lay down, Emma thought about how awkward she felt asking Michael for help; about how kind her childhood friends were to her even though she didn't reach out with a similar generosity. She thought of her father and the grace he'd offered her over the years and across the miles. These were good people. But there were gaps, holes in her relationships with them. Holes she had dug.

"I have no idea how to fix this," she said.

Emma drew a pained breath and reminded herself that in just a couple of days she'd be back in Boston where all of her trials were fought inside a courtroom. At least there she knew the rules, she knew how to solve the problems.

Then she rolled over to face the bedroom window on the second floor and looked out over the farmland, watching the clouds grazing the sky like white buffalo.

~ SEVEN ~

Someday, some way,
you'll realize that you've been blind
Yes, darling, you're going to need me again
It's just a matter of time.

—BROOK BENTON
"It's Just a Matter of Time"

"So, have you agreed to go out with him yet?" Lara Gilmor said. She was the firm's youngest and newest associate attorney, and like Emma, was single. Emma and Lara often took lunches together at a small Thai food restaurant near Chinatown. It was the kind of Boston eatery where you could get in and out in an hour.

"Who? Colin?"

"Yes, Colin. Who else? He's such a hottie and he's obviously smitten with you."

"Lara, I can't believe you," Emma held her cell phone in one hand and a paper grocery sack in the other. "Nothing could be further from my mind these last few days."

"Emma, how is it that even smart girls can become so dense when it comes to the subject of men and dating? Colin is so the one for you. He's a successful lawyer with great teeth and a six-figure, high-rise salary. You'd be crazy to let him stay on the market."

"You make him sound like a prized ham in a butcher-shop window."

"He is, and you need to ring him up in the express lane, get him bagged, and bring him home."

"That's just gross. Get him bagged?"

Emma pulled a bag of fresh tomatoes from her grocery sack and set them on the counter.

"It's not gross, it's practical," Lara said, reaching into the top drawer of her desk and sliding a red Twizzler from its bag. She bit into it. "When you find what you want in life, you just gotta go for it."

Emma tried to picture herself and Colin together. The two of them racing down to Cape Cod in his BMW for a getaway. Colin would talk to clients on his cell phone while he drove, and she would wonder why he had to talk to clients on the way to their getaway.

"I'm not sure he's my type."

"Colin is every woman's type. Tall, rich, and handsome … and rich."

"What's gotten you all excited about Colin anyway?"

"Oh, I don't know. He stopped by the office this morning to meet with Robert. He chatted with me awhile, gave me the news about your dad, and he asked me about you, of course. Want my opinion? He's seriously missing you."

Emma stuffed a head of lettuce and bag of carrots in the refrigerator crisper. She folded the paper grocery bag in thirds and stashed it in a lower cupboard.

"Why did Colin meet with Robert?"

"He didn't say, but it must have been important. Their meeting went on for over an hour. It was business, but I can't tell you what kind."

"Hmm, that's interesting."

Lara bit into her Twizzler again.

"I guess, but now you're avoiding the subject. *If* Colin were to ask you out, what would you tell him?"

"He already has, Lara, and I told him I see us only as friends."

"I can't believe you!" Lara said in mock disgust. "You've got to get back up here as quick as humanly possible so I can talk some sense into you."

Emma watched out the window as the wind shook the leaves from a maple tree.

"I don't know. I've always thought there's one special person out there for each of us, and I think when it happens, we know. I don't think we have to be talked into it."

"I'm not talking you into anything except popping open those eyelids of yours to see this special person who seems to have found *you*. I mean, if you're not gonna go for him, maybe I should … oh, never mind. So when *are* you coming back to civilization?"

"I don't know yet."

"Robert is under the impression you'll be back on Friday."

"I know. I'll talk to him. He knows my situation."

"You're not getting any heat from me. We all just want to see you take care of things, and get back up here where you belong as quickly as possible."

Michael agreed to stop by the Madison farm as soon as he and Bo finished the roof at the Macintosh place, or when rain fell, whichever came first. The following morning all of Juneberry awoke to the sound of a steady September downpour. Michael heard the rain as he lay in bed.

Before the weakened sun rose to reveal the morning's gloominess, Michael called Bo to officially cancel their planned work. He stood at the gas stove in his kitchen and fried eggs, sunny-side up, for breakfast. But his mind wasn't on breakfast. He was recalling one of his earliest memories of Emma. He was in the seventh grade and she was just a fifth grader. During recess, he taught her how to hit a softball. At first, he'd been frustrated by her impatience, but the way she reacted when her bat finally connected with the ball was enough to erase any uncertain feelings.

Their first dance came in high school—after Juneberry won their homecoming game. "Unchained Melody" had started playing when he asked her. They stayed friends throughout high school but didn't fall in love until that summer after she'd graduated. He didn't know the term *soul mates* back then, but thought of the two of them as "cuff-link love," matching pieces made to go together.

"Women are like fine jewelry," Michael told Bo one day. "Men are like the strong black boxes that hold the jewelry. You know the ones I mean? Women are the beautiful works of art, and men are there to appreciate their beauty, to surround and protect them."

The moment he said it out loud, Michael knew that's how he felt about Emma. When he saw her that night after work, he kissed her like she was the most precious diamond in the entire world. If a picture paints a thousand words, a kiss paints what words can never say. When the day came that she told him she was leaving, all Michael could ask was "Why?" It was a question she could not answer. A question she still hadn't answered. But when she asked him to help her father the day before, *his* answer had come easily.

When Michael pushed the doorbell, thunder boomed and rolled a long, seemingly unending rumble. He laughed at the coincidental timing and hoped the weather wasn't a foreshadowing of what awaited him inside. He wore his denim work clothes, but had second-guessed his attire more than once on the drive over. Raindrops darkened small ash-colored dots on his shoulders.

Emma opened the door.

"Michael," she said.

"Looks like a good day to be working indoors."

"Yes, it does. Won't you come in?"

Emma pulled open the heavy front door. Michael came into the foyer and shook the rainwater off, shuffling his feet across a floor mat that looked to be made from some sort of coarse natural fiber.

"I want you to know how much I appreciate this," Emma said. "I'm sure when my dad comes downstairs he'll want to tell you the same thing."

"It's no problem," he said, looking around the entryway. "It's been awhile since I've been inside the old place."

"It hasn't changed much. Do you want to take a look at the room?"

"Sure."

Emma led him down the front hallway. A narrow strip of red carpet ran through the center of the hall. Most of the downstairs was painted white. He remembered the intricate crown molding where the walls met the high ceiling, and the two fluted columns that stood at the entrance to the comfortable living room. He tried to ignore the memories that peeked around every corner, but they came anyway. The house was full of memories.

"This is the space we're thinking of changing," she said. "Dad's still sleeping upstairs, but we've tossed around a few ideas. We really want to hear yours."

The two stepped into the small room.

"It's a lot smaller than I remembered," Michael said.

Emma pointed to the back wall.

"On the other side of this wall is a pantry that really isn't needed. Do you think we could knock it down? The room really needs to be larger if at all possible."

"Maybe ..." Michael studied the room, taking it all in. He saw the closet running the length of the opposite wall.

"You've got another two feet of space if you're willing to take out this closet area."

Emma pulled open the sliding door and looked inside. The closet was jam-packed with old clothes, boxes, photo albums, and other evidences of family history.

"You can see how things stack up in these older closets. If you wanted, we could build new storage areas into the design of the room," Michael told her.

"I didn't know what was in here until just now," Emma said. "I suppose I'll have to sort through everything and clear it out for you."

"Do you have somewhere else to put this stuff?"

"I don't know. I'm not sure how much is stuff to keep and how much can be thrown away."

"Well, we could build a secondary workspace with a counter and cabinets above. It's a great way to include functionality with design."

"I like that."

Michael pointed to the ceiling.

"I think we can match this historic design in the new cabinets, too. As for this window, I'd recommend putting in insulated windows that will let in more natural light. Are you thinking of keeping the carpet? Or can that be removed?"

They examined the flat navy blue carpet beneath their feet.

"Looks like it's pretty worn. I suspect it can go," Emma said. "But I'm not sure what Dad will want to replace it with."

Michael moved the rocking chair to the center of the room and knelt down in the corner. He removed a utility knife from his work belt and pried up the carpet.

"Did you know you've got a hardwood floor underneath this old rug?"

Emma took a step closer to see.

"I thought we might find that, since there are hardwoods running through most of the house."

"Won't it be in bad shape?" Emma asked.

Michael stood, nearly bumping into Emma. She took a step backward to avoid him.

"We won't know until we pull this carpet out, but sometimes the carpet works like a shield and the flooring can look better than you'd expect."

"Do you want to see the pantry now?"

"Sure."

Emma and Michael walked to the back of the house and into the pantry.

"Well, this is it," said Emma. "It's kind of an all-purpose room."

Michael looked in.

"You're right. There's a lot of space in here, and I'll check, but it doesn't appear that the bedroom wall is load bearing. It shouldn't be a problem knocking it out."

"Sounds like you'll have your work cut out for you. Any ideas what a renovation like this would cost?"

Michael looked at Emma. She was looking around the room—anywhere but at him. Their conversation had been all business thus far.

"I don't know. I'll break down the costs for you. It shouldn't be too expensive."

"Thanks, Michael."

"This a great house. How soon do you want me to get started?"

"The sooner, the better. I mean … as soon as Dad agrees, of course."

"Well, we can get started right away if you want. Why don't you give me a hand clearing out the furniture. Once that's done, we'll take some measurements and then I can draw up a design plan. That will help me with the estimate, too."

"I'll get to work on clearing out the old closet."

⁂

Upstairs in the quiet of his room, Will Madison prayed. As he knelt down at the side of his bed, he felt the warmth of his breath against the wool bedcovers. With eyes closed, he uttered softly worded expressions of thankfulness and supplication. He didn't pray for his health, the heart inside his chest that had broken earlier that week. He didn't pray for relief from the broken heart he'd carried for so long. Will Madison prayed for his daughter, the second of two women he'd lost.

Hannah was the only woman he'd ever loved. They'd grown up together in Juneberry. At first, Will thought of their love as a game. He played the role of pursuer, wooing Hannah with his love antics in high school and through four years of college. She was full of beauty and life.

During the fall of their senior year at Clemson, a group of friends and classmates were talking about what they might do after college. When Hannah mentioned the possibility of moving to California, the reality hit Will that he couldn't live without her.

By Thanksgiving that year, he'd asked Hannah to marry him, and over Christmas break, they wed. She never broke his heart until she passed away at the young age of thirty-four. His consolation prize? A five-year-old daughter named Emma who he'd raise as a single parent, with a single-minded hope of never losing her.

Will steadied the wavering sound of his voice before the Lord; his gratitude showing in both words and tears. A decade of unceasing prayers had been answered after his heart stopped beating and he opened his eyes in a hospital bed to the beautiful face of his daughter.

"Lord, You have brought her back to me …

"Thank You for Your goodness. You are so kind to us."

The old man's voice broke as he whispered his heart to His God.

"I don't know how long she'll be here, Lord, but if there's any way You could …"

Will closed his eyes again, pressing out tears, quieting his voice. His prayer sounded selfish to his ears. How much more it must sound that way to God. He lowered his face to the bed, emptied himself of the illusion of control in his life. He thought of the heart attack that nearly took his life. A feeble yet sincere smile came to his lips. In a strange way, he was grateful for his heart attack. He would go through it again for a chance to see his daughter. Yes, God did indeed work in strange ways. He listened for, and heard, The Voice. The Silent Voice:

"I am in control of all things.
I am in control of you, and
I have your best interests in mind.
Rest."

Will Madison sat on the hardwood floor in his bedroom and leaned against the dark Shaker dresser, wiping tears from his eyes. He had confidence in an invisible God, certainty in unfulfilled promises. He drew in a calming, tremorless breath and pulled himself up to sit on the bed.

"Lord, You are so good to me, an ordinary man. How can I ever repay You? I trust You, and I am Yours."

Downstairs, Michael and Emma pulled the top mattress off of the bed, walking it in half steps out the narrow door, and down the hallway to the living room.

"Tell me more about your life in Boston."

"What do you want to know?"

"I dunno. Start at the beginning."

"Well, the beginning was a long time ago."

"Why Boston?"

"Hmm, that's a good question. I guess it sounded beautiful, a Northeastern city on the Atlantic Ocean. All that history. So different than … here."

"A complete change."

"Don't take it personally."

"I won't. Please continue."

"Well, I went to school. I was proud of what I'd accomplished. There are a lot of smart people there—I felt intimidated at first. But then I realized this was a chance to push myself—to find out what I really could do."

"When did you decide to become a lawyer?"

"It was in my third year. I'd seen all the law school students there on campus. Of course, my dad was a lawyer, and I just felt drawn to it. Maybe it was a bit naive of me, but I guess I really just wanted to help people. You know, give a few 'Davids' a chance to defeat the occasional Goliath."

Michael smiled.

They set the box springs next to the mattress in the living room and went back to the bedroom. Michael began loosening the long bolts connecting the headboard to the metal frame.

"How'd you end up at Harvard?"

"By accident, really. I met a Harvard law school professor while doing some volunteer work with inner-city families. He encouraged me to apply."

"Harvard law school."

"Yeah, I'm still not entirely sure why they ended up accepting me. Sometimes coming from a small town helps since they like a diverse student population."

Side by side, Michael and Emma lifted the antique headboard and carried it to the cluttered living-room floor. They set it down, gently leaning it against the sofa.

"I'm sorry, Michael," Emma said.

"Sorry, for what?"

"You know. For leaving to go to law school the way I did. I can't really explain it further than that …"

"You don't have to explain everything, Emma."

"No, but … it wasn't an easy decision."

"It should have been. How could you *not* go? Not everyone gets a chance to go to Harvard."

Emma pushed aside the thin, lacy curtain hanging on the bedroom window … like a bridal veil. The cold autumn rain continued to fall. Unraked leaves slept in scattered piles on top of the cropped green grass. She turned to face Michael.

"I don't know what to say," Emma said. "Some choices are harder than they appear. You can never say yes to one thing without saying no to another. Do you know what I mean?"

"Yeah," Michael said, stopping to look at Emma. "Everyone

knows what that means, but the part I'm a little fuzzy on is what you had to say no to."

Emma gave him a "you ought to know" look, but Michael didn't budge. He stood there, waiting.

"I had to say no to you," she said, like the words had pained her to speak them.

Michael stood unmoving for a moment, then walked over to Emma. Her arms were crossed to shut out the cold. He placed his strong hands on her shoulders, and she saw once again in his face the look of compassion and strength she trusted.

"I loved you," Michael said. "But you made the right decision. You were meant to go and do all the things you've done."

Emma spoke in tones lower than a whisper.

"Don't you ever feel a sense of loss? Like something that could have been wasn't?"

"Yeah," Michael said. "But it drove me crazy. For my own peace of mind, I had to find another way of looking at things."

Emma cleared her throat.

"Which was?"

"That things happen in life for a reason. As hard as it was losing you, I still put it all in the plus column. I mean, why keep grieving?"

Emma fell into Michael's embrace in the light of the window. He took her in, and she wrapped her arms around his waist. They stood motionless in an embrace that said little more than "I remember."

Emma pulled away from Michael and touched at the corner of her eyes.

"One of the partners at the firm has an old Rubik's Cube he keeps on his desk. It's one of those things you can't help but pick it up and try your hand at, turning all the squares," she said. "You try to twist sense out of the disorder. Have you ever played with one of those?"

"Yes," Michael said. "But I've never been able to put it in order."

"Me neither. And that's exactly how I feel about everything. I've tried to turn the scrambled pieces round and round the cube until they all make sense, but they still aren't in place."

"Emma, there are a lot of people still turning scrambled pieces round and round."

Emma closed her eyes, then hugged Michael again, enjoying familiar comfort in the strong arms of Michael's friendship—arms that were once so much more. She rested her face against his chest.

A moment passed. And then another. Then she stepped out of the embrace, gently.

"What about you?" Emma asked. "Are you settled? What's your Rubik's Cube look like these days?"

"I got lucky, I think. The puzzle I started with already had most of its pieces in place."

Emma smacked him on the chest.

"Lucky you. So you earn your living by carpentry. What was left in the puzzle for you to unscramble?" She kneeled at the closet door to begin the work of unpacking the boxes of memories and uncertain treasures.

"I'd rather not say."

Outside, the rain tapped mysterious Morse-code messages on stubborn leaves and ran rivers through the gutters.

"Okay, don't say," Emma said. "So what makes things so good these days?"

"I've got friends like Bo who I've known all my life. I know everybody in Juneberry. My parents still live here. I've worked on a hundred houses in town, so I guess being here makes things make sense even when it feels like they don't."

"I guess some people find what they're looking for in faraway places, and for others it's right where they started," she said.

"Friends make the difference, Emma. There are some things we just can't unscramble on our own."

Emma stood suddenly.

"I think I'll go check on my dad. Do you feel like a cup of coffee this morning?"

Michael nodded, "Yeah, coffee sounds great."

Emma walked out of the room. Her footsteps tapped a hollow rhythm as she ascended the stairs.

"You were the final piece of the puzzle," Michael said to the empty room.

~ EIGHT ~

The only thing that you've ever known is to run ...
but everybody needs somebody sometimes.

—KEITH URBAN
"Everybody"

Christina's writing schedule kept her inside her sunny white office with
the large picture window and the incredible view of South Carolina.
She promised herself breaks through the day—long walks through the
hilly mountain trails helped provide balance when her speaking schedule took her away from home. Airports and shuttles, generic hotel
rooms, and conference centers, those were her *real* workdays. Christina
needed time on the mountain to counter balance time away.

On a break from her writing and the rain, Christina walked her
quarter-mile driveway through the woods to collect letters from her
mailbox on SC59. As she walked the long road, crunching red pine
needles under her feet, Christina embraced the morning. She engaged
her creative literary mind to wonder whether it was possible for forests
to be haunted. The trees seem so endless, like watchers of town history. Silent and mysterious, she imagined the forest keeping a
collective record of all the people it had seen pass through. All good
woods, she decided, seemed a little haunted.

Christina thought Emma might be the keeper of a mysterious
secret too, a woman haunted by the memories of things seen and

heard. It had always seemed just a little odd how Emma had run off to Boston and not been heard from since. Christina had spent enough time ministering to women to know the kinds of issues that made them run. She pledged to be there for Emma if her hunch bore out.

Duke, Christina's four-year-old golden Lab, ran up ahead to the front yard. Overnight, all the maples in Christina's yard had succumbed to the change of season and let go of their leaves. Duke played in a drift of red beneath the dozens of trees in her yard.

Christina's thoughts turned to Bo. She wondered if he'd ever let her completely into his life. She'd known he was the one since the early months of their dating. Bo was wild, but he was also faithful and kind. Rugged and untamable, but Christina held no desire to constrain him. His energy was like the spinning blade of a helicopter. He was a machine of great strength able to lift, drive, and build. She saw herself as a stabilizer in his life, the secondary blade necessary to make flying possible.

At 5'2", the thirty-four-year-old strawberry blonde wondered if men really took her seriously, even with all of her success. Christina was cute, and doubtful most men could see her beyond that. Until she met Bo. He'd become her best friend. After two years of dating, he'd yet to pop the question, but that had nothing to do with Christina. She knew what tied his hesitation toward marriage. She prayed daily for the Lord to bring healing so Bo could be whole, and she could find home.

At noon, Duke's barking clued Christina that Emma had found her place nestled among the trees. Christina looked through the glass front door to see Old Red chugging up the long, winding drive.

"Christina, your place is so beautiful," Emma said, climbing out of the truck. "And so remote. I feel like we're in the mountains."

"Well," Christina said, "you are." She gave Emma a long hug. "How are you?"

"I'm good," Emma said, revealing that she was still in transition from the hectic pace of travel and family illness, and the calm restoration of small-town living.

"Well, come on in. Let me show you around."

Christina pulled on the glass front door. It opened with a swooshing sound and snapped shut behind them.

"Oh, Christina. Your house is amazing!"

"Thanks, I love being out here. It's become a part of me."

They walked through spacious rooms decorated with beautiful architectural details and exquisite furniture, and bathed in natural light.

"This is wonderful."

Christina showed Emma to the kitchen. A window from floor to ceiling showed the mountain view and the elevated back deck.

"I thought the same thing when I decided to build out here. I just love being surrounded by nature."

"You probably hear this all the time, but you've really done well for yourself."

"I can't take any credit. Behind everything you see is a story of God's grace."

"I see."

Emma stood on the opposite side of the marble countertop island while Christina put the last touches on lunch.

"So tell me about your place in Boston."

"I live in an old brick townhouse in Back Bay. It's a three-story place and I've got my bedroom on the top floor because that's where it's the quietest."

"Sounds exciting. Do you like it up there?" Christina asked.

"Yeah, there are lots of great restaurants, theaters, museums, things like that. It's where my work is."

Christina laughed.

"It's like I'm a little bit country, you're a little bit rock and roll." Emma smiled.

"I guess. So, you're a writer? What are you writing?"

"Oh, that is *so* the number one question writers are asked."

"Sorry to be so cliché."

"No, you're not." Christina laughed. "It's just that it takes months to write something, even longer to edit, and only two days to read. The book I'm writing now is called *Four Seasons*. It's about thinking of life in terms of seasons. You know, spring is when we're young and everything is new and life's all about fun. Summer is when we come of age and we work hard to get where we want to go. Fall represents the season when we reflect on our lives and wonder if we made the right choices. If we've chosen to travel the right roads."

"Winter must be when there's a little snow on the roof," Emma kidded.

"Yes, and when you want to find yourself inside with someone, warmed by the memories you've created over a lifetime."

"Sounds lovely."

"Thanks. I set aside time for prayer every morning to ask God what He wants me to say. This past springtime was so busy. I was traveling all the time. Fall is so beautiful on the mountain. The world feels like it's slowing down and tidying up its business before a long winter's slumber."

"I have to agree, Juneberry looks beautiful this time of year," Emma said. "In a way, it *feels* like a time to tie up loose ends, settle accounts, however you want put it."

Christina pulled the cellophane off the dishes she'd prepared earlier.

"I hope you're hungry."

"Christina, this table has so much good food!"

Emma took her seat at the table. On it, Christina had spread out chicken salad, toasted pita bread, grapes, cloth napkins, and flowers.

"Maybe you are Martha Stewart."

"Mind if we say grace?" Christina asked.

"No, of course," said Emma. The two women closed their eyes.

"Dear Lord, we thank You for this day, for the rain and the sun, this wonderful lunch, and for my friend, Emma, who is here today because of Your loving-kindness. Amen."

Christina passed Emma the plate stacked with pita bread.

"So, tell me about Bo. Is he the one you hope to spend your winter season with?"

"Bo? Yeah, he's my best friend. I think I've always known he's the one."

"How long have the two of you been going out?"

"We've been dating for over two years and it's been wonderful. He's just so exactly the opposite of me in all the right ways, and yet we're compatible at the same time. I think we really complement one another."

"Have you guys had the talk yet, about marriage I mean?"

Christina frowned. "Well, yes and no. I'd like nothing more because I'm ready, but Bo isn't, and I wonder sometimes if he'll ever be."

"Uh-oh, is he one of those commitment-phobic men?"

"No, his case is a little different. Bo was married once before. Together, they had a little boy named Jason, and Bo was a very committed husband and father for those six years."

"What happened?" Emma asked.

"She thought the grass would be greener somewhere else."

"That's too bad."

"Yes, it is, but there's more to it than that. When she divorced Bo, she took Jason back with her to Columbia. Bo drove back and forth for visitation, ninety minutes each way, and did everything he could to remain Jason's father. Fast-forward two years later, she remarried and moved away to Los Angeles with her new husband, and took Jason with them."

"Oh my."

"It's unbelievable," Christina said, her emotions pierced. "He was the one who got Jason up in the morning, made his breakfast, and tucked him into bed with a story each night. When she decided to leave the marriage, she just severed Bo's relationship with his son."

"She can't do that. He has visitation rights."

"Yeah, but she has custody rights, and she chose to move Jason twenty-four hundred miles away. Bo was willing to do anything to stay Jason's father, he even tried moving out there. But he couldn't make life work in California, and she made it as difficult as possible for him to see Jason."

"And now he's gun-shy."

"Can you blame him? I mean to lose your only son …" Christina's voice faded into a sad sigh. "When we first started dating, he'd told me up front that he couldn't go very fast, which was fine with me. He said it was like his heart had been frozen, then dropped to the bottom of the lake through a hole in the ice. That's pretty cold."

"Does he ever see Jason?"

"He flies out to California twice a year, stays in a hotel. And Jason comes back to South Carolina for a month each summer. He was just here in July. It's so sad. There's no way short visits and phone calls can replace how great they were together for six years. Bo told me Jason doesn't remember much of when Bo lived in the house with him."

"Sounds like he needed a good lawyer."

Christina shrugged her shoulders.

"That's the reason he doesn't want to marry again. He wonders if he could survive me doing the same thing to him. Can you imagine losing a child that way?"

"Do you think he'll come around?"

"I hope so. He said the whole experience 'fried his wires.' I'd like to think he'll learn to trust me over time 'cause I would never do that to him. So I just pray."

"That he'll come around?"

"No," Christina said. "That God will heal him. I only want what's best for Bo."

Christina's love for Bo puzzled Emma. In Boston, Lara talked about men as if they were items for purchase in a mail-order love catalog. Emma didn't know it until that moment when she heard Christina's words and saw the caring expression on her face exactly why Lara's perspective had always seemed shallow.

"Christina, I've never heard someone say that before. You want Bo to be yours more than anything, but you don't pray for God to give him to you. You pray that he'll heal?"

Christina set down her silverware and leaned in to speak.

"I'd love nothing more than to wake up in the middle of the night and see Bo sleeping in bed next to me. I think about watching him across the dinner table each night, and knowing he's there because we're married, and I dream about us going somewhere as husband and wife. I'd just love those things, but most of all, I love *him*. I can't think of love as being anything else but my desire to place his well-being above my own wants, and see him become the whole man God wants him to be."

"What if he never marries you?"

Christina let out a nervous laugh.

"Don't scare me like that. It's best not to think about it, but I have confidence in God. I know whatever He has for me will work out for the best."

Christina took a sip of ice water. Emma watched her in silence. How could she love someone so much and just be willing to let him go?

Christina set the glass again on the table and smiled to Emma. "Okay, my turn. Tell me what's going on with you and Michael?"

Emma raised her shoulders and shook her head.

"I don't know that *anything* is going on. He's helping renovate a home office space for my dad. We talked some the other day."

Her voice trailed off.

"That's all?"

Emma hesitated.

"Well … we had a good talk this morning, too, while we were moving furniture. I don't know what else to say. He's an incredible man, but there's nothing going on between us. That was a long time ago."

Christina dotted the corners of her mouth with a napkin, folding it again on her lap.

"I agree with you, Michael's a really good man," she laughed. "It's funny how the two of you just ran into one another."

"Yes, it was kind of strange. I saw his truck when I was crossing the street and it struck me just how new and clean it looked parked next to Old Red. I was just reading his name on the side when he appeared from out of the hardware store. I think the strange part is that it was a complete surprise, but on the other hand … I don't know, I sort of expected it?"

Emma laughed a nervous laugh.

"I'm sorry, I realize that must sound completely irrational and stupid."

"Oh, I don't know about that. Perhaps Michael's been on your mind?"

"I don't know," Emma said, shrugging. "It was just one of those weird moments. I don't know anymore beyond that."

"Were you happy to see him?" Christina asked, taking a bite of her salad. Emma thought about it for a moment.

"Yeah, I was. I felt like there was unfinished business between us, and it seemed like a good time to settle things up."

"My gosh, Emma. You make it sound like a business transaction," Christina laughed, picking up her napkin and holding it against her mouth.

"Well, I don't mean it that way. I just … felt like there were things that needed to be said, mostly by me. It's not easy, Christina. Life isn't easy. We make choices sometimes without any earthly idea how things will work out. Sometimes we make the right ones, and sometimes we just blow it."

"What choices are you referring to?"

"Going to college in Boston when everyone else I knew and loved was staying here," Emma answered. "Starting a new life in a new world."

"Anything else?" Christina asked.

"You're intuitive, Christina," Emma said. Emma set her napkin on the table, and slid back her chair. "Maybe you want me to add, 'never coming back to the old life' too?"

"There's nothing I want you to add, Emma. We were a group of friends who loved each very much once. You left … and then you didn't come back. We still love you, but we don't understand why you disappeared. Why you didn't want to keep in touch when we tried reaching out to you. I would like to understand someday … if you'd be willing to tell, I mean."

~ NINE ~

And it's sure good to know that love still remains.

—SARA EVANS
"Some Things Never Change"

It was nearly three thirty when Emma climbed into Old Red to head home. The sky's dark clouds were finally giving way to the sunlight. Crimson streaks appeared along the horizon like mellowing shrouds cruising westward, handing day over to night.

The midafternoon air felt cool. Emma wasn't surprised to see an elderly woman walking her small dog along the country road; she was enjoying the sunshine, but had enough good sense to wear a sweater.

Emma switched on the headlights and accelerated to a brisk 45 miles per hour. The yellow lines on the country road popped vibrantly in contrast to the muted colors of the woods on either side. Everything in nature was blacks, browns, silvers, and reds. South Carolina looked as if unseen hands were shutting off the world of summer, sealing it up for next year's spring blossom. The fading colors were nature's fond kiss good-bye.

Emma's cell phone rang, a discreet three-tone melody that she hadn't taken the time to replace with something more pleasant. She picked it up, looking at the caller ID. It was Michael.

"Hello."

"Hi, Emma. This is your dad."

The sound of her father's voice surprised her. He was in a jovial mood, and his humor made her smile.

"Michael suggested it would be a good idea for me to call and prepare you for what you're gonna see when you come home."

She took her cue to play along.

"All right, what are the two of you up to?"

"Honey, I came downstairs to find Michael tearing up carpet. I liked what I saw so much I asked him to show me the big picture."

"And?"

"Well, we kind of got carried away, and ended up knocking out the wall in the bedroom. You know that window against the outside wall?"

"Yes."

"It's gone too. We've completely demolished the entire room."

Emma saw a family of deer in a grassy field adjacent to the highway. A buck, doe, and fawn grazed in a clearing, moving only to raise their heads and watch the truck go by.

"You're right, I don't believe it, but I think it's great. I didn't know you were ready to move full steam ahead."

"Once things got under way, and I understood the floor plan you two had laid out, I told Michael to go for it."

"I don't want to sound like a mother hen, but you aren't overexerting yourself, are you?"

"Ah, I'm going as easy as I can, you're not to worry. Hold on a minute, Michael wants to talk to you."

Emma listened as the two men shuffled the phone between them. She couldn't help but laugh when she thought of how much fun they must have had demolishing the room together.

"Emma? Hey, it's Michael. Listen, your dad really seemed gung ho about moving forward with the demo, so we just tore into it. I think you'll be happy with all that's gone on. We've really got a lot done today."

"I can't wait to see it. How's he doing anyway?"

"He just stepped out to the kitchen to get us a couple glasses of water. Don't worry; he's serving in a more supervisory capacity. I didn't ask him to do any heavy lifting."

"He did just have a heart attack on Monday."

"I'm set to pack up in a few minutes, so if you don't see me when you get back, don't think I'm abandoning you. In the morning I'll be here as early as you can stand it."

Don't think I'm abandoning you.

"How early is that?" she asked, momentarily lost in thought.

"Can you handle six thirty?"

"Umm, better make it seven, and Michael …"

"Yeah?"

"Thanks. I could hear the excitement in my dad's voice. I think he's really happy."

"Lots of people are happy this week, Emma."

Emma said good-bye and punched the red button, shutting off her phone. The last few minutes of daylight were still present in the sky to enjoy.

"Lots of people are happy this week," he'd told her.

"Yes, and I'm one of them," she said out loud, feeling good about the life that was hers to live, feeling blessed to have her father still in it.

Emma drove in the dark, thinking back over her day, recalling the elegant lunch at Christina's house. She was surprised at how easily they'd fallen back into their friendship. That was true with Samantha, too. Maybe things weren't as broken as they'd seemed. Perhaps everything would be sorted out in a matter of days and Emma could fly back to Boston knowing all issues past and present had been solved.

Over a distant hill, two white pinpoints of light pierced the dimming twilight. They approached Emma on the opposite side of the two-lane road.

Emma's cell phone rang again. This time she answered it without checking the caller ID.

"Yes?"

"Emma? Robert Adler."

"Hi," she said, still not used to bouncing back and forth between two disparate worlds.

"How is everything down there? How's your dad?"

"He's doing better. He's out of the hospital and home now," Emma said, switching gears from Juneberry cordiality to the harefooted pace of an East Coast law firm.

"That's exactly what I wanted to hear. When do you expect to depart for Boston?"

Emma hesitated. The dark car in the opposite lane drew closer. Its headlights were set on high beams and gave off a bluish tint, so bright they were blinding.

"Robert, I'm not sure yet. Things are progressing as fast as can be expected, but there's still more I need to do."

On the narrow strip of SC59, the mysterious car swerved dangerously close to Emma. She pulled the steering wheel to the right until her tires left spun in the loose gravel of the shoulder. The other car passed close enough that Emma could have seen the driver were it not for the tinted windows.

"Hmm," Adler said. "I thought we'd agreed you'd be here by Friday. Maybe the details have been lost in translation this week, but the meeting with John Tenet of Northeast Federal is a go. John's on the verge of changing their company's representation. It's about a two-million-dollar contract."

"He's coming into the office?"

"Yes, and I very much need you to be at this meeting. The back-story is Tenet called within twenty-four hours of your Interscope victory; that wasn't coincidental. He and I have been discussing business over dinners and cigars for a year, but his call on Tuesday was unexpected. He'd like to meet you. They have a lot on their plate right now and they think we're just what they need."

Emma felt a sudden, sharp anxiety. Her pulse had already quickened because of the close call with the speeding car.

"Isn't there any way we can meet next week?" Emma asked. It seemed a reasonable enough request given the distance she'd traveled, the importance of her father's health, and the loyalty she'd exhibited to the firm over the past nine years.

"Not with John Tenet. He sets when a meeting is going to take place. That time he's set is this Friday at twelve thirty Eastern time. That's why I'm going to ask Helen to charter a corporate jet to fly you out of Columbia tomorrow. That will help avoid any delays."

"Robert, I came home to help my dad get back on his feet. He's not totally there yet."

"I really don't want to rush you, Emma, but Northeast Federal is more than just a new client. As we've discussed, they're a gateway to a whole new world of corporate litigation for us. You said your dad's doing better. It's time for you to get back to work."

Emma thought about her response for less than a second.

"Robert, I can't come back to work just yet. I'm needed down here. My dad's home from the hospital, but ..."

"Emma," Adler interrupted. "We don't gamble with clients like NF. We play every ace we've got, and right now you're the high card. Just come back to Boston. We'll nail down this account and before you know it, it'll be Thanksgiving, and you'll be back home for a visit."

Emma thought of how she'd taken on every legal assignment handed to her during her years with the firm. She'd lived and breathed its culture, its fourteen-hour workdays, its workload that helped to bury an uneasy past in the dark, cool depths of her mind. She thought of the unscrupulous clients and protracted courtroom battles that tested her intellect, her emotions, and her morals, and how she'd done everything ever asked of her. Foremost on her mind was what she'd been given, employment with the firm fresh out of law school and a full partnership all by the age of thirty. Robert had opened those doors for her, and in return asked only for her loyalty.

"Robert, I can't leave tomorrow. I'm sorry, I just can't," Emma said. There was no easy answer. "I know how important this meeting is with Northeast Federal, but I'm right in the middle of things here, and I can't leave."

Emma knew Robert Adler was unaccustomed to hearing the word *no* from anyone, especially from his protégée. There was a long pause before he finally spoke.

"Give it to me in numbers. How long do you intend to be there?"

"I don't think I can give you a number, Robert. I've been thinking probably mid next week."

Adler spoke in a voice low in volume, high in compressed tension. "Wednesday is ten days, Emma. I'll tell Tenet you were called out of town on a family emergency but will absolutely be back in Boston on Wednesday morning. You can do that, right?"

The yellow lights of the Madison farmhouse appeared from out of the darkness, welcoming Emma. She slowed the truck.

"Robert, I'm trying to find the balance between two of the most important things in my life. Please don't ask me to rubber-stamp an expiration date on this trip."

"You don't expect business to just stop until you get back, do you?

When my son died, I took two days off. One to plan the funeral, and one to attend. Then I was back to work. In fact, I think I worked part of that second day."

Emma pulled Old Red into the drive, put the truck in park, and shut off the lights.

"I've given nine years to the firm, Robert. You know how important it is to me. I've rarely taken a vacation. There's never a good time to take a break, but this break picked me."

"Don't think for a minute that I'm not supportive of you and your personal life, Emma, but this race we're in is like a marathon. You've been running it for nine years, and I've been running it for over forty. It's times like these we learn our greatest lessons. I'm trying to coach you to stay focused and keep running because you have no idea how much personal success is waiting for you just around the corner."

Emma heard something peculiar in the sound of Robert's voice.

"What do you mean?"

"Opportunities. You've got a bright future, Emma. There are opportunities out there that haven't even crossed your mind yet."

"What are you saying?"

Adler paused.

"Let's focus on one fire at a time. For now, I'm going to plan on your being here in the office on Wednesday morning. You let me know Monday if you see a problem with that. Take this weekend to think things over and finish up what you've got to do."

The phone clicked off. Emma sat in the darkened truck trying to figure out why she chose to stay when Robert had just handed her the perfect excuse to leave. In the half-moonlight she could see Michael's truck still parked in the drive. She closed her eyes. She'd never said no to Robert, and the act left her with the bitter aftertaste of betrayal. Her instincts as a lawyer and law partner confirmed the importance of a client like Northeast Federal. Robert was right—the timing was critical. Despite her emotions, Emma trusted his judgment. The only solution that made any sense was to take these extra days, finish up everything in Juneberry, and get back to Boston as quickly as possible.

Emma opened her eyes and was startled by the shadowy figure of a man standing outside the driver's-side door.

"Oh!" she shrieked.

"You all right in there?" Michael said. Emma opened the door and climbed out. "You look a little frayed at the edges."

"You scared me."

She put her arms around him and Michael did the same, wrapping her in the arms of friendly support.

"Sorry, just a rough phone call from work. I guess with all the travel, Dad's heart attack, and everything, I'm just a little wiped out."

"Everyone has their breaking point," he told her.

The night air felt cool, and Emma could smell burning leaves far off in the distance.

"I think I've met mine."

Michael continued holding her and Emma felt something she hadn't known in a very, long time: safe.

"Why don't you come inside and see what we've been doing?" He stepped back and turned Emma around, walking her up the steps and into the warm house. "It will either cheer you up or really knock you over the edge."

Inside, the Madison house was a total disaster. Every downstairs light was on, making the mess all the more impossible to ignore. A plastic tarp held in place by five-gallon containers ran the length of the hallway. One container held a sledgehammer. Another pail had been loaded with assorted power hand tools. Drywall dust had escaped the downstairs bedroom, and despite the tarp, the thinnest layer of powder the color of ash dusted the floor and furniture in the den.

"Oh my," Emma said.

Inside the space formerly dubbed the guest bedroom, it looked like a bomb had exploded. The matted navy blue carpet had been completely torn out. The entire wall that once had stood between the small bedroom and the pantry behind it had vanished, leaving behind only a rough, exposed surface where a wall used to be. Wires dangled, and the cool outdoor air drifted in through a hole where there used to be a window. A double-thick sheet of construction plastic hung partially attached to the frame. The floor waved with an uneven ocean of plastic and cotton drop cloths, and everywhere eyes looked or noses sniffed, a thin layer of demolition dust settled.

"Where's the rest of the wall?" Emma asked.

"We tossed it outside," Will said, pointing to the hole where the window used to be. He seemed rather pleased at the ingeniousness of its disposal.

"This is the worst of it, right?" Emma asked them both. "I mean, it starts looking better after this, right?"

"Right. We'll put it all back together soon enough."

"This room is a total mess," Emma laughed. "But at least it's under way.

"I think I'm going to take a picture of this," Will said. "Before and after, er, during and after."

He stepped out of the demolition site through the door in the hallway, the plastic rustling as he crept over it.

Michael turned to Emma.

"Still stressed?" he asked.

She rolled her head, stretching the aching muscles in her neck.

"A little. I'll bounce back."

"Maybe dinner would help you get your bounce back."

"Just what are you suggesting?" Emma smiled.

"Nothing, no big deal. Just thought you could use a night off. By the looks of it, you haven't started the natural unwinding process that is supposed to take place in a small town."

Before Emma could respond, Will reentered with a digital camera and took a snapshot of the room. He clicked the picture, and although the room was bright, the flash went off.

"I can't get over how different this room looks with that wall out of the way," Will said, keeping his eye to the camera. Another flash. Will stepped inside. Another flash strobed behind them, like a bolt of light at a fireworks show.

"It's funny how one small change can make such a huge difference," he said, shifting to where Michael and Emma stood in the west corner of the room. "Hey, you two stand together and let me get a picture of you."

Emma and Michael turned around to face Will.

"That's good. Move a little closer so I can get you both in the shot," Will instructed. The slightest hint of reluctance held them in place for a moment. Then Michael and Emma scooted toward each other, keeping their eyes focused on Will and his camera.

"3-2-1 ..."

The camera flashed. A memory flashed in Emma's mind of another time they'd posed for a picture together—at the dance during Michael's last year of high school. Even with Christina there that warm May evening, Emma felt geeky and awkward. There she was, a sophomore, hoping someone she liked would ask her to dance. Then Michael spoke to her in the dark cafeteria, the only light coming from the bright soda vending machines lining the wall. He was a senior who "ruled the school" that year. They slow danced together in the middle of the room. After it was over, an overzealous student photographer from the yearbook committee asked them to pose for a picture. Embarrassed and not knowing what to do, they'd both made silly faces, Michael's idea, and turned the whole thing into a joke. The photo never made it into the yearbook.

"Dad, Michael's asked me to have dinner with him tonight," Emma said, making the statement sound matter-of-fact. "Would you be okay if I made you something to eat and went out for a while?"

"Emma, you don't have to make my dinner," Will said, lowering the camera. "I'm going to get something light and turn in early."

"You'll be okay if I go out then?"

"With Michael? Go, have fun."

Will left the room.

"I'll need a shower first," Emma said. "What time are you thinking?"

"How about seven thirty?"

"Perfect."

"We'll have dinner in Juneberry at 310 Wilshire."

"What restaurant is that?"

"Michael's Grill," he said. "It's a quaint, exclusive, table-for-one kind of a place, but I can find another chair. I think you'll like it."

"I'm sure I will."

They walked together out of the room and down the hallway. Michael reached for the doorknob, then turned to see Emma at the foot of the stairs and Will stepping out of the kitchen.

"I'll be back tomorrow—weather permitting—and we'll start putting this house back together," he said. "Emma, see you 'bout seven thirty?"

"I'll be there," she said, and disappeared up the staircase.

~ TEN ~

Love, look what you've done to me
Never thought I'd fall again so easily.

—BOZ SCAGGS
"Look What You've Done to Me"

Michael couldn't remember the last time he'd had a woman over to his house. The white cottage at 310 Wilshire, the first house on the corner, welcomed visitors to the neighborhood with a beautifully landscaped lawn, and a large, friendly maple tree. A white plank rancher's fence marked where the yard met the blacktop driveway.

Bo Wilson often pulled his truck into that drive on those mornings when they'd decided to commute to a work site together. Michael's brother, James, was no stranger on summer days when the Atlanta Braves played baseball. They hung out on the deck out back, watching the game, distracted only by an occasional cardinal cooling itself in the birdbath.

But a woman in the house? That was a rarity. Michael had imagined Emma in the house before. He'd pictured her in every room. He could see her standing at the kitchen sink in summer, rinsing fresh strawberries, while sunlight streamed through the window. He'd thought of her lounging in the den in the comfy tan chair by the bay window. He'd wonder if Emma would enjoy the back gardens, or listening to the sound of flowing water from the small fountain.

Sometimes he could even see her climbing the stairs at night, tired from the labors of a long day, just before she disappeared into the recesses of his mind.

"Hi," Emma said, standing on the front porch. She looked beautiful in a silvery V-necked sweater, and a brown leather jacket that somehow made blue jeans look elegant against the backdrop of the porch-light-tinted yard.

"Come on in," Michael said.

The town knew Michael as a lifelong resident, the carpenter with the smart sense of humor and a talent for building. Friends recognized his cultured side, his love of baseball, grilling steaks on the barbecue, and long days boating on the quiet lake. Few knew him as the man who had fallen deeply in love one perfect summer night. Someone had opened his chest while he slept and stitched love inside his heart. It had hurt like a saw cut when she'd told him she was going back to Boston.

He knew then he couldn't keep her. There was no sense in trying to tether her to Juneberry. He could see Emma longed to fly free or escape.

A month after Emma moved, he and James made a road trip to Beantown to catch a Red Sox game, barely surviving Boston's insane traffic. They had great seats behind first base, but Michael spent the day distracted, knowing Emma was somewhere just on the other side of the Charles River. What started out as a fun road trip, with a half-baked plan of running into Emma, turned out to be nothing short of slow torture. Michael drove back without seeing her, even after multiple promptings from his brother.

But that was long ago.

Now Emma Madison stood in the center of his living room admiring three ears of Indian corn placed on the mantle above the fireplace.

"I love your house, Michael, and these recessed bookshelves. Did you build them?" Emma asked.

"Yeah, back when I first bought the place. That's the only major change I made, other than some landscaping in the backyard."

Emma slipped off her jacket, and Michael hung it on a peg in the entryway.

"I'll bet you're hungry."

"I'm starving," she laughed, following him into the kitchen. One lamp was lit in the dining room. Recessed lights hidden underneath the kitchen cabinets brightened the rest of the space.

"Thank you for inviting me over," Emma said. "I needed this."

She pulled out a bar stool and sat at the kitchen island. Michael poured her a glass of sweet tea.

"I've got steaks marinating in the fridge, and I'm going to toss them on the grill with some veggies," Michael said, running over the menu with Emma. "Does that sound all right?"

"Sounds delicious."

Michael opened the oven door and in a moment Emma could feel its warmth. He reached in, and pulled out a CorningWare dish filled with something wrapped in foil.

"How do you feel about fried shrimp?"

"Michael, you've really gone all out."

"Not really. The shrimp is from Allen's Place. He's usually got fresh seafood from the coast, so I asked if he could make these for us."

He set the shrimp on the island in a serving dish, and brought out a small bowl of cocktail sauce from the refrigerator.

"Go ahead, dig in. I'm just going to put the steaks on."

Michael pulled the glass pan with the steaks from the fridge and carried them through the sliding door to the grill on the back deck.

"How do you like your steak?" he called back through the partially open door.

"Medium well," Emma replied. She got up from the island with her drink and followed Michael outdoors. The night air was cold, and Emma rubbed her arm with her one open hand.

"Brrr, it's getting cold out here."

"Not if you stand next to the grill. Here, come closer."

She walked down the step toward the grill, its fire heating the cozy patio. Michael transferred the first of two steaks from the glass dish to the surface of the hot grill with a set of chef's tongs. It sizzled.

"You've become a gourmet, Michael."

"I got tired of eating fast food a long time ago," he said. "That stuff will kill ya."

"Didn't you ever consider just finding a girlfriend to cook for you?"

"There have been a few," Michael said, setting the second steak on the grill. The patio awning above them was lined with festive, oversized green and red Christmas lights, and they added a soft, warm glow to the surrounding trees.

"I feel like I should be doing something," she said.

"I think you're missing the point of this evening. You're *not* suppose to be doing anything," he told her. "Where's that shrimp?"

"Oh, still inside."

Emma headed back into to the kitchen island and returned with the shrimp and sauce. She set the serving dish on the patio deck table and took a seat, the metal chair scraping the cement as she slid it forward.

"Mmm, I love the smell of steaks grilling."

Michael smiled, happy that she was happy. Emma peered around the edge of the patio awning, craning her neck to look up at the stars.

"It's a clear night after all that rain. I can see a few stars up there."

Michael walked to where Emma sat, placing his hands on the back of her chair. He peered up at the autumn sky with her. Bright evening stars framed by patches of dim, shadowy clouds were shining like a child's drawing, pinpoints of brilliant white against a backdrop of construction-paper black. Wind chimes rustled from a neighbor's yard.

"It's beautiful," he said, dropping his hands from her chair and returning to the grill. A spatter of grease fell into the open fire and hissed the flame higher. Michael set foil-wrapped vegetables on the grill.

"You really seem to have it all together, Michael. How is it no one's ever come along to sweep you off your feet?"

"How do you know no one hasn't?" he said, seasoning the meat with a shaker.

Emma shrugged. "I don't know. Doesn't the Bible say it's not good for a man to be alone?"

"I don't feel alone, Emma," Michael said, turning off the grill and moving the steaks onto a new plate.

"Thanks again for …"

"Hey, enough thanks already! You're wearing me out. Tonight's your night for getting a break. From what you've told me about your life in Boston, you don't get much of a chance to unwind up there."

"No, I don't," she said.

The night blew a gust of cold air through Michael's yard.

"Let's get inside."

They went back inside and shut the cold night air behind them.

Emma pointed to a candle that was sitting on the counter. "Michael, would you like me to light this candle with our dinner?" she asked.

"Yeah, that'd be great."

"I love this room," she said, when the candle's flame rose to its fullness. Michael's kitchen took on a flickering glow.

"We can eat in here, if you want," he said. "We don't have to sit in the dining room."

"Now *that* would be relaxing," she said.

Moments later they were enjoying their meals seated at the counter.

"Mmm, now that's good steak," Emma said. "Michael, this dinner is wonderful."

"I'm glad you like it," he said, taking a drink of tap water without ice. "Okay … I'm going to turn the tables on you. How is it you've never married?"

Emma nearly choked on a sprig of grilled asparagus.

"Me? I don't know. It isn't that I haven't wanted to."

"No boyfriends or admirers?"

"There's one admirer, but I think I've been focused on career for so long, it's hard to find the time to fall in love."

"Maybe your standards are too high."

"I don't know, I keep thinking there should be some way of knowing, something that tells you when you've found the right one. I'm waiting for a bell to ring, that says 'This is the one for you.'"

Michael felt a twinge of compassion for Emma. The beautiful woman eating steak in his kitchen had a weakness that he couldn't put his finger on. He thought maybe it was only his imagination, but part of her seemed to have been washed up on the shore of his island. Her boat striking a hidden reef under the blue of the ocean, sinking and setting her adrift in the sea. The ship's bell falling down beneath the blue of the water, coming to rest in silence in the sandy coral below.

"Maybe you'll hear it one day."

"I hope so," Emma smiled. "So you just never found the right one?"

"I didn't say that."

Emma's voice softened.

"I hope you find her, Michael. You're a good man. You deserve that."

"Emma," Michael said. "There are a lot of things in life I don't control. I came to terms with that a long time ago."

Emma stared at Michael in the candle's glow. There was a surprisingly strong bond between them. She'd felt a similar bond yesterday morning with Samantha in her dad's kitchen despite the passing of so many years. The link was there too with Christina, a connection that transcended their teenage high school antics. Now, as the evening grew long, she found herself staring into the eyes of the only man she'd really ever loved. The man she'd chosen to leave so she could survive.

For an hour after dinner, Emma revealed to Michael her history of the past dozen years. They'd moved to the living room and sat on the sofa, sharing stories filled with purpose and laughter.

"It's getting late," she said, finally. "I should probably go." She stood and went back to the kitchen to carry the dishes to the sink.

"Emma," Michael said.

"Yes?"

"You don't have to do that."

"I know. I'm happy to, though. It's my way of saying thanks to you."

He watched her rinsing off the dishes in the sink, just like he'd seen Emma do in his mind. It both amazed and overwhelmed him.

"You know when I said I'd come to terms with the things I don't control?"

Emma shut off the water.

"Yes."

"The part I control is *who* I love, not who loves me in return. That gives me a certain amount of peace."

"So, who do you love?" Emma asked.

"My family, friends, the folks at church. I know a lot of people in this community, so it's a pretty long list. How about you?"

She thought for a moment, standing in the center of the kitchen, looking into the blue and white ceramic tiles behind the stove without really seeing them.

"Can I tell you a secret? I don't love anybody, Michael. I only love the *idea* of love. It all seems so beautiful, but no one ever lives up to its expectations."

Emma left the room to retrieve her leather jacket. She slipped her arms into it, and turned back to see Michael following her into the entryway.

"I don't think that's true, Emma."

"I left everyone I knew here in Juneberry. How else can you explain someone doing that, other than to say they don't care?"

"You came back, Emma," Michael reminded her. "When your dad needed you, you came back. How else can you explain that, except to say you do?"

"His heart attack was a wake-up call, that's true," she said, standing at the door. "When I was twenty-two, the only thing I knew was that I wanted to go to law school. I really believed if I could succeed, then success would be like a moat around me. It would protect me. But you know what?" As she spoke, the truth dawned on her for the first time. "That same moat you build for safety can trap you, and keep everybody else shut out."

Emma put on a brave smile.

"I'm sorry, I don't know where this is all going," she continued. "It really is getting late, Michael, and I'm suddenly very tired. Thanks for everything. The dinner was wonderful."

Emma placed her hand on Michael's arm, held it there for a moment, then ran it down the length, over the outside of his shirt sleeve, feeling the soft flannel under her fingers, before gently squeezing Michael's hand.

He watched as she walked through his yard, paused when she came to Old Red, then climbed in as she'd done years before. Even as she drove away, he noticed electricity in the air. Whatever it was, he trusted it because Michael Evans had learned just because *he* didn't control everything in his life, it didn't mean his life wasn't controlled by Someone.

When the sound of her truck faded into the distance, he heard the distinct sound of wind chimes again, coming from somewhere behind the tall wooden fences of the neighbors' house. He wondered if she'd noticed them earlier. He wondered if she, too, had thought about how much they sounded like someone ringing a bell.

~ ELEVEN ~

You may be their pride and joy
But they'll find another toy
When they take away your crown
Pick me up on your way down

—DAVID BALL
"Pick Me Up on Your Way Down"

"Hey, it's me. You're hard to reach these days."

Emma pulled herself upright in bed, knocking a pillow sham to the floor.

"Colin? Hi, what time is it?" Emma looked at the bedside clock with one eye partly open, and the other completely shut.

The clock read 7:59 a.m.

"Sorry, I didn't think I'd wake you. You're usually up and running at full speed by this time," he laughed. "You must be getting a little too used to having time off."

"Is something up?"

"Oh, no. I just called to check in on you. Last night, I tried calling, but couldn't reach you. I was worried … a little, anyway."

Emma ran a hand over her face and through rumpled hair, trying to rouse herself.

"I had dinner with a friend and left my cell phone in the truck. Where are you?"

"On east 90 heading through Boston. It's snowing. Almost looks like Christmas already. Did you say truck?" Colin asked. "I have a hard time picturing Emma Madison behind the wheel of a truck. Well, listen, I'm not going to keep you. I just wanted to see if you thought you'd be back by this weekend."

Colin's heavy Boston accent wrapped around his words like wire around a pencil.

"It's looking more like next week. Wednesday, I guess."

"Really?" Colin said, surprise contorting the word. "What did Robert have to say about that? I'm just curious."

Emma climbed out of bed, finding the robe she'd borrowed from her dad over the back of her vanity chair. She stretched her arms through the sleeves.

"It wasn't what he wanted to hear, but it's workable."

"Huh," Colin said, sounding more like a lawyer and less like a kid from South Boston. "I'm just trying to see your situation as a strategist, Em. Four days ago, you win the biggest trial of your career. Then you're called out of town on a family emergency, which you have to attend to, of course. But you're taking another week off?"

"Well, Colin, things still are unsettled here. We're renovating a downstairs bedroom into an office for my dad. That project only started yester—"

"That's fine, that's a great idea," Colin broke in. "But do you really need to supervise that? I mean, look, taking a few days off before a weekend is one thing, but a law partner is irreplaceable, especially if you've got new clients knocking at your door."

"How do you know about that?" Emma asked.

"Robert may have mentioned it. We met this week to talk about some things, and I ..."

"Colin, I appreciate your concern, and believe me, as a partner

I'm completely invested in the firm's acquisition of new clients, but Robert and I have talked about it. This will hold until Wednesday, then I'll be back."

"All right, you know what you're doing. I just thought I'd be a sounding board for you. I'm at the office again pulling into another parking garage, so I'm about to lose signal."

"Well, at least say good-bye this time."

"Thought I did last time, I ..."

The cell phone went dead. Emma closed the lid and tossed the phone onto her bed. Was it selfish to take all this time with her father? Robert and Colin seemed to think so, maybe Lara, too. She fought the temptation to rethink everything.

Emma heard the muffled sounds of two men talking downstairs. She found the last pair of clean pants she'd packed, an old pair of indigo blue jeans and slipped them on. Then she picked out a cream turtleneck and put on a flowered button-up to wear over it.

Emma stepped across the hall to the upstairs bathroom. She pulled her hair into a ponytail, washed her face with the special soap she'd remembered to bring from Boston, and dried off with the clean towels her father had left for her by the sink.

She came downstairs with only her white cotton socks on her feet, her presence announced by the creaking boards. Emma stopped halfway down the stairs and leaned over the railing.

"Good morning," she said.

"Good morning, sweetheart," Will said. "I was afraid we'd wake you with all our banging around down here."

"Banging around down here first thing in the morning is a good thing. Anyone else in the mood for pancakes?"

Will looked like a contractor in work jeans and T-shirt. Michael stepped around the corner holding a white Styrofoam cup of coffee.

"Morning, Michael," she said, her eyes remembering the night before.

"Morning, Emma," he said, tipping his head like a cowboy wearing a hat.

"So, are we to understand you're volunteering to make pancakes?" Will asked.

"Well, I want to make some contribution. Besides, pancakes, bacon, and coffee just sound so good." She breezed by Michael. "So what's up with Bo this morning? Aren't you both supposed to be doing some roofing project?"

"We're dividing the work. He's continuing with the Macintosh place. Depending on how quickly things go here, I'll probably help him wrap up roofing first part of next week. But today? It's all about the home office. This is where it starts to get fun."

"Well, you know where you can find me when you need a woman's opinion."

Emma walked into the kitchen. Will had started a fresh pot of coffee, and she could smell it as soon as she walked in.

In a kitchen on the other side of Juneberry, Samantha Connor placed her hand on her stomach, feeling the baby kick inside her womb.

Two more weeks, Samantha thought to herself while she unloaded warm clothes from the dryer. Samantha found the portable phone they'd lost track of the night before sitting on the washing machine, then silently chastised herself for her absentmindedness. Pregnancy, she told Jim, had numbed her mind. She dialed Jim's number.

"It's me. Sorry to bug you, but I just wanted to call and see how your day is going."

After more than twenty years of marriage, Samantha knew Jim would hear the feelings behind the words. He knew all of the reasons she might be calling. He knew about her insecurities, her fear of spiders, that she'd never learned to swim, that she cried sometimes while watching greeting-card commercials on TV.

"Things are fine here, honey. How's everything at home?"

"Oh fine, Noel's upstairs playing his guitar and Beth's already left for school. I'm downstairs folding laundry."

"Anything on your mind?"

"No, I'm just thinking I'd give Emma a call this morning to see how she's doing. I'm so glad we got a chance to talk this week, and Christina says they had a good time yesterday. I was considering inviting all the ladies over here on Sunday afternoon. What do you think about that?"

"Sounds fine as long as you feel up to it."

Samantha opened the lid to the washing machine and tumbled in a new load of laundry.

"I'm just thinking about a small ladies' tea. Nothing fancy. Just some sandwiches on the deck if it's warm enough. Otherwise, we'll have it indoors."

"Sure, I think that's a great idea. I'd just make sure Beth helps you with the cleaning. Noel and I can pitch in too, then bug out so you have the place to yourselves. You just don't want to take it all on yourself."

Samantha shut the top of the washing machine and picked up a powder blue laundry basket filled with warm clothing. She carried it into the living room cradling the portable phone against her shoulder.

"I won't do too much, but I want it to be nice. I'll have to check the weather and see what's it's going to do that day."

"I'm sure you'll have a lovely time."

Samantha set the basket on the sofa and sat down next to it.

She wore an old pink robe and slippers, the only things in her closet she could really feel comfortable in. She backed her feet out of the heelless slippers and felt the coarseness of the carpet against her toes.

"Jim?"

"Yeah."

"Are you still glad you married me?"

"Yes, of course I am. Why do you ask?"

"I don't know. When I compare myself to Emma and Christina, I just feel like I haven't done very much with myself."

Samantha scooted back, letting herself sink a little deeper into the cushions of the old couch. She felt as big as a house, unattractive, and unlovable.

"Why is it women always compare themselves to each other? Sam, we have a wonderful marriage, two nearly grown children, and a new baby on the way. Instead of asking whether you've done enough, why don't you ask yourself if you're happy and if you enjoy your life?"

"I'm grateful for all that, I am, but they just lead such adventurous lives. Emma's a successful lawyer, Christina writes books and gets to travel around the country. I feel like all I ever get to do is fold clothes and make babies."

"Samantha, that's not true. You've stayed at home so our kids can have a full-time mom. You make the house a pleasure for all of us who live there, and your cinnamon coffee cake is the envy of the office here. Our family wouldn't be the same if you weren't there doing everything you do."

"I know, but I want to do something special with my life too. I want to make a difference."

"Noel and Beth are something special. In just a few weeks, we'll have another special creation in our home to love and enjoy. You get the privilege of helping grow that new baby into all God wants him to be."

Samantha let out a long, exasperated sigh. She propped her arm on the basket like an armrest, feeling its warmth against her skin.

"Then why am I so down on myself? I love our family and I really do like being a mom."

"Because what we're doing is hard work, Sam. Everybody has the same fantasy of dropping everything and going off on some grand, exciting adventure."

Samantha laid her head against the back of the sofa wishing it was Jim's shoulder.

"Do you ever dream that? About going somewhere away from the pressure?"

"Heck yeah! But the difference is I get to escape from my pressures at a place called *home*. It's what you do for me and everyone in our family that makes that possible."

A smile appeared on Samantha's face. Jim's words had worked their wonder, renewing Samantha's spirit just like the time he'd brought her a bouquet of yellow jessamine, her favorite flower, that day in July. He always seemed to know just what words to say and it startled her to think where she'd be without him.

"I love you," she told him simply, because it was never easy for Samantha to find the right words. Not the way Jim could.

"I love you, too, hon. We're still going to the Whitfields' barn dance on Saturday night, right?"

"Oh my gosh, I'd completely forgotten about that."

"Well, there's your fun and excitement, Sam. Country music, hayride, apple cider. Some of your favorite things. Sounds pretty wild and crazy to me."

"I wonder if Emma knows about the dance. It sort of snuck up on us with everything going on this week. I know Christina and Bo are going."

"There's another reason to call Emma."

"Yes, it is," Samantha laughed. It wasn't a cruise down the Riviera, but she knew she loved her life.

"Okay, I feel much better. Gotta go."

"What a second! Now that you're back to normal and don't need me anymore, you're just going to throw me aside?"

Samantha got up from the sofa and peered around the corner, taking the phone with her, making sure Noel hadn't come downstairs.

"No, I'm going to cook you pork tenderloin tonight," she said in a whisper, "and think up some *other* ways to show you how much I love you."

"Right back atcha."

Emma tunneled through the stacks of canned and dried goods, boxes of Wheat and Corn Chex that had been carried in from the pantry. She carved out a space to cook breakfast and a place at the table for the three of them to eat.

It was after nine when Emma called her dad and Michael in for breakfast, but she barely had to call—the smell of bacon frying in an iron skillet spoke loud enough to draw them away from work. A stack of silver dollar pancakes rested on an antique serving plate she'd found in the china cabinet.

"If it feels like we're on a camping trip in here, I'm sorry," Emma said, apologizing for the state of the kitchen.

"I'm impressed you were able to make breakfast at all," Will said, as the three of them sat down at the table. "It all looks so nice, does anybody mind if I say grace?"

Will offered thanks for the meal. A loud boom of thunder clapped just as they opened their eyes from prayer. In the darkening skies above them, a familiar rain began pouring again.

"Looks like Bo's done for the day," Michael said. "Glad I have somewhere indoors to work."

"Looks like this storm is going to hang around for a while," Will remarked.

"I hope it clears out by tomorrow," Emma said. "Samantha called to invite us all to the Whitfields' barn dance. Do you know anything about that?"

"Honey, everyone knows about the Whitfields' fall dance," Will said. "They've hosted one every year for the last six or seven. Michael, you've been before, right?"

"Can't say I have," Michael answered, cutting into his pancake.

"What did Samantha say, Emma?"

"She just said she and Jim were going, Christina and Bo, too, I guess."

"Why don't the two of you go?" Will said. "If the rain clears, the Whitfield farm will be beautiful. Frank really takes care of the place."

"You want to go?" Michael asked.

On the surface the question seemed to ask for an easy answer, but scratching a little deeper, this had all the markings of a real date, a second date.

"Sure," Emma said. "We can all go as a group."

"I think you're in for a wonderful time," Will said. "Once this rain stops, it's going to be a beautiful fall. Speaking of rain, I just remembered leaving my bedroom window cracked upstairs."

Will carried his breakfast plate to the sink. "I like the fresh air at night, but I don't much like a soggy bedspread."

Will left for upstairs.

"Michael ..."

"Emma, don't worry about last night or tomorrow night. They don't have to mean anything. We'll go and have a good time, and that's all it has to be."

"This feels awkward," she admitted. "I don't mean to presume anything. I'd love to go to the Whitfields' with you, but I'm going back to Boston next week. Can we just say we're going as friends?"

Michael stood up. Following Will's example, he took his breakfast plate to the counter near the sink and set it down.

"You're right, Emma, this is awkward. And we are only friends. I'm helping your dad because it's what folks in Juneberry do. Well, that, and we agreed on a fair price so it's a good job for me, too. I asked you to dinner last night because you looked like you'd fallen into a shredder and needed some down time. As for the Whitfields' tomorrow night, it's like square dancing—everybody needs a partner and it just makes sense for us to match up."

Emma studied his face. His brow scrunched up just a little before he continued.

"Emma, I learned long ago that we're different people. I'm as attached to everyone here in Juneberry as an oak tree is rooted to the earth. I think you're more like a leaf. When the wind blows, it picks you up and carries you someplace far away. I guess there's nothing wrong with that. It's your life, but you don't have to explain to me how it all works and how you've got to go back. I don't expect you to do anything less."

Michael exited the kitchen and went back to work. Emma sat at the kitchen table, her mind spinning thoughts of Michael like she was flipping through channels on TV. She cleaned up the kitchen and went upstairs to take a shower. As she dressed afterward, she heard her cell phone ring. She had to dig through the unmade bed to find it.

"Emma? Hey, it's Lara. How's it going down there in Hooterville? Seriously, we're all starting to miss you up here in civilization."

"Hi, Lara. I miss you, too. So, what's the latest at the shop?"

Emma sat on her bed brushing tangles from her wet hair.

"Well, you're at the top of Adler's poo-poo list. He's not used to *not* getting his way around here, and the meeting with Northeast Federal today is huge! Just *what* were you thinking when you said you wouldn't be here?"

"I just couldn't make it, Lara. I'm right in the middle of things."

"Well, that's not how it's going over here. I just thought you should know people in the office are divided over whether you're quitting your job, or making some power statement with Adler after your amazing victory in court this week. Odds are three to one on the latter."

"This has nothing to do with that," Emma said, defensiveness creeping into her voice. "I'm helping my dad put his life back in order. I wish I could make it sound more complicated than that, but it isn't."

"Hey, I get it, but saying no to Robert and missing this meeting has got everybody in the office talking. I think he sees your not being here as some kind of betrayal."

"That's ridiculous. I've taken some time off for a family emergency, that's all. He knows that."

"Honey, I totally understand, but Robert's hung a star on your door and he expects you to perform. Today's meeting is like opening night at Carnegie Hall to him, only his star, you, says she won't go on. Do you get it?"

"Okay, I get it."

Emma dropped the hairbrush onto the bed and stood to pace the room.

"Lara, I've never realized how hard it is to balance work and family," Emma confessed. "Until now, this hasn't been an issue."

"Well, to be completely honest with you, Em, until now, you haven't had a family."

Emma made a sound like air was stuck in her throat.

"Lara, I've always had a family, it's just that I've made work my priority. It blows my mind that it's only taken four days of shifting my focus to completely upset the apple cart."

"Well, I know of a way to get the cart back on its wheels."

"What's that?" Emma asked, standing in the stormy light of the bay window, looking out over the farm damp with fresh rain.

"Robert wants you patched into the meeting this afternoon via conference call. He instructed me to call you this morning to set it up."

"Ay, yi yi, doesn't anybody understand the meaning of time away from work?"

"I wish there was such a thing, Emma, but for law partners, that's an illusion. So, can I patch you through?"

~ TWELVE ~

Do you remember when
things were really hummin'?
Come on, let's twist again.
Twisting time is here.

—CHUBBY CHECKER
"Let's Twist Again"

The Whitfields' farm was spread out over a hundred acres and it felt more like two hundred the day Frank Whitfield's tractor broke down on the far side of his land and he had to make his way back to the farmhouse on foot. The Whitfield estate was built a century earlier a half mile off Scatterfield Road, where the land was hilliest. It was done this way because hills were less farmable, but the effect was that the house stood out like a monument, surrounded by a rolling landscape and a sprawling, broad-branched oak tree.

Several barns had been raised on the property over the decades. The smallest of these was approximately the size of a three-car garage. The largest barn stood three stories tall and had been painted barn red, with a brown shingled roof the color of auburn hair.

Acres of apple trees on the estate's horizon were sketched in mystery by the setting sun. The untamed woods growing on either side of the river gave the farm just enough mystery to hearken visitors back to the fictional world of Ichabod Crane and a party he attended two hundred years before. Perhaps more than one party guest would recall the night of Ichabod's ghostly encounter with a headless horseman on his ride home, and the grim reality that he was never heard from again.

A round, bright moon hung between the barn and the farmhouse as Emma and Michael lead a three-car convoy up the Whitfields' long, dirt driveway. Michael parked his truck in an open field where cars, trucks, and minivans were parked willy-nilly, an impromptu community undertaking. Bo and Christina parked his Blazer next to them, and Jim and Samantha claimed the next spot for their minivan.

The Whitfields had decorated the barn with care. Its large doors were thrown open and a welcoming yellow light emanated from inside. Colored Christmas lights strung on nails glowed around the square entrance making it clear to first-time guests which barn held the party.

The night air was cool and crisp as they walked through the grassy field. It was the first moment of twilight. Samantha threaded her arm through Jim's as they walked.

"I'm just amazed at how the Whitfields are able to put all this together every year," Samantha said. "It must take them weeks of planning and days just to do all the decorating."

"It looks amazing," Christina added, adjusting her gaze from the barn to Bo hiking through the field beside her. Bo's everyday workman's attire naturally resembled the Western look of a barn dance. Christina took hold of his arm, giving it a squeeze as they walked.

Michael and Emma walked side by side too, but with a buffer zone between them that made physical contact unlikely. Michael had worked at the Madison farm all day Friday and Saturday morning. He and Emma had chatted a bit, but only briefly.

Mrs. Whitfield stood inside the open barn doors greeting guests as they arrived. Esther Whitfield was a lifelong farmer's wife, committed to keeping on with the old traditions, and to whom entertaining came as second nature. She'd started hosting "the great barn dances," as she called them, several years earlier when she had begun to worry that Juneberry was losing its sense of community. She crafted the dance idea based on a memory she had of going to barn dances as a teenager when the men came back to the farm after fighting the war in Europe.

"Welcome, everyone. Won't you come in?"

"Mrs. Whitfield, I don't know if I've ever seen the farm so lovely," said Christina.

"You know, this old barn dance has given us an excuse to dress the old place up and have some fun. We all need a night just to enjoy our neighbors and have a good time.

"Emma, how's your father doing?" Mrs. Whitfield asked. "I felt so badly when I'd heard the news."

"He's doing much better, thank you. I'll tell him you said hello."

"Please do, and tell him our prayers are with him. Now, go on inside and help yourselves to some food. There's cider and doughnuts, apples from the orchard, cakes, and lots of fresh pies."

"Thank you, Mrs. Whitfield."

Emma turned and whispered in Samantha's ear.

"How did she know who I was?"

"Mrs. Whitfield knows everybody, Emma."

Inside the cavernous barn, brown and orange paper streamers floated down from the plank rafters. Bales of straw had been stacked around the edges for seating in addition to a dozen card tables with folding chairs set up underneath the loft. Loose straw had been strewn across the barn's makeshift dance floor giving the wood planks a Gilley's-honky-tonk feel. In the far corner the Whitfields' youngest son, Tommy, acted as DJ behind a long table set up with audio equipment and post-mounted speakers.

Along the side wall, two banquet tables covered with pumpkin orange tablecloths displayed the pies, cakes, punch, and plates all arranged with care. The most popular objects in the room were two space heaters radiating heat throughout the barn. Forty people were already milling around, making the large space feel cozy and full of life. Country music poured through the speakers.

"I love country music," Bo said. "It gets you feeling all Cracker Barrel inside."

"I'll bet they don't do this in Boston, Emma," Christina joked.

"Not for the last hundred years."

"How about a glass of cider, ladies?" Bo asked.

"Perfect!"

Michael, Bo, and Jim swaggered to the refreshment tables dressed from hat to boots like cowboys while Samantha, Emma, and Christina searched for a place to perch. Tommy Whitfield switched on his microphone and brought it to his mouth.

"Ah, as you can tell we're not real formal around here," he said. "If you've got a request, just ask and I'll try to play it for you. Otherwise, I'll just try to keep the place hopping."

With the timing of a pro, Tommy brought up the lively sound of twin fiddles underneath his short and sweet introduction, and the room came alive. The men returned with six cups of apple cider, setting them on the table, and Christina jumped up to take Bo by the hand.

"Come on, let's dance!"

Before Bo had a chance to voice his agreement or objection, he and Christina joined a dozen other couples pouring into the middle of the barn to form a country line dance. Samantha and Jim soon followed, she doing her best to teach her rhythmically challenged husband the four basic steps to country line dancing in the equivalent of the slow lane on the dance floor.

Emma scooted closer to Michael, who leaned against the barn's post support beam closest to their table. His white cowboy hat threw an angled shadow across his eyes.

"Do you still know how to dance, Michael?" she asked.

He tilted his head back, lifting the shadows away from his face.

"I've always been more of a slow dancer," he said, looking and sounding like a real cowboy. "I like to think what I do has a little more soul."

Emma admired the way he looked just then, standing there in the glow of red and green lights in jeans, white shirt, cowboy hat, and a larger-than-life oval belt buckle any rodeo rider would be proud to call his own.

They watched the other couples dancing in rhythm and step. The irresistible sound of a new song brought more partygoers to the dance floor. The room was full now, the music loud and thumping, and the mood festive. Jim was just getting the hang of the Electric Slide when Samantha needed a break.

"He's trying his best out there," Samantha laughed. "But I think he'd better keep his day job."

"Are you okay?" Emma asked Samantha, whose cheeks looked a little flushed and splotchy.

"I think so. I just got a little worked up."

Samantha sat down with Jim at the table and drank some apple cider. Emma pulled out the metal folding chair next to hers and sat.

"I had no idea Bo could dance so well," Emma said, leaning in so Samantha could hear her over the music. "They look great together."

"She thinks he's Garth Brooks and Patrick Swayze all wrapped up in one," Samantha said.

Christina and Bo line danced in perfect rhythm on the dance floor through the first three songs. On the fourth, Tommy Whitfield slowed things down with a country waltz.

Michael leaned down to whisper in Emma's ear. She got up without answering and took Michael's hand. He led her to an open spot in the dance floor and touched his hand to her waist. Emma rested hers lightly on top of Michael's shoulder while their other hands clasped together. Slowly, soulfully they began to move with the music. She could feel strength and warmth in the way he held her hand.

The singer's voice was familiar as love itself, and Emma recognized the song; she'd always loved it. Michael had sung it to her once that summer sitting outside at her father's farm, watching for falling stars. She wondered if he remembered as they waltzed along in their own private space.

"Are you lonesome tonight?
Do you miss me tonight?
Are you sorry we drifted apart?"

Her eyes locked with his and Emma couldn't help but think how the song's famous lines mirrored their own story.

"You're right," Emma said. "This dancing definitely has some soul to it."

"Yep," Michael said, in the relaxed voice of a cowboy. "Slow dancing's like that, ma'am. In fact, anything you want to see turn out right you gotta take slow."

"I hope you're not saying great dancing is just about tempo," Emma said, having fun with their banter. "I think it's all about knowing you're dancing with the right partner."

"Well, some would argue that the secret to truly great dancing is all in having an ear for hearing the music," Michael said. "If one of the partners doesn't know it's time to dance, they'll both just be sitting it out until it's too late to move."

Emma smiled at him, surprised by how effortless it was to be with Michael. It'd been that way at dinner, and while they carted furniture from out of the spare bedroom together. It had been effortless that entire summer; like that time they fell asleep in each other's arms out by the lake one afternoon. She could still feel the soft fleece of the blanket against her face and smell the coconut scent of the suntan lotion.

"I'm sorry for what I said, Michael. I mean, not that any of it made much sense. You deserve my gratitude, not my clumsy attempts at trying to clarify things. Would you forgive me?"

"Emma, would it hurt your feelings if I said you were like a carrot on the end of a stick? Every time I make a move toward you, you get one step farther away. Forgiveness is easy when it comes to you. It's all the rest that's hard."

"What's hard?" she asked.

Michael paused, questioning just how much he should tell her.

"Doin' the right thing, Emma," he finally said. "It's the easiest, hardest thing there is."

They swayed and turned inside the pulse of the waltz. Tommy segued one slow classic into another, newer country ballad. Emma and Michael remained on the dance floor moving in time with the music, while Bo and Christina joined Jim and Samantha at their table. They all watched Emma and Michael continue slow dancing.

"What do you think of Michael and Emma tonight?" Samantha finally asked.

"I don't know what to think," Christina said between sips of cider. "They look good together, I know that."

Samantha turned to Christina, raising her eyebrows, conferring not so subtly to her that she'd missed the most important point of her question.

"She's going back in a few days," Samantha said, emphasizing each of her words. "He's still going to be here."

"I think the hopeless romantic in me believes love can make it somehow," Christina said.

"Christina, can't you see he's falling in love with her? I love Emma too, but there's every chance she'll break his heart when she goes back to Boston. Again! He'll be stuck in Juneberry doing the same old thing, wishing he could see her, and she'll be getting on with her life. Doing all the exciting things she gets to do."

The song began to fade as the overhead lights came on. It was a stark, raw light that lit up everything. Michael and Emma held each other's hands for a moment or two after the song ended.

"You're right, that's a possibility," Christina said. "But when you love somebody, things don't always go the way you want them to. Sometimes you have to stick through adversity and not give up. You know, I think love can be a test. When it gets difficult, that's when we learn if our love is real, and if we have the devotion to be true to it in spite of all the heartaches."

"Are we talking about the same thing here?" Samantha asked. "I just don't want to see him get hurt."

Mrs. Whitfield took Tommy's microphone, untwirling the cord. Emma and Michael wandered back to the table where the group sat.

"If I may have your attention," Mrs. Whitfield began, "I want to welcome everyone here tonight. Mr. Whitfield and I hope you're all having a good time."

The barn lit up with hoots and hollers of appreciation from the seventy or so guests. Men took off their cowboy hats and raised them in the air. Bo stuck two fingers between his teeth, letting out a loud, clear whistle until the applause ended.

"We're not going to stop the dance for long, I just wanted to let those of you who are interested know, Mr. Whitfield is setting up the tractor and trailer behind the barn right now. Hayrides will be starting in just a few minutes. One word of advice if you want to go out on a hayride, make sure to bundle up! It's getting chilly outside."

Mrs. Whitfield waved to the crowd with both hands before exiting the stage.

"Where does the hayride go?" Emma asked.

"Part of the ride is out in the open air, and part of it goes through the spooky orchard," Christina said with delight.

"I know what I'll be doing for the next forty minutes," Bo said.

Christina turned to face him.

"How do you know *I* want to do that?" She feigned mock irritation.

"Christina, the word *hayride* has your name written all over it."

"Yee-haw, you've got that right. Come on, baby!"

Christina pulled Bo up from the table. They grabbed their coats and bundled up for an extended ride in the cold night air. From her seat at the table, Emma watched Christina take Bo's hand as they made their way outside. It was the smallest of romantic gestures, but something in it stirred her. She thought about how much Christina wanted what she couldn't have, but she did have Bo for the dance.

"They are such a cute couple," Emma said.

The music started again and the lights went down. Partygoers ambled back on to the dance floor illuminated entirely by strings of lights hung and wrapped around nails and rafters.

"They were made for each other," Samantha said so that Emma could hear her. She locked eyes with Jim's as if to tell him, *just like us.*

The exhaust from Frank Whitfield's John Deere tractor launched billowing smoky puffs away into the night air. The temperature had fallen to somewhere in the low forties. Bo and Christina felt the chill instantly as they left the comfort of the heated barn.

A flatbed trailer as tall as Bo's chest was hitched to the tractor. Bales of straw lined the edges, and loose hay filled the middle two feet deep. An old wooden ladder had been propped up against the side of the trailer for riders to climb into the back, and as they did, they sank into the stacks of hay.

Bo and Christina found a spot in the front on Farmer Whitfield's right. They sat and leaned against a bale of straw facing the others.

"I just love this kind of stuff, Bo. I don't know why the others didn't follow our lead."

"Not everyone's as adventurous as you are." Bo pulled a piece of straw out of Christina's hair.

She snuggled closer, tighter against Bo's side for warmth. The tractor's engine sputtered, and Farmer Whitfield, dressed in a thick armor of warm winter clothing—hat with flaps, wool scarf, thick gloves—shifted the tractor into first gear, jerking the trailer forward.

Bo saw from the expression of childlike delight on Christina's face, it was the little things in life that made her the happiest. The faces of the other partygoers on the hayride were soon in shadows as the tractor moved them out into the fields.

"I'm glad you're as adventurous as me," she said, snuggling her face in the warmth of his neck.

"Christina," Bo said, wrapping his arms around her. "I wouldn't miss this for anything in the world."

They watched as the scenery around them changed, drawing

them back to an older, simpler time. Red-painted barns and tall silos, white-roofed chicken coops and grain storage containers, cows standing in the fields, their breath looking like fog in the moonlight.

The rumbling chug of the tractor drowned out the sound of all other conversations aboard the hayride. It made the whispers between them private.

"You seem especially happy tonight," Bo said.

"I love being outdoors. I love being with our friends, having us all together," Christina breathed. "And I love being with you."

She punctuated her response with a kiss to Bo's cheek.

"Sounds like you've got everything you need," he said.

Christina looked up at Bo, into eyes that were the color of faded denim. "I just want the one piece that's missing."

The hayride jostled over a bumpy trail that led into the shadowy orchard. The apple trees' cragged branches stretched out to the trail as if to reach the riders. Moonlight perched the color of bone on the edges of leaves, illuminating them. The tractor turned wide, its headlights chasing rabbits off the orchard trail.

"Let me rephrase that," she said in a soft voice of confidence. "I want to wake up every morning with you sleeping beside me."

Christina lived with a conviction that if ideas could be expressed in words, they could be understood, but Bo liked things he could touch, see. He needed Christina to explain her feelings in ways he could wrap his mind around. He knew she was a jewel, long before his dad had pointed it out to him that first Thanksgiving. Christina was smart and beautiful and successful, but that wasn't Bo's attraction or his problem. He knew how rare a thing it was to really click with someone. He knew he loved Christina more than his own life, that he'd never stop loving her, and that he'd never be loved more by someone else. But Bo remembered the bitter marriage of his youth. How he'd invested himself heart, body, and soul to its continued existence, and how he eventually lost himself and then his son in the bargain.

"As long as I'm the last man you kiss before you go to sleep at night, we're good. You aren't seeing someone else after I drop you off, are you?" he joked, doing his best to fake a serious expression.

"Yes, Bo. I'm keeping him in my laundry room."

Christina turned her soft, cold face toward him in the darkness. Her eyes closed in the dark night, and she kissed him.

Farmer Whitfield turned the tractor down the final loop of the shadow-filled trail, its headlights piercing into the apple trees like beams of daylight penetrating an unsuspecting night. Christina stretched to whisper in his ear again.

"Hey, after the dance why don't we invite everyone back to the house? We can have hot chocolate or cider, anything warm."

"Sure, if people still want to do things. I think you're just getting cold." Bo tilted his head back, staring into the night and gauging the distance back to the heated barn. Across a field of cold earth, he could see the lights in the distance. Not even Mrs. Whitfield was waiting for them.

"I am cold, Bo, but I think it could be fun. I love these times when we're all together," Christina confided. "And I love the times when it's just the two of us. You know I love you, right?

"I think so."

"You know so. I couldn't make anything more clear."

Bo kept silent. He enjoyed listening to Christina's voice. The way she expressed her passion, her enthusiasm for life, feeling little puffs of breath on his neck when she spoke.

Bo looked into the deep pools of Christina's eyes, almost certain he could see the pale clouds above reflected in them. Or maybe they, too, were like piercing beams of daylight penetrating into an unsuspecting night.

She remained still, a warm unblinking statue before him. He knew she wanted more from him, and even he believed she deserved it. In that moment, he allowed himself to wonder how it'd be, if he fell into her eyes. Would he drown there, or would they become the passageway to a marital island paradise he believed in once long ago?

He kissed her again, a deep long kiss, knowing full well the cost of falling into her, and the deepness of her love for him.

The tractor pulled under the bright outdoor lights of the farm. Farmer Whitfield shifted into neutral and stomped down the parking brake. He climbed down from the tall seat of the John Deere, stacking several bales into a makeshift staircase for the riders. Passengers debarked almost instantly, darting into the barn's warmth and the company of friends happy to see them return.

Once inside, Christina walked up to Frank Whitfield, who was opening his wool burgundy scarf, coughing into his right hand. He looked like a 1950s movie actor, one of those foursquare men who acted in Westerns and who could survive harsh winters whether on film or in real life.

"Mr. Whitfield, that was by far the best hayride I have ever been on." Christina extended her hand to shake his. The color returned to Frank's face and he smiled like he'd just gotten a compliment from one of his granddaughters.

"Well, thank you, thank you," he said. "I'm so glad you enjoyed it."

Bo took Christina by the hand again. The party looked to be breaking up. The overhead lights were on now, Tommy had stepped away from the DJ table, and the music had stopped.

"Is anyone in the mood for a late-night hangout session at my place?" Christina asked, now that the three couples were back together again at the same table. "We can make it the first official lighting of the fireplace."

Samantha looked at her watch.

"Oh, it's so late, hon. We'll see each other again tomorrow. You're both still coming to our ladies tea party after church?" Samantha asked Christina and Emma.

"Oh, yes. What can we bring, Samantha?" Emma asked.

"Nothing at all. Just plan to meet over at my place around one o'clock."

"Yes, it's getting kind of late, Christina," Emma said. "Maybe we should all call it a night. Who all are you expecting at the tea tomorrow, Samantha?"

"It's just going to be a small group. You, Christina, my daughter Beth, my friend Janette, and me. Do you know Janette Kerr, our resident movie star?"

"She wasn't a movie star, Samantha," Jim said, tearing the corners off a paper napkin left on the table.

"She was too! She made movies in Hollywood. I'd say that's a movie star."

"I've never seen one of her movies."

"Yes, you did," Samantha said. "Remember that old Western you and Noel were watching with that gunfight in the saloon? She was the blonde who worked there."

"Oh yeah, okay," Jim said. "Did she have any speaking lines?"

"She did in other movies," Samantha added, standing. "Anyway, she's the nicest lady and she goes to our church so I invited her to come."

Jim fished his keys out of his pocket.

Samantha reached for her purse on the floor beside her.

"Sorry if we're being party poopers," she said. "I don't go very long without running out of steam anymore."

"Oh, we totally understand," Christina said, summing up the feelings of the group. The three couples made their way out the way they'd come in. They thanked Mrs. Whitfield as a group, shaking her hand, before walking out into the cold, dark fields together.

The night air felt colder after being inside the barn all night. Jim put his arm around Samantha while they walked, stepping over the ankle-tall grass that was wet with fog and rain. Christina and Bo laughed and held hands. Emma and Michael walked side by side, talking in a quiet, private conversation. Christina looked back and thought she saw Emma reaching out to hold Michael's hand, but it was impossible to be certain in the misty, dark fog.

Michael parked his truck in the dirt driveway underneath a grand oak tree that swayed and creaked above them, shaking and dropping its leaves in the autumn night. The dashboard lights gave off a soft glow and the heater hummed warmth into the cab. Emma clicked on the radio and turned the volume down, the country music becoming a quiet accompaniment to their good night.

"So, did you enjoy your refresher course in South Carolina good times?" Michael asked.

"I did," Emma said, turning toward him.

"I'm glad we went. It may have been because—like square dancing—everyone needs a partner, but it was nice."

Michael studied her face, tinted blue by the dashboard lights, trying to read her thoughts. It had been twelve years since he last thought he knew what she was thinking, but then he'd been proven wrong. Twelve years. They'd lived such different lives. "It's been nice having you home. Your dad is glad to have you back. Samantha and Christina seem to feel the same way."

"Everyone's been so good to me."

Emma reached for Michael's hand.

"Especially you. You're helping my dad, you made me dinner, you took me to the dance. Thank you, Michael."

"You're welcome. It's no big deal."

"It *is* a big deal, Michael."

Emma folded one leg under her and leaned toward him. "I didn't know what to expect when I came here, but everyone's made me feel welcome. No, that's not the right word," she said, pressing her index finger against her lips. "They've overlooked my sudden departure and been gracious in a way that's more than what I deserve. Why are they doing that? Why are you?"

Michael rested his left hand on the steering wheel, leaned against the driver's door. He sighed.

"Do you really not know?" he finally said, letting his question hang in the air like a ball tossed up that wasn't going to fall back down.

"I ..." she said, when she realized he was finished with his answer. "No, I don't. It doesn't make sense. Tell me why."

"No."

"No? Why won't you tell me?"

"Because you need to figure it out for yourself."

"Okay, I can accept that. But there is an answer, right?"

"Yeah, definitely." Michael was quietly tapping his fingers against the steering wheel along with the background music. "You'll figure it out. Eventually you'll understand."

Emma drew in a deep breath and let it out slowly.

"What can I say? I'll try to figure it out. You're right, I mean, that's the least I can do."

Emma reached her hand over to adjust the truck's thermostat. She spun the knob with the tip of her finger, dialing the temperature back several degrees. "Seems like I have a lot to figure out these days. Too much."

"You want to talk about it?" Michael said, directing the air to the window defroster.

"Well …" she began. "My office has called every day, upset that I'm still here. Yesterday, I was ordered to take part in a conference call with a potential client—all part of being a partner, I know, and it's an important client and how do they not understand that I 'get' that anyway? It's not like I haven't lived out the credo that 'the firm comes first' for the past nine years. The thing is, they're making it sound like I signed some sort of agreement to prioritize my life that way. I don't remember signing that agreement. Things change, right? I've come to realize it takes only four days of making family a priority to lose nine years of equity at work.

"I needed to come to Juneberry. I understand that. And since I've been here I realize how things have changed so much in so many ways—Dad's getting older, two of Samantha's kids are practically all grown up and they've got another on the way, Christina's got her dream career. I've missed so much, you know? It's not like I can just pretend all the years didn't happen."

"Every choice we make has a cost, Em. Yesterday's choices and today's."

His voice was calm, and though the words could have stung, Emma sensed they were spoken out of kindness. She squeezed Michael's hand, pushing away the lamentable thought that he was part of the price she'd paid.

"I feel like I'm caught between two different worlds. Does that sound funny? And I feel like I'm failing in both of them."

"Emma," Michael said. "It's not that bad. Things will work out. They always do."

"Then why am I suddenly so conflicted about all this? My life in Boston is everything I wanted. I love it there. And my career—assuming I still have one when I get back—is only getting better. I should be happy about that, right?" she said.

"I think you'll have to figure that out on your own too. But not tonight; it's getting late. You need some rest."

"You're right. I think maybe you're right about a lot of things. Another mystery to solve, I suppose."

Emma pulled open the door. An instant rush of cold air hit her. She grabbed the front of her jacket and pulled it tight around her, waving good-bye with frozen fingers. Then she turned and climbed up the steps to the side porch and vanished inside.

Upstairs in her room, Emma saw her cell phone on the nightstand and picked it up, checking for voice messages before going to bed. There was one—a number she didn't recognize, 508 area code. Cape Cod. She pushed the message retrieve button and sat on the bed to listen.

"Hello, Emma? It's Colin. I'm looking out at the Atlantic Ocean from a client's beach house, and it's absolutely magnificent. I had to call you to say, wish you were here. It's relaxing, and I think you'd love it. It's warm here today and from the terrace I can feel the breeze coming in off the ocean and smell the salt water. I'm just down here for the day on business, but I thought I'd try to reach you ... anyway, if you happen to get this message tonight and it's not too late, call me back at this number. My cell phone's out of juice and I won't get the chance to recharge until I'm back in Boston tomorrow. And, Emma ..." Colin's voice reached for the right words. "Come back soon. Ciao."

She rested the cell phone under her chin and closed her eyes. Life was so like a spinning puzzle cube, only it didn't matter who spun the corners. It always wound up looking scrambled, a confusing jumble of pieces that never seemed close to falling into place.

~ THIRTEEN ~

Praise the Lord, I saw the light.

—HANK WILLIAMS
"I Saw the Light"

On her first Sunday morning in Juneberry, Emma woke to the sound of her father's electric razor—a steady hum, then the rhythmic tap of his hard-soled shoes walking across the hardwood floors in the upstairs hall. He had tried to be quiet, but every sound seemed to be amplified on this particular day.

Will Madison was accustomed to regular church attendance every Sunday. He was religious about it, a phrase he often used in conversation just to get a reaction from others. From their response, he could usually gauge their comfort level with church ... and sometimes what they felt about faith itself. He wasn't about to let something as small as a heart attack keep him away from church today.

Will dressed in a blue suit and tie, then set about the routine of combing short, silver-black hair that really didn't need fixing at all. He didn't feel comfortable in the ultracasual look so prevalent in many churches. It didn't bother him if others dressed down, but he preferred to continue practicing the respect and reverence for church he'd experienced as a young boy.

"Emma," he called from outside her bedroom door. He knocked twice on the wood post and the sound reverberated in the hallway.

"Emma, I'm going to go to church this morning. Do you want to go with me?"

He heard nothing, no shuffling feet, no snoring, not even a plea for more sleep. He considered whether Emma was used to a different Sunday-morning routine, a leisurely rise from bed perhaps, hot coffee and bagels with the oversized Sunday-morning paper sprawled out on the floor. He knocked again.

"Emma, are you awake? I didn't think to ask last night, but would you like to go to church with me this morning? Are you up?"

The door opened and Emma appeared, fully dressed. She was wearing a stylish skirt with an orange and brown pattern and a simple pullover sweater. Her hair was pulled back and held into place with a gold band that matched her necklace.

"What are you doing?" he asked.

"I'm going to church with you," she said, fitting a small hoop earring into her ear. "Is that okay?"

"Yes … yes, of course," Will responded, surprised that she was going, and delighted she was almost ready. "Are you hungry for breakfast?"

"Not really," she said. "Maybe can we pick up a coffee on the way into town?"

Hope Community Church was the big church a block off Main Street. Its white-planked steeple rose above the elms; it was tall enough that Christina could see it from her place. The building had served Juneberry well for more than 150 years, with only a few modifications—a blacktop drive and parking lot, a community room added in the early 1980s, a modernization of the sound system, and every fifty years or so, a remodeling of the main sanctuary.

Will parked the Cadillac in the back, the recently repainted yellow lines still looking fresh and bright against the blacktop. They entered the church through the community room, passing by the children's classrooms where groups of preschoolers colored at tables and snacked on Goldfish crackers and apple juice.

The community room was like a modest public-school cafeteria with cream-colored tile flooring, fluorescent overhead lights, and a half dozen windows hidden by colorful floral curtains. A Baldwin upright piano stood against a wall, and a huge bulletin board served the dual role of church information center and children's art exhibit.

They arrived right at the break between Sunday school and the main worship service. Fellowship time. The smell of hot coffee and promise of doughnuts drew congregation members like a swarm to the community room.

Will turned to Emma. "I guess we found a place that serves coffee on a Sunday after all."

Emma poured herself a cup of coffee, bypassing the plate of glazed doughnuts. She caught sight of Samantha, Jim, and Noel Connor sitting together at a round table near the bulletin board. Samantha waved from across the room, and Will and Emma set out to join them.

"Good morning! It's been awhile," Samantha joked. "Will, you look really good. How are you feeling?"

"I can't complain, Samantha. I feel pretty good, all things considered."

It was the first time Emma had seen Noel since their day at the airport and then the hospital. He looked even more grown up, Emma thought, in black dress pants, white dress shirt, and a dark jacket.

"How's the rest of your week been since we last saw each other?" Emma asked.

"Not nearly as exciting," he joked.

"Noel got an acceptance letter from SEBTS yesterday," Samantha said. "He didn't remember to tell us until this morning. There must be too much going on that boy's mind."

"Noel, that's fantastic! I didn't know you were thinking of going to seminary."

"We sent out an application in August to start next fall," Samantha informed the Madisons. "I was pretty sure he'd get accepted, but we are all thrilled."

"Do you know what you'd like to do after seminary, Noel?" Will asked.

"I think I'd like to be a minister here in Juneberry."

Samantha beamed. "He's so *smart*. That's exactly the answer a mother wants to hear."

Emma was once again spellbound by the maturity of Noel's response. She wasn't surprised that he knew what he wanted; it was what he wanted that impressed her. How could he be so sure at such a young age?

"You certainly were that to me on Monday."

"He's leading worship at the service this morning," Samantha told them.

"Which reminds me," Noel said, getting up from the table with his parents. "I need to get inside before the service begins."

Wooden pews ran along either side of the sanctuary. A caramel-colored carpet covered the floor in the aisles. At the front of the church stood a podium that matched the natural stain of the pews. A green velvet cloth hung over it and a garland of Indian corn and assorted squash decorated a table in the back.

It was quiet in the sanctuary and the stillness granted Emma a degree of peace from all the turmoil she'd described to Michael the night before. Will led Emma and the Connor family to seats midway back on the left side. Beverly Williams, the volunteer Emma had met at Wellman Medical, sat nearby.

"Glad to see you on your feet again, Will," she said as the worship music began. They all rose to their feet.

The worship that morning was stirring and inspired. Noel and two twentysomething women led the singing, accompanied only by Noel's guitar. Emma listened as the group sang, marveling as Noel's rich, full baritone resonated through the sanctuary. She didn't know the songs, but there was something about the singing that transcended words. Instinctively, she knew this was what worship really meant. They sang about God's greatness with resolute conviction. The second song was about placing trust in Christ. Emma wondered, What did that feel like? The worship leaders and members of the congregation lifted their hands in the air as they sang, reaching up to touch a heaven that seemed to near in response to the music.

When worship concluded, a young pastor named Brian Collins walked to the podium. He had short brown hair parted on the side and wore blue jeans and a short-sleeved blue tartan plaid shirt. In the front row directly ahead of him, a lovely woman of about thirty corralled three small children all under the age of eight.

"Is that your pastor?" Emma asked.

"Yes, and that's his wife and family," Will said, pointing out the mom and their kids.

"How's everyone doing this morning?" he asked. There were about two hundred people in the congregation, and a few enthusiastic members answered back they were well.

"I'm glad to hear it, because that's precisely how I feel when I wake up on a beautiful fall morning in a house with my wife and children and come to church knowing I'm going to spend time with all of you.

"I'm just going to jump right into the sermon today. No lame jokes, for which I'm sure you're especially thankful." A quiet ripple of laughter punctuated the pause before he continued. "Do you know what the Bible tells us about heaven? It says heaven is a place where we are *with* God. It tells us for all time, even before the earth was created that God the Father, Jesus Christ the Son, and the mysterious Holy Spirit were all together alive in community. Can you picture that?

"Consider this—throughout the Bible we're taught that *we're* to come together for one another, to love one another. And then, right there in the last book of the Bible, we see a description of all those who believe and trust Jesus Christ coming *together* to live forever with the Father, the Son, and the Holy Spirit. Us together with God. That's the way God's Word describes His creation when it's running the way He designed it."

Emma listened intently, distracted only by wondering when was the last time she'd been in church and heard a sermon? Eighth grade?

"The end. Well, not really, but you've just heard the shortest sermon I'll ever bring to this pulpit because there's really nothing more I can add to it—except to summarize!" Pastor Brian said, his right finger going up in the air along with a smile on his face.

"Community, community, community. It's *all* about community. That's the explanation of why it *pains* us when we find ourselves isolated from others. That's the reason *why* it hurts to say good-bye to those we love. That's the answer to the question, 'Why do people crave intimacy?' It's the reason sin is so destructive, because sin separates us from God, and from each other—sin destroys community."

Pastor Brian spoke in such a casual style she felt as if she were just listening to someone reason through the cultural issue of loneliness.

"Nothing you purchase can replace community with your friends, family, or God. No position at work can fill the void. Wealth can't take its place, and fame won't make any difference."

Emma saw pictures inside her mind of the person she was, but they were incomplete pictures, half-sketched like a child's unshaded coloring book. Just black and white outlines.

"In church we talk about a relationship with Christ, because relationships are an essential part of community. To have a relationship with someone, first you have to meet that person."

"I'm as attached to the people in Juneberry as an oak tree is rooted to the earth," Michael had told her at breakfast. *"You're more like a leaf—the wind picks you up and carries you far away."*

"Have you ever really been a part of a community?" Pastor Brian asked. This time, no one replied.

"Anyone can be a visitor, people can even be long-time residents, or citizens, but that's not the same as living in community.

"Community takes commitment. Otherwise, it's only temporary. If you're a Christian, you're part of a community called the church, God's family, and that doesn't ever go away."

When Emma tried later to recall just how the church service ended, her memory was fuzzy and unclear. She remembered her dad putting his arm around her as they walked through the community room, and how she'd rested her head on his shoulder as they walked to the car. She remembered the sun shining gloriously bright and the breeze at noontime blew warm and mild.

"Are you in the afterglow?" Will asked her on their drive to the farm.

"What?"

"The afterglow," Will said. "You're so quiet. That's the way I feel sometimes after church. I just want to enjoy the solitude without getting worked up about anything."

"Maybe," Emma said. The entire week had been part of her undoing, and church had only pushed her uncertainties closer to the edge. She felt somehow different than just a week before, something she attributed to being out of her usual groove. She thought of it as a bottle that's barely balanced, about to fall. She was standing on a point so tiny that she knew she'd have to fall one way or the other before long.

Before they'd reached the farm, Emma heard the sound of her cell phone ringing inside her purse.

"Please tell me they're not calling you about work on a Sunday," Will said.

"It might be Samantha calling about the party."

Emma took out her phone and looked at the caller ID.

"It's Colin," she said, flipping open the lid of her cell and placing it against her ear.

"Hello."

"I can't believe you've only been gone seven days. It feels like a month."

"Where are you? You sound like you're running to catch a bus."

"I'm at the club on a treadmill. Some of the members complained about not getting clear cell phone reception in the fitness center, so they made some structural changes and now we can use our phones while we workout."

The whole idea sounded farcical. "Why would you want to?" Emma asked.

"Just one more way to do business," Colin said. "I hope you're okay with me calling you. I tried to reach you last night again, but I couldn't get through."

"I'm sorry, Colin. We worked on my dad's home office all day, and last night there was a big community event here and a group of us went together."

Emma listened to Colin's breathing, a short choppy sound as clear as if he were in the car with them.

"How's the office coming?" he asked.

"It's almost finished. It just needs a little drywall work, a polish on the floor, new paint, and we'll be done."

"Furniture," Will added.

"Oh yeah, I promised to take my dad to look at office furniture. I think that's tomorrow," she said, looking at Will to confirm. He nodded. "I want to get him a cloth chair for his office, not one of those sticky leather ones."

Will rolled the Cadillac up the drive and parked it under the carport. He nodded at Emma and went inside through the kitchen door.

"Good, sounds like everything's come together. It will be nice having you back in Boston," Colin said.

Emma swung open her car door and walked out into the sunshine. She kicked off her shoes to feel the grass underneath her feet, enjoying a lackadaisical stroll after church.

"Colin, can I ask you something?"

"Yeah, go ahead," he said.

"Do you believe in God?"

She heard his surprise in the silence. Faith had never been a hot topic in their discussions.

"Yeah, I guess so. Everybody believes in God to some degree, most do anyway. Why? Did you spend the morning in a Southern revival tent or something?"

"Something like that," she joked. "I went to church with my dad. I just thought I'd ask you because I trust your opinion. You seem to know a lot about everything."

"Enough to be dangerous, I suppose," he laughed. "I believe in God, went to Mass as a kid. I think there definitely are some things that are right and wrong. Yeah, you're hearing that from a fellow lawyer. The bottom line is, I think religion's fine, unless people take it too far and fall over the edge. That's the CliffsNotes version of what I believe. What about you?"

"I think there might be more to it than that. It seems to give some people a greater sense of community."

"Like I say, I'm not an expert. I think religion is like medicine. When life gets you down, it's there if you need it."

"Christina probably has some thoughts on the subject," Emma said, her eyes drawn to dozens of yellow wildflowers still in bloom, growing on the side of the barn.

"Who's Christina?"

"A friend of mine. She's a Christian author and speaker. Travels around the country talking about things like this."

"Maybe you should talk to her about it."

"Maybe I will," Emma said.

"Okay, let me ask you a question," Colin said.

"All right," she said, carrying a handful of wildflowers back to the house to put in the kitchen window as a gift for her dad.

"Aren't you the least bit curious why I've called you so many times this week?"

~ FOURTEEN ~

You've already proved it to me time and time again
Baby you're one good friend.

—GEORGE CANYON
"One Good Friend"

At two o'clock that Sunday afternoon, Emma parked Old Red against the curb in front of the Connors' quaint Juneberry home. She noticed the ornate Victorian porch, recognized Samantha's touch in how it was decorated behind the waist-high wooden handrail. Corn stalks, straw bales, a small kitschy scarecrow, assorted pumpkins and gourds greeted visitors and gave them a friendly welcome.

Emma climbed five porch steps, walking up to the open door feeling like a kid trick-or-treating. She knocked, but just as she gave the door her first tap, Jim was getting up from the recliner.

"Am I the first?" she asked.

"No, no, there's a couple already back there," Jim said, opening the glass door and escorting her through the Connors' homey family kitchen.

Samantha greeted her at the patio door, all smiles. She wore not a trace of anxiety, which impressed Emma. The thought of running around to set up a tea party after spending all morning at church was daunting to her.

"Samantha, this looks beautiful," she said, standing on a step at the back patio doorway.

The enclosed patio ran almost the full length of the house. It was kind of a hidden treasure, a screened-in sanctuary overlooking Samantha's backyard garden. Latticework capped the farthest porch wall, providing privacy and some separation between houses. Samantha had decorated the space in white wicker, including rocking chairs and a love seat, a bookcase filled with plants along the house wall, and baskets containing large green ferns hanging from the ceiling.

She'd warmed up the room with pink decorator pillows and a beautiful ruby red carpet.

"Hi, Emma." Samantha welcomed her with a hug.

"I'm so glad you could make it. Let me introduce you to everybody. You know Beth; she's a little taller than the last time you saw her."

Beth said hi with a wave, somehow managing to pull off looking grown up enough to be invited and too cool to be there all at the same time.

"And I'd like you to meet Janette Kerr," Samantha said, gesturing toward the smiling older woman sitting in one of the wicker rocking chairs. "Janette has become such a good friend through our ladies Bible study at church."

"How do you do?" Janette said, in a voice sounding both gracious and sociable. Her face looked familiar. The blonde-haired woman with a gentle hello and unhurried manners radiated peace. Emma wondered but didn't think she'd ever seen one of Janette's movies.

"Fine, thank you. It's a pleasure meeting you. I understand you're an actress?"

"Oh, ho, that was a *long* time ago."

Emma sensed she was neither proud nor ashamed of her

Hollywood career, weary perhaps of having the same conversations about it. Emma took her answer as a hint and sat down with her at the table.

"Sure is a pretty dress you're wearing," Emma told her.

"Thank you. I wore it to church this morning."

"We're still waiting on Christina," Samantha said. "But I'm just so glad that you're all here today. I wanted to throw a welcome-back party for Emma since we love her and haven't had a chance to see her in a while. Now that the weather's cooler and the bugs are gone, I thought we could all get together and just have some snacks and girl talk."

From the other room, they heard Christina's voice.

"Looks like we're all here!" Samantha said.

After hugs and hellos and compliments on the patio's decor, everyone was seated for tea.

"As you can see, we have a couple different kinds of hot teas, fruit tea, unsweetened tea, and just plain old water to drink."

Beth rolled the teacart into the center of the patio. The center-piece of the impressive display was a ceramic teakettle—white with blue and purple wildflowers, surrounded by matching cups, creamer, and sugar bowl. The cart was stocked with everything from milk to cream, honey, and cakes.

"At first, I thought about asking everyone to bring a dish to pass, but then I thought maybe Beth and I could just bake a few things."

"A few things?" Christina laughed, and the others joined in. The table looked decked out for Thanksgiving, with pumpkin pie, choco-late frosted brownies, sliced turkey and bread for sandwiches, and banana bread.

"Samantha, Martha Stewart would blush in embarrassment if she were here," Christina said. "This table looks incredible."

"Yes, Samantha, you've completely outdone yourself," Emma said.

"I'm just so glad to be invited," Janette said.

Samantha smiled and joined everyone at the table and Beth began serving the tea.

"Beth, we hope you'll feel at home with us," Emma said, watching as the teenager served the hot tea with practiced poise.

"I feel like I'm with the Juneberry all-stars," she said. "You ladies have done it all."

"I'm not sure how to take that," Samantha joked.

"I'm taking it in the best sense," Christina said.

"I'll bet you all have some great stories." Beth poured another cup of hot tea and offered it to Emma.

"Stories we've got!" Christina said. "I'm not sure we're going to tell them, but ..."

The four ladies laughed, and Samantha coaxed the seated women to help themselves to the food.

"Oh, come on. Mom says you and Emma went to high school together and used to hang out at her house all the time. What kind of teenagers were you? Did you ever get into any trouble?" Beth asked.

"We were actually pretty good girls," Christina said. "Your mom made sure of that. Emma was on the track team, and I was in student council."

Beth poured a cup of tea for her mother after serving everyone else, then poured herself half a cup. "What about boys?" she asked.

"We dated some in high school," Christina said. "Mark Barnes—do you remember Mark?" she asked Emma. "Mark asked me to the junior prom, and I dated a foreign exchange student from Ecuador my senior year."

"Ricardo!" Samantha and Emma belted out, laughing at the memory.

"He was nice," Christina said. "Okay, a little weird, but nice."

"What about you, Emma? You must have had lots of boyfriends."

"Not really," she said, pouring cream into her tea and stirring it. "I was more of a tomboy in high school. I dated some, but it was on and off."

"You dated Michael in high school," Samantha reminded her. "Everyone thought you two made a nice-looking couple."

"We were never that serious," Emma said. "We went to a couple of dances, and he asked me to go to a game and watch him play baseball that spring. But really we were all just part a big social group. Somehow, we managed to escape the entanglements of awkward teenage romances."

"Speak for yourself," Samantha said. "I *married* my high school sweetheart, although to be honest, our relationship was never that awkward. My parents liked Jim right off the bat, and I got along with his mother so well that by the time June came around after graduation, we were already talking seriously about a wedding that upcoming fall—and no Beth, don't *even* think about it."

"You and Michael were never serious?" Christina asked. "You got along so well that summer during college, I would have expected that was sparked by a trace of something from when you dated before."

"Hmm, you're really asking me to go way back, aren't you," Emma said. "He'd asked me to dance with him my sophomore year, that was the first ... no, he'd helped me open my locker—oh this is funny, I'd forgotten. He helped me open my locker my freshman year. Remember how hard it was to open those old lockers with the combinations—turn right, turn left. I could not get mine to open, and then this arm reached over my shoulder and whacked the door by the handle and it popped open. Turned out it was just stuck."

"How did you two get back together that summer before law school?" Samantha asked.

"It was sweet, really. I had taken my dad's truck to Dudley's car wash on top of the hill—is it still there? I don't remember seeing it. Anyway, my dad offered it to me for the summer and I wanted to wash off the farm dust and vacuum the inside. I think I'd graduated from BU only a few days earlier. It was May, warm and sunny, I was so happy to be done with school for a little while.

"Michael and his friend Terry drove up to wash his Blazer and we just started talking. He was already working in construction at the time. Michael and I just started hanging out all the time. We loved to go out to the lake and look at the stars. He'd bring me flowers, listen to me tell all my dreams, and I wrote him letters ..."

Emma drifted back in time on a wave of memories, as buoyant as a raft on a summer lake. She wondered when she started signing those letters, "I love you."

"I don't think there was a day that entire summer that we didn't spend at least some time together. He was on my mind all the time."

Her eyes bore through the glass-top wicker table as she spoke. A single finger rocked back and forth across the edge of her teacup. The other women listened in silence.

"Every week our love grew deeper and wider. By the Fourth of July, I knew I was over my head in love with him. We thought we were perfect together, and I never doubted it, not once."

Emma stopped. Her testimony, and then her silence, only deepening the mystery. Around the table, the ladies' collective curiosity built into a crescendo.

"You can't stop there. What happened?!" asked Christina.

Emma ran her small delicate hand over her blue and white cloth napkin next to her plate, feeling the coarse fibers, tracing its patterns. Christina was right, she'd gone too far into the story to stop telling it now. She owed it to them. She took one last look over the figurative rocky cliff—the interruption in her story—then made the decision to dive into the deep blue lake.

"At my dad's house, we're remodeling an old room, the guest bedroom downstairs. Michael suggested we could gain some extra square footage if we knocked out the closet. It was being used for storage, so first we had to empty out all the boxes. We moved them into the living room along with all the bedroom furniture and other debris from the renovation.

"Friday afternoon, while my dad was upstairs resting, I went through the boxes for the first time." She looked around the table. The other women were spellbound, motionless at the table.

"He'd stored all my mother's things in them, some of it trivial, things I guess he didn't want to throw away. Old birthday cards, photographs, love letters, their high school yearbook. I found two photo albums, one from their wedding. The other had pictures of their first house, in Juneberry I guess. On another page there was a faded photo from when they purchased the farm. There was snow on the ground and the biggest smile on my mother's face. She was all red lipstick and peg-leg slacks. On the last pages, there were pictures of my parents bringing their newborn baby home from the hospital. It was so long ago, the three willow trees weren't even planted in the front yard yet. There were a few photos of me as a little girl, then the pictures stop."

Emma's story stopped too, paused while she allowed her thoughts to pool again.

"I spent my childhood looking for my mother and never finding her, wanting something I couldn't have. *Someone to watch over me*," Emma said, in a whisper like it was a joke, but one that brought pain instead of laughter. "We lived in a house filled with obscure, hazy memories, and an almost indescribable heaviness because someone was missing. There was an empty place in my heart, and I'm sure in my dad's, too. One day she was there, and the next …"

"I guess I was about twelve when I came to terms with it all, accepted the fact that my mom wasn't coming back. I just decided the best thing to do was to put it all behind me, 'cause I couldn't handle it. Does that sound weird? I took those things of hers that I had—a small, framed picture I kept by my bed, a ring handed down to me that I used to play dress up with, a bronze key chain from Clemson, stuff you'd give a kid," Emma said, and sniffled.

"I put all those things in my jewelry box, and loaded the box in a canvas bag. I rode my bike out to Close Point at the lake, to where it's swampy and remote. I took a gardening spade with me, and I began to dig in the mud and clay. I must have dug for half an hour, and when the hole was big enough, I dropped the canvas bag with the jewelry box into it, and buried it up in the mud."

"My gosh, do you think it's still buried there?" asked Samantha.

"That was the year I moved to town, right?" Christina said.

"Yes," Emma said. "And for the rest of junior high and high school, things went pretty well.

"One day when I was in the library, during study hall, I found a shelf with college catalogs. When I saw one from Boston University, I just connected with it. I remember standing there between the bookshelves thumbing through its pages. Later, I asked the guidance counselor, Mrs. Garrish, if she thought Boston was too far away for me to go to college, and I remember she told me, 'No, it's just up the coast.'"

"It's like, what, eight hundred miles?" Christina said.

"I needed a break. I needed to get away, and put it all behind me. I found I could do that the farther I got away."

"And Michael?"

"That summer with Michael … It was the first time I'd been back in the house for a whole season. Sometimes, when Michael and I would go out to the lake, I'd remember what I'd buried in the mud there as a little girl.

"I'd go home at night to a dark house and feel her presence, the memories, and I'd try to push them away again until morning. As the summer wore on, that got harder and harder to do. I loved Michael, but I also felt trapped here … not because of Michael, but because of painful memories, things I never talked about to anyone. And the draw of Boston became so strong because it made them go away, mostly anyway. I had built a good life there. And a future, too. In the end, that was what I put all my trust in—the future I was pursuing in law. I knew leaving came with a price. I guess … I just didn't know how costly it would be."

"What did Michael say when you told him you were leaving?" Christina asked.

"We talked about my future a lot and how it would affect us. You know, he said all the right things. But when it came down to the last few days before I was scheduled to depart, I just decided to book an earlier flight to save us both the pain of a long good-bye."

Samantha raised her eyebrows.

"I know, not the way I would choose to do it today, but I thought it was like pulling off a Band-Aid. Then I got busy at law school, and Christmas came and went and the next summer I took an internship rather than come back to Juneberry. We can fast-forward through the rest, but basically I graduated, passed the bar, and was hired at Adler & McCormick and continued my fourteen-hour workdays," Emma said, looking at Samantha. "The next thing I knew, I was answering your phone call about my dad. Nearly a decade had flown by."

"So you never really said good-bye to Michael?" Christina asked.

Emma nodded. "Sadly, that's true."

"I remember my mom coming home from the funeral and crying in her bedroom," Samantha said. "Hannah was her favorite sister and she always took care of her. I can remember her saying to me, 'Who's gonna love that little girl now? Who's gonna take care of that little girl?'"

"I wanted to escape the memories of my mom," Emma replied. "I didn't think of it as running away, though, because I really was running to something. A good something. But ... yeah ... the more I think about it, the more I realize that's what I did."

"Emma, I'm sorry you felt so alone. I feel like if only we'd have known somehow," Samantha said. "We were all so close. We could have done more."

"I don't know, Samantha. I couldn't talk with anyone about it. Even Michael, who was so good to me."

"Christina, help me out here, but, Emma, I think you're missing an important part of the story," Samantha said. All of their teacups were empty, but no one moved to refill them.

"I *so* know where you're going with this," Christina said, creaking back in her white wicker chair, pleased that it all made sense to her now.

"I think it's the most obvious part of your story. It may be the part that's eluded you for all these years: Emma, Michael Evans is the one. He's your soul mate," she said.

"Absolutely."

"Even I can see that," said Beth.

Samantha noticed the empty cups. "Honey, can you go heat more water for more tea?"

"But this is the best part!" Beth protested, but Samantha motioned her inside with her eyes.

"Emma, people can do the craziest things, make the most horrible decisions at the worst times, and they can *not* act when the timing is critical," Christina said. "This is the first time I've really heard what really happened between you and Michael. I think Samantha might have seen it—"

"Yeah, I did."

"—but I didn't realize the scope of it all, not until I heard you tell it. Now I'm wondering, Emma, if you see it."

All eyes looked to Emma, who was sitting with her back to the patio screen. The sun had just passed the top of the world, starting its descent into late afternoon, and the air felt breezy and warm.

"I don't honestly know what I see. Michael's a great guy, but that was twelve years ago. We had a wonderful time last night, but I'm leaving again for Boston this week. However I got there, I have a life in Boston now. A good life. And a career, too."

Emma's answer sounded sensible and resolute. She didn't bother to present other evidence to her friends that contradicted sensibility and resolve, such as the way she'd felt there on Main Street the first day she laid eyes on him. Or how when she'd thought of him in Boston, and she did think of him sometimes, she hoped he still resembled the man she'd fallen in love with. And when she'd seen him, standing at the tailgate of his white Chevy, it was like he was everything from before, only better. Emma chose not to mention how it felt to dance with Michael, to be held by him surrounded by timeless tradition and by friends who had loved her—even if from eight hundred miles away—for a lifetime. She didn't mention any of these things, because she didn't want to think of them. She wanted to stuff them in a canvas bag and bury them in the mud because it was easier that way. It was easier to leave a day earlier rather than hang around and listen to someone you love ask you to marry him. Faraway places offer the irresistible gift of silence from the voices and the memories.

Beth returned with more hot water, and Samantha suggested they brew a pot of chamomile. While the group watched young Beth opening and setting the tea to brew like a skilled barista, Janette spoke up for the first time that afternoon.

"I didn't know your mother that well," Janette said. "In fact, I don't think I ever spoke to her except once at the grocery store, but Emma, I'm going to pray for you because I feel like there's more going on than you realize. I can't say what exactly, 'cause I don't know, but I'll be praying."

"Thank you," Emma said, feeling better for having shared her story, but tired of being the center of attention. "Can I just suggest we change the subject now?"

The women laughed, and Beth poured the new pot of tea.

"What about you, Christina," Samantha asked. "What's happening in your story?"

"Oh, I'm just in love with a wonderful man who's been deeply wounded and lost his family. He's afraid of moving forward, and I'm not willing to give him up, so I'm praying and waiting, not worrying or pushing. It's hard, but I'm confident God will work it out somehow."

"How long has Bo been divorced?" Janette asked.

"Eight years."

"That's a long time. Are you sure you aren't waiting in vain for something that'll never happen?"

"I think the something that happened is, I met Bo Wilson. I didn't meet someone who's potential husband material; I met my best friend and I can't imagine living life without him."

"I'm hearing a lot of new things I can pray for," Janette said. "I'll pray for you, too, Christina,"

"You better watch out, Christina. Janette is a real prayer warrior," Samantha said. "If she's praying for you, you've got a real ally on your side."

"Beth, what about you?" Christina asked. "Remind us how the world looks through the eyes of a high school senior."

"I like hearing your stories," Beth said, sitting on a wicker hassock near the teacart. "They're funny and sad."

"What do you hope your story will be, Beth?" Christina asked.

"Well, one worth telling. I know I want to be a somebody."

"What's a somebody?"

"A somebody is a person who's successful, and everyone knows who they are. An actor, a singer, the guy who invented the iPod. That's a somebody."

The ladies let out an audible groan.

"We've had these discussions before," Samantha said, turning her attention to Janette. "A lot of people in Beth's generation don't think they're important unless they possess some level of celebrity. They're using the Internet to draw attention to themselves so they can feel important, not for something they've accomplished, but just to be seen in a make-believe celebrity medium."

Beth sighed and shook her head. It was clear to Emma that she'd heard this argument more than once.

"Beth, dear, I was an actress in Hollywood. Back in the days when stars really were glamorous," Janette said. "It's not what you think it is."

"Maybe you could talk a little about that, Janette," Samantha suggested. "I'd appreciate any wisdom you have on the subject."

Janette turned her chair toward Beth.

"I won't give you the long version, but I had dreams too when I was your age. Eighteen, nineteen. I wanted to go to Hollywood and become an actress. It was in the early 1960s, and against my mother's wishes, I went to California and worked my way in the Hollywood system. I appeared in movies, on television. I met lots of the really big stars, and one day—*phfft!* it was over."

"The people who have their names up in lights aren't any different than anyone else. All the time you're either struggling to get somewhere or working hard to hang onto what you've got. Some of the most famous people in movies don't feel famous on the inside. They feel like they're faking it. Sure, I had a lot of fun out there, especially when I was young. People just assumed I was rich because I was in the movies, but I barely made any money at all. It's all an illusion. Make-believe. You're somebody because God loves you, not because you happen to become famous for a short time, and that's all it is—temporary. I don't know if you'll believe me, but you'll never find a greater audience than the crowds in heaven who look down and want you to have the life God has for you."

"I have to agree with Janette, Beth. I've met lots of musicians and artists in my work," Christina added. "Peter Thomas is a friend of mine. He has a *great* voice, but he's just a normal person."

"You know Peter Thomas?" Beth asked, her eyes filling with celebrity stardust for the man whose worship songs were sung in churches around the world. "Oh my gosh, he's awesome."

"Beth, Peter's a totally regular guy. He doesn't live a better life just because he's famous."

"I think he does," Beth said. "Being famous tells everyone you're important."

"Honey, I was once on the cover of a magazine that sat on newsstands all over the world, but at the same time I lived in a tiny apartment in West Hollywood with a roommate—another actress under contract with the studios. We worked hard attending premieres and parties, rubbing shoulders with the famous. Then we'd go home to our apartment and wonder how we'd pay next month's rent."

FIFTEEN

You're climbing mountains, I'm on the hill
You're always running, I'm standing still.

—VINCE GILL
"If You Ever Have Forever in Mind"

It was late Sunday afternoon when the ladies' tea finally ended. Sam insisted Emma take the fruits and veggies for her dad—grapes, orange wedges, cherry tomatoes, and some avocado—wrapping them up in ziplock bags.

"When are you leaving to go back to Boston?" Janette asked Emma while she slipped into a bright red wool coat with black faux-fur lapels.

"Wednesday morning," Emma said, taking hold one shoulder of the coat and helping Janette into it.

"If you have time, dear, come see me before you leave, okay? I'd like to talk with you." Emma wasn't sure she'd have time, but something about Janette's invitation conveyed it was more important than just a social call. She'd almost gotten the words "I'll try" out of her mouth, when the storm door closed and Janette was already out of earshot.

"Samantha, I'm just amazed by this day," Christina said. "Thanks for getting everybody together. It couldn't have been any nicer."

"I'm so glad you enjoyed it." Samantha hugged Christina and Emma at the front door. "A week ago I would have never believed we'd be here having tea today. There's a part of me that's been unsettled, and now I feel so much better."

"I think I've been feeling that way too," said Emma, stuffing the last snack bag into her purse.

"What are you all going to do for the rest of the night?" Christina said.

"Bo and I have a movie date at home. It's part of our new Sunday-night strategy to hang out more. What about you, Emma?"

"I don't know," Emma said, thinking out loud. "I've thought about calling Michael."

Samantha smiled. "To talk about the renovation I suppose," she ribbed. "Emma, are you even considering the possibility that Michael means more than you've come to terms with?"

"I'll think about it," she said, just before Jim and Noel opened the front door from the outside and Emma slipped through it.

The sun had dropped behind the tree line, lowering the temperature by ten degrees. A gust of wind wound inside her coat, and she hurried to the shelter of the truck. Emma pushed the key in the ignition, the green Sinclair dinosaur key chain bouncing back and forth like a hypnotist's watch. She switched on the heat, pushing the level all the way into the red zone before heading toward town. The wind had picked up, blowing leaves through the beams of her headlights as the bleak October sky closed out light and color. One thought tumbled round and round inside Emma's mind, but she wasn't sure she wanted to admit it: She wanted to see Michael again, and soon—that night.

She got out her phone and dialed his work number, but there was no answer. She opted not to leave a message, unsure of what she'd say.

"Wouldn't you know it."

Emma tossed the cell phone back on the seat, and it bounced end over end into shadows. She returned her attention to the drive back out to the farm. *Why couldn't Michael just be at home? And what is this urgency to see him all about anyway?* She considered swinging by his place, then decided that would be lame.

Except for the local grocer and a BP station on the end of West Main, all the shops in Juneberry were closed. Emma didn't feel like closing so early on a Sunday. She felt energized and not in the least bit ready to call it a night.

Christina and Bo had their planned movie night. Samantha and Jim had each other. Emma felt like something was supposed to be happening in her world too, but what? The musical pulse from her cell phone chimed in the dark and she felt around on the truck's long front seat to find it. With a long, right-leaning reach, her hand bumped against it. She grabbed the phone just before it slid between seat and door.

"Hello?"

"Hey, it's Michael. Did you call me?"

"Yes, I did. Thanks for calling back," Emma laughed with a mixture of surprise and relief. "Do you have plans tonight?"

"No, no plans. I'm unhitching my boat right now, but that's about it."

"I didn't know you had a boat."

"It's just an old fishing boat. I was out on the lake this afternoon until the fog rolled in and the fish went deep."

"Did you catch anything?"

"Not this time. It was too late in the day. I just wanted an excuse to be out on the water."

A misty spray of rain landed on Old Red's windshield as Emma drove the winding country roads. She liked listening to the sound of his voice in the dark, like FM radio at night.

"Sounds like you won't be having fish for dinner."

"Not unless I open a can of tuna," Michael said. "Dinner sounds good, though. I'm starved."

"Well, what would you say to having dinner with me?"

Michael was silent for a moment on the other end of the phone, and Emma entertained the painful possibility that he might say no.

"Give me thirty minutes. I've just got to stow the boat and tackle, clean up."

This felt right. Emma smiled.

"Hey, is it raining where you are?" she asked, finally turning the knob that switched on Old Red's wiper blades.

"It's rained off and on at the lake all day."

"How about going someplace warm for dinner, where there's a fire. Do you know of a place like that?"

"Not around here, but there's a Sportsman's Lodge in Anderson."

"Anderson? Isn't that too far to drive in the rain?" she asked, as the truck's headlights carved a tunnel of light from the rainy darkness on SC59.

"I don't think so," Michael said, unwinding the crank on the boat hitch, slivers of rain hitting him in the dark. "Where are you now?"

"I'm about five minutes away from the house."

"Great. I'll pick you up in forty minutes."

❦

Noel Connor worked underneath his Dodge truck inside the Connors' garage, removing the oil-pan cap. He'd slid an old, stained aqua-colored blanket beneath the car to lie on while he changed the oil; the cement floor was too cold for comfort.

Noel saw his dad's feet step inside the garage door. The radio was on Q98 Country, but the volume was set low.

"How's it coming?" Jim squatted down to peer underneath the truck.

"Fine. I'm just puttering around out here tonight. Helps me relax."

"Your mom just sent me out here to tell you we're having leftovers from the party tonight. They look pretty darn good too. Why don't you take a break, come on in for supper."

"I'll be right there," he said. Noel reached for a faded red rag next to the toolbox and wiped grease from his hands.

"Panthers are playing tonight too if you feel like watching the game."

Noel tilted his head to look at his dad. "That sounds great too. I won't be much longer. This is the last thing I've got to do."

Jim lowered himself down even farther to get a better look at Noel's work on the truck.

"You know, I'm proud of you."

"For what?"

"I guess for a few things you've done this week. If I were a rich man, I'd give you a hundred dollars and tell you to go have fun with your friends."

Noel joked, "Make it a fifty."

"I don't think I have that either," Jim teased. He lay back on a mechanic's rolling sled and wheeled himself underneath the truck next to Noel.

"Fancy meeting you here, Dad," Noel said, smiling.

"Hey, I've always thought it was better to have conversations face-to-face whenever possible. What I was going to say was … your mom and I are proud of your decision to go to seminary, for helping Emma at the airport, leading worship today at church, lots of things. You've got a lot on the ball for someone your age, even for someone my age."

Noel just nodded. "Thanks, I guess I feel like God's got me where He wants me. I'm kinda excited to see what's next."

"Your mother really liked your answer today about coming back to Juneberry to work someday. You scored some major mama points, Son.

"It's rare that people receive a calling so specific. Your mother and I have prayed a long time, that your faith would grow more important to you, and that God would show you what He wants you to do. Sounds like He's done just that."

Noel stopped tinkering for a moment to look directly at his dad. "Sometimes it's like He's telling me what I need to pack for a trip before I ever set out on it. I mean, I just follow basic instructions and find myself standing in the place where God's working."

Noel's answer silenced Jim. He waited a moment before saying anything, watching his son work on the old truck.

"I imagine there are more than a few of us who wish we could hear God as clearly. I know one thing, though: Your mom and I sure heard Him right when we decided it was time to start a family. We love you, Son."

A strong wind sent the fallen leaves scurrying like packs of spiders clacking along beneath the streetlights. The air was chilly, like Friday-night football weather, on the starless night, and corn stalks from the harvest lay broken in the fields.

Few vehicles were on the main highway as Michael and Emma piloted their way toward Anderson in scattered rain. In the time before Michael picked her up, Emma had changed her clothes, touched up her makeup, and fixed her hair in a new way that she actually thought looked good.

The lights of the Sportsman's Lodge emerged from out of the dark like a warmly lighted oasis. Inside, the rustic restaurant looked like it'd been carved from wilderness timber a hundred years before. A fire glowed in the fieldstone fireplace, freshened by new logs. The dining room was nearly empty, with many patrons kept away by the night and the weather.

The drizzle outside only enhanced the cozy atmosphere inside, making the surroundings all the more alluring. The hostess seated them in a wine-colored booth by the fire.

"Michael, this is so cozy. It's *exactly* what I imagined when we talked on the phone tonight."

A young waiter, no older than Noel, approached from the server's station. He came bearing gifts: two glasses of ice water carried on a round tray. He greeted them with a friendly "Good evening" and joked that they should expect dazzling service since they were his only table. He was wearing a plastic nametag that said AARON.

Emma asked for hot tea with honey, a taste she still had from the afternoon, and Michael ordered black coffee, which the waiter brought to him in a tall white mug.

"Do you need a few minutes to decide?" Aaron asked.

"Yeah, I think so," said Michael, who was watching Emma read her menu instead of looking at his own.

"Take your time," he said. "Our specials tonight are sea bass with vegetables and rice, and filets wrapped in bacon. I'll be back in a few minutes."

He disappeared through a set of double doors into the kitchen.

"What were we talking about?" Michael asked, pushing the laminated menu to the edge of the table.

"I don't know. I might have been saying how happy I was that you called me back. Your timing was wonderful."

"Sorry I missed your call the first time," Michael said. "I had just stepped outside the truck to unhook the boat trailer. It took a little longer than normal because of the rain, but I saw you'd called when I got back in the truck."

The waiter returned, topping off Michael's coffee. They ordered the specials, one of each, eliciting compliments from Aaron, who took their orders to the kitchen without writing them down. When he was gone again, they sat without speaking, merely looking at each other.

Emma felt as though her heart had been flipped like a pancake since she first arrived in Juneberry. She wanted to tell Michael about the changes somehow but wasn't sure how she'd put it into words. She wanted to tell him about the morning worship service, the conversation at Samantha's—and how everything felt new and uncertain. Emma decided to temper her emotional earthquake with the wisdom of allowing the night to run its natural course.

"Tell me about fishing," Emma finally asked.

"After church, I like to go to quiet places where I can be alone. I hadn't been out on the water in a few weeks, so I hitched up the boat and drove over to Lake Greenwood for the day. I got such a late start that most of the other fisherman were coming in as I was going out. I saw that the clouds were getting dark to the north, but they were slow moving. So I headed out and was able to fish for about two hours before the first raindrop fell. Got a few bites, but no fish."

"What do you do when the fish aren't biting?" she asked, watching the light from the fireplace flicker on his forehead.

Michael thought for a moment. "I listen to the water lapping up against the sides of the boat. I think about things. Let all the stuff from the workweek fade away for a time."

"It sounds relaxing."

The waiter brought out the filet and sea bass, and a basket of oven-warmed bread that he placed on the table with a small container of honey butter.

"Is there anything else I can bring you tonight?" he asked.

"I think we're good," Michael said. Emma nodded her agreement and he was gone again. Michael asked if he could pray for the food and Emma agreed to that, too. Then he offered her a piece of bread and the two began eating.

"Why don't you tell me about your day?" he said.

"I'm not sure I can put it into words. More than anything else, I think I've been moved by a sense of gratitude, Michael."

He looked up at her, surprised. There was something about her that was different, tranquil perhaps, like she'd de-stressed enough from small-town living to have at long last caught her breath.

"What happened today to prompt that?"

"Not just today. It's been happening all week, one day cascading into another. I can't put it into words, but I feel *different*. I've been thinking back on the way you looked after me in high school and even how we felt about each other that summer, and I see what an incredible man you've become … and …"

"And it's made you feel … *grateful*?"

"Yes. But saying that somehow seems smaller than it is." Emma leaned her fork against the dinner plate, her eyes taking on the wandering look of searching for the right words. "Something's going on with me; I just don't know what it is. I knew it would sound confusing when I tried putting it into words."

Emma reached across the table and took hold of Michael's hand.

"Michael, don't you feel sometimes like you're part of a bigger story? Like there's more going on that you can see or touch?"

Michael didn't say anything. He just stared at Emma trying to read in her eyes just how much of the bigger story she had absorbed. He'd been aware of the larger story his whole life.

"That's how this feels."

It was 10:00 p.m. when the movie Christina and Bo were watching ended. Bo found the remote control next to the half-empty popcorn bowl and pointed it at DVD player, then the TV, shutting off the electronics.

"I think it's time to call it a night," he said, setting the remote down and squeezing Christina's hand to rouse her.

Christina stretched. "I did pretty good there for a while, only dozed off right near the end."

She yawned, stretching out her arms full length before dropping them gently around Bo's neck.

"So was this Sunday a lonely one, or did we fix that problem?"

"I think we fixed it. How was yours?"

Christina gazed at him through sleepy eyes. "My entire weekend couldn't have been any nicer. The barn dance, church this morning, Samantha's party, and a movie night with you. All of my favorite things all wrapped up in one weekend. How did I get such a blessed life?"

Bo touched Christina's face, twisting a strand of golden blonde hair around his finger.

"Because you're a good person."

She closed her eyes, resting her cheek against Bo's hand.

"I don't think that's it, but I'm so glad God's blessed me with you."

She opened her eyes and kissed Bo.

"My favorite moments are the ones when it's just the two of us," she whispered in a voice so low he had to bend his ear to her lips to hear her. "I never feel more complete. I never feel more alive than when I'm with you."

"You know I love you, too, right? Just don't expect a lot of fancy words, 'cause you know I ain't got 'em. But it would be a shame, probably a sin, if you never knew how much you mean to me."

Christina closed her eyes, a smile curling up the corners of her pink lips.

"I'm not trying to be a pushy chick, but with all this good vibe going around, do you ever think about our being able to do this all the time? Do you think about us …" she paused. She knew Bo wasn't particularly confident expressing his emotions.

"I think about it," he said. "It's like there's two parts of me. One part wants us to be together, and another part just doesn't want to lose you. I had a family once. I had a son, a commitment. I lived in a totally different way than you see me right now. And then, whack, one day it was all gone. She took a part of me away. I'm still not all here, Christina."

Christina's heart broke for Bo. "We could do it *together*," she pleaded with him. "I could help you heal. I know God wants to restore you."

"If I didn't think that was possible, I'd have to let you go. I couldn't keep you hanging on, but I'm not ready."

Christina drew in a long breath, and let it out slowly. After two years of dating, it was so dispiriting seeing how much distance there still was to go. She closed her eyes for strength.

"I'm going to pray, Bo, that God will work this out."

Christina started to sob. "I'm sorry, Bo, I don't know why I'm crying. It's just so strange how God can work out really complex problems with such grace and ease, and yet our situation remains unfixed."

She wrapped her arms around the man she loved but couldn't have. Closing her eyes tight, she prayed for God to break through.

~ Sixteen ~

Fall into these arms of mine
I'll catch you every time.

—Clay Walker
"Fall"

Monday morning opened with a brilliant sunrise, a burning yellow-orange ball rising like mercury in the east. Along the mountain ridge, and on every tree in the valley, colors popped with an awe-inspiring vibrancy from the touch of a fiery sun.

Michael took note of the colors on his drive to the Macintosh house, high in the hills above Juneberry. He parked on the gravel construction drive and, opening the door of his truck, stepped outside, breathing in the crisp morning air.

The coffee tasted just right, even if it was from a paper cup. It was strong medicine to help him sift through something Emma said to him the night before.

It was a much different time when the twenty-two-year-old Emma talked of "feeling grateful" under a Juneberry moon, just days before she disappeared. *Grateful. For their relationship? Or for the opportunities that awaited in Boston?* She left him days later, leaving only memories of their love behind.

Last night she said she was grateful. She said she felt *different*, too. *How different?* he wondered.

He thought back to their dinner, watching her talk in the honey-eyed firelight. He'd never seen a more beautiful woman in all his life. He never loved another woman as he'd loved Emma. Even in the dry years, those dozen distant summers when no one had heard a word from her and he'd doubted he'd ever see her again, the flame continued to burn inside him. He was certain it was this ongoing, unrequited love that doomed all of his dating relationships during the past dozen years.

Bo hadn't yet arrived at the work site. The sun broke free above the horizon line, pouring warmth against Michael's face and neck to soften the bite of the chilly autumn morning. He pulled on a pair of heavy leather work gloves and lifted a bundle of roofing shingles from his truck. With any luck, they'd finally finish the Macintosh roof that had been twice delayed by rain.

Noel Connor strummed his Taylor guitar on the patio in the quiet of morning, singing worship songs. The Bible rested open in front of him on the glass-top wicker table where the day before, Christina, Emma, his mom and sister, and Janette had sipped chamomile tea and chatted. Noel read a few verses from David's psalms and made up his own songs, conversations between God and him. The sound of the pick against the guitar strings danced through the screens, reverberating into the yard with its birdbath, fountain, and stone walkway. God's creation was majestic and alive to Noel. He closed his eyes and prayed to hear the Silent Voice.

Will lay in bed that morning watching the sun come up in his window, a prayer of thanksgiving moving silently on his lips. One week earlier, a Monday morning, he had sipped coffee alone at his kitchen table, not yet dressed for work, when he felt a tingling pain shoot down the length of his left arm. As crazy as it sounded, he'd do it all over again if he had to. He thought as he lay in bed, how life was better because of the heart attack. His prodigal daughter had come home.

He rolled out of his warm bed, and knelt down on the cold wood floor. "Thank You, Lord," he said, eyes pressed shut, feeling the stitched patchwork of the quilt Hannah made them against the palms of his hands. "Thank You."

Bo Wilson pulled in late at the Macintosh house. Usually, they could set each other's watches by their routine. He was always on-site by sunup with a drive-through breakfast in hand and a well-fed dog hanging his head out of the passenger side window.

"You beat me this morning," Bo conceded. He tossed Bear the last of his breakfast burrito. "What time did you get here?"

"About a half hour ago," Michael yelled down from atop the roof.

Bo put on his tool belt and carried his coffee to the ladder; it made a hollow aluminum clanging sound as he fixed its position before climbing up.

"Why so early?" he asked when he'd reached the rooftop.

"Let's say, I had an interesting night last night," Michael said. He attached the compression hose to the nail gun. "When I woke up early this morning, I just didn't feel like lying in bed and decided to avoid passivity."

The aluminum ladder bumped and clanged against the side of

the house again as Bo climbed off it. On the slanted roof they worked with care, securing their footing by walking against two-by-fours nailed into the rooftop.

Near the chimney of the four-thousand-square-foot home was the last, large section of unshingled roof. The flashing had already been installed and the sheathing was in place. Michael projected that about four hours of work lay ahead of them to attach the last of the roofing shingles.

"Let me guess; could Emma Madison somehow be involved?" Bo asked, kneeling down to work where he'd left off previously.

"You got it. She called me about five o'clock last night and we drove out to Anderson for dinner."

"She called you? And you went to Anderson? That's a long way to go for just a meal."

Michael shot a nail into the top of a shingle, just touching the feeder tip to the upper corner, feeling the weight of the hydraulic gun tug. "We didn't mind."

"Why doesn't that surprise me?" Bo said. "Anything out of the ordinary happen?"

"Well … she said she felt … different. I don't know, is that out of the ordinary?"

Bo placed the next shingle flush against the one before it. He touched the nail gun to the corners. They worked left to right, overlapping a new row over the old.

"Different, huh? Good different?"

"I think so. She's a tough one to figure out these days. We get along great, you know? Almost like old times … but …"

"Yeah, 'but' is right, Michael. Look, she's only been in town a week, right? And how long does she plan on being around?"

"Not long."

"Right, not long. So be careful. About the time you put your trust in somebody, you turn around and find they're gone."

Bo shot another nail in the roof.

Michael heard a deeper bitterness in his friend than he ever had before. "Is that how you feel about Christina?" he asked.

Bo grunted. "No way. She's the exception to the rule. She's the exception to every rule," he said. "There aren't a lot of women like her."

"And you don't think Emma's cut from the same cloth?"

"I don't. She left town once before, left you high and dry. Has she ever apologized or explained why she did that?"

"Apologized, yes. Explained, no."

Bo shook his head.

"And she's leaving in a few days …" Bo said, tapping the nail gun against the hard rocky surface of the roof. Michael knew Emma's story touched all the dark places in Bo's fears about the opposite sex.

"I'm not gonna say anything else, Mike, 'cause I want you to be happy, but I wouldn't read too much into it. Even though she says she feels 'different' doesn't necessarily mean she's falling in love with you."

"Yeah. But is it so wrong for me to find out what she means?"

Christina walked the quarter-mile hike to the end of her driveway, whispering a prayer for the restoration of her true love's heart.

"Dear Lord," she spoke in the quietness of early morning, "I praise You for the morning. I praise You for this day. I love You dearly and I trust You unquestionably. I pray for my love, Bo, whose heart was broken. Will You restore what is broken? Will You pick up the pieces of his shattered heart and mend them together again? Please remove the bitterness and hurt that's choking out the life in this wonderful man. I believe in him, and I believe in You. May Thy will be done. I give my love for Bo over to You. I surrender it, and I give You Bo. I would gladly give myself for his healing. I love and trust You, Lord, and surrender him into Your loving hands."

Emma took her coffee upstairs to the bedroom and set it on the table next to the bay window; a small wedding photograph of her parents balanced the other side. She sat on the red cushion in the window seat, parting the sheer nylon curtains that made the bay window the perfect place to think.

She heard a knock on the open bedroom door and saw her father standing there when she looked up.

"I just thought I'd check on you," he said, standing at the doorpost. "How was dinner last night with Michael?"

"It was great," she said, her voice sounding soft and reflective. "We had a really good time."

"Why do you look so sad then?"

"I'm not sad," she said, feeling more transparent than normal. "I'm just confused."

"Do you want to talk about it?" Will said, stepping into the room, closer to where Emma sat in the bay window.

"No, I don't think so."

"That's fine, we don't have to talk."

An antique Victorian chair rested between the two windows. Will drew it across the floor closer to Emma, making a scraping sound that was oddly comforting. He sat down on the needlepoint cushion a few feet from Emma. Outside, they heard the sounds of birds chirping, finches who normally stayed in Juneberry all year round. Emma sipped from her coffee cup, setting it back down next to the picture.

"I went through the stuff in those boxes, from the bedroom," she said, pulling her feet up on the cushion and wrapping her arms around her legs.

"I'd forgotten all the stuff that was in there," Will said, rubbing his hand back and forth across his chin.

"It's impossible to be in this house and not think of her," said Emma. "You keep pictures of her everywhere." Emma pointed to the photograph. "I found your wedding album, and the copy of the *Juneberry Register* from the week she died. All my life there's been this hole, this place where all my memories should be. But I never got the chance to really know her. You have so many memories with Mom, boxes full of them. Everything I have is a fuzzy, faded picture of someone I'm not sure I'm even remembering right."

"I understand your loss. I feel it every day too."

Will got up and walked over to the window and sat next to Emma.

"But you ought to know, your mother loved you more than anything in this world, Emma. We'd tried to have a baby for the longest time. Doctor visits, prayer. When you finally came along, you were the delight of her life. You slept in a bassinet in our room, and we would lie awake at night unable to sleep because we worried you might need us. Your mother fed, bathed, dressed, and treasured you for five years. When she got sick, she couldn't understand why God would allow something to come between the two of you. It was so sad. I felt helpless to change what was happening."

"I remember when she was in the hospital and they wouldn't allow me to see her," Emma said, murky pictures fading into view.

"Your aunt Annette was a lifesaver just like Samantha is today.

She stepped in to help with you when I was at the hospital with your mom or had to go to work."

"I remember eating dinner over there, spending the night," she said. In her mind's eye Emma saw an image of herself brushing her teeth next to Samantha, giggling together at the bathroom sink.

"Your mother died in July and you started school in September. I worked all day while you were at school, and I made sure I was home when you got off the bus. We did that until you were in high school."

"You were always here. I do remember that, Dad. Then I left for college." It was the end of one kind of sadness, and the start of another.

"It was a very empty nest," Will said. "Until now."

"Yes, until now," she told him, reaching for his hand. "I'm so sorry that I waited so long to come back. I won't do that again."

"Emma, it's okay. You don't need to apologize. I feel like everything's being put back together again.

"Emma, your mother was the love of my life, and you were the love of hers. She'll always be a part of this farm, because she'll always be a part of us. Just like we'll forever be a family. And we'll always be a part of Juneberry, too."

"I don't know, Dad. I'm not so sure I fit in Juneberry."

"Emma, you'll always fit in a place where people love you. Besides, this house is the place she hoped you'd always think of her."

"What do you mean?" Emma asked, puzzled.

"She just asked me before she died to keep some pictures of her on the walls while you were growing up so you'd know who your mother was and how much she loved you. She wanted you to have some things that were special to her, stuff I gave you a long time ago. Do you still have those things?

"What things?"

"Oh, let's see, that was a long time ago. She wanted you to have a little Clemson key chain from when we were in college together because she always hoped you'd go there. And the ring I gave her the night I proposed because she always hoped one day you'd find true love. And there was a framed picture of the two of you. She said she always wanted you to see her holding you."

Emma burst out crying, "Why didn't you ever tell me any of this? I didn't know the meaning behind any of those items!"

"Explanation? Honey, are you serious? Explain why you have a photo of you and your mother, her engagement ring—what does that symbolize? A Clemson college key chain? Honey, it's obvious. Haven't you ever noticed there are three weeping willow trees in our yard?"

"Yes, but …"

"Before she died, your mother asked me to plant those trees to represent the three of us. Always together on the farm."

From the crows' nest–like view atop the Macintosh house, Michael watched the dark, foreboding clouds approaching from the west.

"How you coming?" Michael shouted. Bo was at the other end of the roof, finishing another row of shingles. They'd been working for an hour longer than Michael had planned.

"Perfect timing," Bo said. Rain began to fall—big, fat drops. There was a flash on the horizon, then the rumble of distant thunder. He pressed the nail gun's metal tip against the last shingle—once, twice, three times—and stood to stretch his back.

The wind whipped Michael's T-shirt like a flag. "Let's get off this roof before it starts to get slick."

Bo lifted the nail gun to unplug it from the air hose. A sudden gust of wind struck Bo in the face and he wobbled backward on his heels. Instinctively, he raised his arms to balance himself, with the heavy gun still gripped inside his right hand. Michael saw a look of horror on his face. Bo was too close to the edge of the roof, and he knew it. It was the last time Michael saw his friend Bo before he fell blindly off the high pitch of the house, leaving behind only his image in the irregular light of the gathering storm.

Michael rushed across the wet roof to the place where Bo had fallen and peered over the edge. Thirty feet below lay the body of Bo Wilson, his face pointing skyward, his limbs stretched out in the shape of a star. Bo lay motionless with the tears of the sky rolling down his sun-browned cheeks.

~ SEVENTEEN ~

I'll always come back,
come back baby to you.

—K. T. OSLIN
"I'll Always Come Back"

The afternoon rain cascaded down Samantha's kitchen windows in heavy jagged lines. She was busy washing a few dishes when the phone rang. It was Emma.

"Samantha, it's Emma. Michael's just called. Bo's fallen off the roof of the house they were working on this afternoon and they're rushing him to Wellman by ambulance."

"Oh my gosh. Is he badly hurt?"

"They don't know yet. Michael said he fell a long ways and that he wasn't moving when the ambulance got there."

"Oh my gosh ..." Samantha gripped the edge of the countertop with a hand wet with sink water. "Where's Christina?"

"I just called her. I'm on my way over to pick her up right now. I'm trying to get in touch with everyone I can while I drive."

"Who do you need me to call?" Samantha asked, hearing the news like a fire alarm and springing into action.

"Could you call Bo's parents? Christina is *really* shook up. I'll be at her house in about three minutes, then we're going directly to the hospital."

"I'll call them and be on my way," she said.

Samantha hung up, leaving soapy water in the sink, and ran through the house.

"Noel!" she called. She heard noises outside in the garage. Samantha grabbed her purse from the table and moved quickly through the back door, nearly slipping on the slick back steps.

Samantha walked with quick, little steps toward the garage, hitting the soggy grass with her shoes as often as the slate stones of the footpath. The garage door was ajar and she could hear music from the radio as she approached.

"Noel!" she hollered. Noel peered around the open hood of the truck. He switched off the radio.

Samantha spoke in controlled, urgent tones. "Bo Wilson has fallen off the house he was working on and is being taken to Wellman. I need you to start praying and I need to get down there."

She turned back through the door without waiting for Noel's answer and headed toward her van. Noel darted out the side door after her.

"Mom, let me take you. The truck's almost ready to roll. I just need to …"

"There isn't time, Noel. I have to go right now. I'll be fine," she said, opening the driver's-side door. She climbed into the vehicle and searched through her purse for her keys and cell phone.

"Come on, come on," she said to the purse.

Samantha overturned her purse, dumping the contents onto the seat next to her. She sorted through the pile with her fingers until she found her key ring—the one she bought at Myrtle Beach the summer before—and started the engine. The van revved to life. She backed out of the driveway, switching the wipers on high as she drove.

Once in the street, she shifted the van into drive and pressed down on the accelerator. Samantha punched Jim's office number on her cell's speed dial and by the time she rolled through the first stop sign, Jim picked up.

"Honey, I need you to start praying," Samantha cried.

"What's happened?"

"Bo fell off the house he and Michael were working on," she said. "He's unconscious and they're taking him to the hospital by ambulance right now. Honey, I'm scared. My heart is beating about a hundred miles an hour."

"Slow down, Sam. Where are you?"

"I'm driving to the hospital. Christina is a wreck. Emma is going to get her and I …" Samantha voice collapsed, falling into a long, uncontrollable sob. "I'm so sorry, I just don't know what to do. I can't believe this is happening!"

"Samantha, I need you to pull over to the side of the road."

"Jim, I can't. I've got to get to the hospital."

"Sam, I need you to pull off the road. Do it now."

Samantha brought the van to a stop along the curb on Agnes Street in front of the elementary school. The buses would be here in half an hour to take the kids home.

"Are you parked?" Jim asked her.

"Yes."

"Okay, now just take a few deep breaths and relax a minute. You know you have to keep your blood pressure from going up. Are you breathing?"

"Yes, but I can't … can't slow down my heart."

"Samantha, listen to me. You're just overexcited. You need to do the things Dr. Sharron told you to do, the things we practiced."

"I can't. Can't make it slow down."

Samantha started to cry.

"Honey, I need you to listen to me. Focus on the sound of my voice. You're having one of your attacks and you need to slow down your breathing." Jim lowered his voice, calm and steady, the way he always did when Samantha's emotions rose like a thermometer set in boiling water. "I want you to take three very long breaths."

Samantha took three breaths. The first one sounded choked and nervous. On the second breath, Samantha relaxed, and the air went in and out clearer. The third breath seemed almost normal.

"How are you feeling?"

"Better," Samantha said. "But I have to call Bo's parents. Will you meet me at the hospital, please?"

"I'm leaving right now and should be there in twenty minutes. Tell me what your heart rate is doing?"

"It's slowing down, but something else just happened."

"What?"

"I think my water just broke."

<hr />

Emma and Christina entered Wellman Medical through the emergency room doors. The two women were dripping wet. They saw Michael waiting for them at the registration desk, his T-shirt soaked with rainwater, soiled with dirt from helping the EMTs lift Bo onto the stretcher. Christina read the seriousness of the situation in Michael's face.

"Where is he?" Christina demanded.

"They took him directly up to surgery. We're to go up there and wait," Michael told her.

Christina pushed through the ER doors without waiting for the others, searching for the nearest elevator, Michael and Emma following a step behind. She entered the elevator and pushed the button for the fourth floor three times in rapid succession, then drew in breath. She pressed the "Close" button and the doors finally closed.

"What happened?" she asked Michael in the elevator.

"We were finishing up the roof just as the rain was starting. We got up to go and then there was a gust of wind and he just lost his balance."

Christina's face contorted and she bite her bottom lip. "How far did he fall?"

"About thirty feet."

Christina forced her eyes closed, praying for sanctuary inside her wounded soul from the horror of the news. Emma held Christina's arm, steadying her.

The doors opened and the three hurried down the hallway looking for answers. A woman wearing green surgical scrubs walked toward the restricted doors.

"Miss, Miss," Christina called out. The woman stopped and looked back.

"Yes?"

"Do you know what's happening with Bo Wilson? He was just admitted to surgery."

"I'm sorry, you'll have to wait in there," she said, pointing to the waiting area. She continued her scurried walk through the set of double doors to the OR.

Emma and Michael escorted Christina into the room to wait. There were twenty empty leather chairs. Judge Judy was sorting through the messes of some poor soul's life on a muted TV mounted in the corner. They sat down in chairs next to one another, then Christina immediately stood and started to pace.

"Was he breathing? Was he breathing on his own when they brought him in?" Christina asked.

"Yes."

"Tell me everything you know."

"When the paramedics brought him in he was unconscious, but alive. They had a mask on his face and he was breathing. But when I got down from the roof, he wasn't. He was just lying there. I thought for sure he was …" Michael stopped short of saying the word. "Mrs. Macintosh came running out and told me she'd already called 911 and the ambulance was on its way. I knew not to try and move him, so I called his name and felt for a pulse, but there wasn't any. So I started to administer CPR. Paramedics were there in ten minutes or so. He started breathing on his own in the ambulance. They took him up to surgery as soon as we got here."

"You rode in the ambulance?"

"Yes."

"Did he regain consciousness?"

"No."

Christina's body wilted into her chair. She lowered her head. Emma reached out to touch Christina's hand and held it. It was cold as ice. Christina moved her lips in silent prayer, her eyes closed.

Emma couldn't help notice the way Christina seemed so comfortable praying. It seemed more of a two-way conversation than a plea to some unreachable being. Sometimes it looked like she was reminding Him of something. Sometimes it looked like pleading, or praise, other times she would sit still, hardly breathing.

Ten minutes later the OR nurse entered the waiting room.

"Are you with Bo Wilson?"

"Yes," Emma said. The woman walked to where they were all sitting in the waiting area, her green scrubs swooshing as she approached.

"My name is Valerie Sala. Dr. Timbrook asked me to tell you that he and Dr. Jenkins are doing an initial diagnostic evaluation on Bo right now. They're waiting on X-rays to determine broken bones and the possibility of internal bleeding. They'll be in surgery for a while yet, but Dr. Timbrook will be out to talk to you as soon as he knows something."

"What are they saying about his condition?" Christina asked. "Is he going to come out of this okay?

"His condition is listed as critical," Valerie said, in a calming tone. "But Drs. Timbrook and Jenkins are excellent surgeons. They're doing everything they can. Right now it's too early for us to know much of anything, but as I can, I'll come back out and let you know what's happening."

Christina drew in a long, shaky breath nodding in a herky-jerky way.

"Thank you."

Christina's voice weakened into a thin whisper of resignation, and Valerie turned to exit the waiting room. There might be no news on Bo's condition for hours. Emma wondered how Christina would last another minute.

On the top floor of Wellman Medical Center, Samantha Connor started the first stages of childbirth. Jim had arrived at their private birthing suite on the fifth floor, sopping wet from the rain. Samantha was ecstatic to see her husband step through the doorway, wet or dry.

"Oh, thank goodness. I thought there was a chance you wouldn't be able to get here in time."

Jim hugged Samantha as she lay in the bed, excited and scared. "I'm here. How are you doing?"

"They just put in the epidural for pain, but I don't think this is going to take that long."

Jim smiled, putting his arm around Samantha's neck in support. "You're going to be a mama again."

"Jim, there's so much going on."

"Shhh, just focus on this," he told her. "There's enough going on right here."

Samantha leaned her head on Jim's shoulder, staring at the second hand on the wall clock above the door. She worked her breathing—short puffs, in and out. "Jim, I love you."

They squeezed each other's hands. For twenty-two years they'd been each other's best friends, they'd been everything to each other. Samantha couldn't imagine her world without Jim in it.

"I love you, too," he told her.

Despite the suddenness of the contractions and the fears floating up from the fourth floor, the mood inside the room seemed sacred, shaped into something rare and godly by the devotion of a committed partnership and the sanctity of welcoming a newly created life.

Jim's cell phone chirped, the sound it made when one of the kids called him on the two-way pager. He answered the cell.

"Yeah."

"Hey, Dad, I'm at the hospital. Where are you guys?"

"Noel, we're up on the fifth floor."

"Do we have a new brother yet?"

"Not yet. Here, your mom wants to talk to you."

Jim handed the phone to Samantha.

"Noel, honey. Have you found Christina? She and Emma should be somewhere … oh!" Samantha felt a strong contraction. She gave Jim the phone and he stepped out into the hallway.

"Listen, Noel. If you find them, call me back on the cell, not the two-way radio, okay? I'll have it on vibrate. Your mom's got a lot on her hands and I don't want her to feel overwhelmed by any news you may have."

"Sure, no problem. I'll call you if I find out anything."

"Thanks."

Noel shut off his phone, walking into the lobby at Wellman. He stepped into the first floor elevator and pushed the lighted circle with the black number four. Noel was comfortable in hospitals. He had interned one summer at Hope Community Church during high school. That internship included lots of hospital visitations at Wellman, and before long he knew the floors as well as the doctors.

He found Michael, Emma, and Christina in the fourth floor waiting room, saw them through the glass wall as he came down the hallway, his shoes squeaking on the polished floor. When he entered the doorway, he gave the hushed group a quick tip of his straw hat. He looked like a cowboy who'd just rode in from rescuing a lost calf.

"What's the latest?"

Emma gave him the facts in a way that didn't come off as either too positive or unduly hopeless.

"He's in surgery. They've taken X-rays. They're checking for broken bones and other things. We're really just waiting for updates."

Emma didn't say what she felt everyone might be thinking—that Bo was in critical condition and they could get word any minute that he'd died.

Christina sat motionless in a chair next to Emma, on her face she wore a nearly catatonic expression. Noel walked up to her.

"Christina," he said, believing that words could be like medicine.

"I called the church about Bo and asked them to contact everybody on the prayer chain. I think some of the pastors are getting together in Brian's office to pray right now."

Christina's eyes continued to stare, unblinking, into the dull brown carpet. Her head nodded in the smallest, almost undetectable, way.

"I also called a group of guys at Clemson from my fraternity. I told them what was going on and asked them to pull together some of the guys there to pray. I hope that's all right."

Her eyes made contact with Noel's. He continued.

"And I remembered you telling me about Southwind Christian Fellowship in Raleigh, and how you'd spoken there once and you said they'd just really connected with you. I called them too. Do you know a Jeannie Harmon?"

"Yes," Christina said in a dry whisper, tears welling up in puddles.

"She's e-mailing or calling all the women you spoke to and she's organizing them for prayer at this very minute."

Two tears streamed down Christina's face from her watery blue eyes. It was the first sign of life they'd seen in an hour.

Christina coughed, clearing her throat.

"Thank you. Excuse me," she said, getting up from her chair to leave the room.

Emma looked at him. "Noel, I can't believe you did all that. That's amazing."

"When my mom told me the news, I knew we needed prayer. I think God just put some of those people in my mind to call."

In the small restroom down the hall, Christina wept and prayed.

"Father, thank You for the prayers. Thank You for Noel Connor. Thank You that You supply hope in the midst of the storm."

When Christina reentered the waiting room her eyes were red from crying, but she looked alive again.

"Can I ask you all something?" she said. "Can we just pray for a minute?"

Michael sat up taller, nodding. Christina knew Noel hadn't ceased praying for the last hour. She smiled when Emma agreed. Yes, of course they'd pray.

They joined hands in a circle, closed their eyes, and bowed their heads, huddling together in the quiet, nearly empty waiting room.

Christina prayed.

"Our heavenly Father ... we come before You now in great humility. Our dear friend Bo has fallen. Father, whatever Your will is, that he should live or go on to be with You, I surrender myself, my feelings, to Your greater will trusting that You only have the best in mind for us."

Emma opened her eyes and looked at Christina as she continued.

"Father, as Your child, I ask You with every ounce of energy I have for You to heal Bo. You know I love him. But, Father, not my will, but Your will be done."

If the world could be seen from the perspective of heaven, and prayers were like candles lit by vibrant faith, the landscape of Juneberry, even greater South Carolina, would have appeared like a forest of Christmas trees strung with strands of white lights.

The four waited in silence, praying for the miraculous, while surrendering themselves to the will of God.

~ EIGHTEEN ~

When you figure out love is all that matters after all
It sure makes everything else seem so small.

—CARRIE UNDERWOOD
"So Small"

"Okay, Samantha—push!" Abbey Kellogg, the midwife who'd assisted Samantha throughout her pregnancy, coached her now during delivery. Samantha took two short breaths and pushed.

"Ohhhhh …"

"That's good. You're doing fine. I can see the baby's head. I just need you to bear down on your next contraction, okay?"

Samantha nodded, gripping Jim's hand and squeezing it with all her might.

"Come on, hon. One more good push."

"Ohhhhh …"

"Bear down, Samantha. You're doing great. Keep pushing …"

One final push and Abbey lifted the Connors' newborn baby boy for his awestruck parents to see. Jim cut the umbilical cord, and in what seemed like less than a minute, the birthing team had cleaned and tested the wrapped-in-a-blue-blanket baby before handing him to his mother.

"Oh my, he's so beautiful."

Samantha's eyes began to tear up.

"Have you named him yet?" Abbey asked.

"Yes," Samantha said. "His name is James Connor. We'll call him Jimmy."

They hadn't decided on a name yet, not until that moment. Samantha wanted to send a message to her husband in a language only the two of them would understand. Jim smiled with pride. He kissed his wife on the forehead, and they wiped the tears from their eyes.

Jim called Beth at home and reached Noel on his cell phone with the good news. The Connor family had a new member.

Valerie Sala, the OR nurse, reentered the fourth-floor waiting room and waved for Christina to join her outside. Three hours had passed, one painful second after another, since Christina and Emma had joined Michael.

The long surgery only confirmed what they already suspected: Bo's situation was desperate. The wait was agonizing, but it meant at least Bo was still alive. Secretly, they thanked God no one from the OR had come out—until now.

Christina rose from her chair, her legs stiff and weak from long hours of sitting. She walked to where Valerie waited, expressionless, in the hallway. Christina had already thought about every possible outcome—that he would die, or be crippled, or vegetative, or that God would spare him, or that he was already dead and they just hadn't told her yet. The only conclusion she'd arrived at was how unprepared she was for any of them.

Emma, Michael, and Noel watched from their seats, trying to read each woman's body language. Valerie was no help. Only her lips moved with the occasional slight tremor of her head. Christina was a mirror of Valerie. Her red, puffy eyes blinked now and then. Christina listened until Valerie finished speaking, nodding to convey she understood. Whatever the news was, Christina had heard it.

Christina came into the room and stood wobbly before the group. She shaped words on her trembling lips, but rejected each of them as fast as she thought of them. Christina looked like a woman surrendered to events completely outside her control, like someone who'd lost her best friend.

"What is it, Christina?" Emma asked.

She struggled getting out the words.

"Bo's alive. He's out of surgery. He's going to live."

A surge of pent-up emotions befell Christina. Her body buckled, a cry of fear escaped her lips—the kind that comes after the scare is over. Michael and Noel rose from their chairs to catch Christina and helped her sit down.

"I just praise God," she cried, shaking her head from side to side. "She said they almost lost him a couple of times. I think it was the prayers. I don't know what else to think. I'm just so glad God spared him."

Emma wrapped her arms around Christina, but as soon as she did, Christina shot up from her seat in realization.

"She said I can go see him," she blurted.

"Do you want me to go with you?" Emma asked.

"No, but I don't know where I'm going and I don't know if I can walk … so, Noel … could you …?"

Noel stood and escorted her out of the waiting room. When they'd gone, Emma turned to Michael and wrapped her arms around him.

"I'm so glad Bo's going to be all right, and I hurt so badly for Christina, but …"

Emma pulled back from Michael's embrace and looked into his eyes.

"It crossed my mind while we sat here today that it could have been you."

"Hey, it's all right. Everybody's all right," he said, brushing a strand of brown hair away from her eyes.

"I don't know what's in store for the rest of the night, Michael. I'll probably stay close to Christina, but I'd like to spend some time with you … if you're okay with that. Can we find some time just to talk?"

"Sure," Michael said. "But for now, let's just go find Bo."

Noel and Christina found their way to room number 312. "Do you want me to go in with you?" Noel asked.

Christina didn't answer. The door was open and she walked through. Bo Wilson lay unconscious in bed, bandaged, swollen, but alive. His surgeon, Dr. Timbrook, stood next to Bo, looking ragged like he'd just been through a battle.

"Are you Christina?" he asked her.

"Yes … Christina Herry."

"Come on in," he said. Dr. Timbrook finished jotting a note in Bo's chart, pushed up his glasses, then set the chart on a tray table. "We had a close call today. He's been unconscious for quite a while, but Bo told me about you before we put him under the anesthetic."

"He was awake after his fall?" Christina asked.

Dr. Timbrook smiled a tired smile. "Not for long, but he told me that I should tell you he loved you."

Christina moved closer and reached for Bo's hand.

"Our main concern beyond broken bones and concussion was the possibility of internal bleeding. Bo's X-rays showed a broken femur in his left leg. It's a severe break that required wire cables and screws. His left ankle was also shattered. He's suffered neck, back, and leg injuries, fractures in one wrist, and he sustained some blood loss."

Christina examined the white plaster cast on his leg. It was elevated in a sling suspended by hospital rigging.

"He's going to spend a couple days with us so we can watch for blood clots and infection. Then Bo will need some significant recovery time, somewhere in the vicinity of six to eight months. Does he have family? Someone who can help with that process?"

"I will," Christina said.

"He'll have to wear this cast for eight weeks, and then he'll have to undergo physical therapy for another eight weeks to regain muscle loss due to atrophy."

"Dr. Timbrook, when will the anesthesia wear off?"

"Probably some time in the next hour or so."

Dr. Timbrook started toward the door. He stopped and turned to Christina.

"Do you have any more questions?"

Christina stepped toward Dr. Timbrook, wrapping her arms around him and squeezing him. She let go without saying a word.

"You're welcome," he said, and exited the room.

Michael and Emma came by Bo's room a few minutes later.

"Do you want some company tonight?" Emma asked.

"I'm going to stay with him," Christina said, conviction running through her voice like a steel rod.

"Can we bring you some dinner? What can we do?"

Christina hugged Emma, who reacted with less shock than Dr. Timbrook.

"Thanks," she said. "Noel's already volunteered. You can just let me say thanks. It's been a long day."

Emma looked at Noel. He smiled, keeping his secret that he was some sort of angel. Not the kind with wings, but a twenty-two-year-old man who had given up his life for something, no, Someone, bigger than himself. *What better way to chill than to hang out here? It's quiet, and I've got a good book out in the truck.*

"You can reach us on the cell phone if you need me tonight," she told him. He nodded again, the brim of the straw cowboy hat falling and rising like that of a nameless hero behind a mask in a matinee Western movie.

"Emma, I'm so glad you were here, glad we were all here today. I've been given so much strength from you all," Christina said.

———

Michael and Emma walked out the front doors of Wellman. The rain had stopped, and sunlight pierced through a patch of cumulus clouds. The storm had brought with it the warm weather of an Indian summer.

"I feel like everyone I know is in this hospital," Emma said.

"It's been a heck of a week."

They left her father's Caddy in the parking lot. As they climbed into Michael's truck, he suggested they grab a drive-through dinner. Two cheeseburgers and Dr Peppers later, Michael drove out on old Highway 90 toward Christina's place.

"Here, I want to show you something."

"What?"

"You'll see."

They drove up to the hill country where they'd gone so many times that summer. Michael drove off the road and followed a path of tire tracks to a ridge, then stopped.

Emma climbed out, the hillside catching the last light of day. A grove of old oaks and pine trees fused with a golden meadow of songbirds. A gentle evening breeze waved through the tall grass. Miles below them, pleasure boats still sailed on the lake.

"Oh Michael. It's so beautiful up here."

Emma shut the heavy truck door and stepped into the clearing. Michael leaned against the truck, letting Emma rediscover the site for herself.

"I remember this place," she said, fading back to another time, walking where they'd walked before.

Emma turned to Michael.

"Remember that night we camped here?"

"Yes."

"The sky was so blue, so clear."

"So cold."

"It was freezing! You built a fire and we stayed up all night and at sunrise we watched the fishermen sail out onto the lake. We drank coffee we brewed over the fire."

"You always loved the outdoors, Emma."

"I didn't realize how much I missed it," she said, looking into the woods, hearing a woodpecker clacking on the side of a tree.

"It hasn't changed much in the last fifteen years. I could throw out a blanket like we did that night. We could stay out here awhile, looking at the stars."

Emma spun around, giving Michael a "do you really think we should?" look, but underneath it was a "that's a great idea!" look.

He pulled back the seat hatch, removing a rolled-up red plaid blanket and walked to Emma. Michael opened the warm blanket, letting the gentle breeze catch it, then wrapped it around her.

"It's big enough for two, Michael," said Emma, offering the blanket to him with an outstretched arm. He moved next to her, pulling the blanket over their shoulders. They stood shoulder to shoulder, staring up at the first stars of the evening.

They were motionless for a long time. When they did move, their actions were subtle, instinctive. She leaned her head against his shoulder. He slipped his arm around her. Slowly, they found themselves in a warm embrace. Emma buried her face in his chest, breathing in a scent that simultaneously took her back in time and pointed her to an uncertain future. He whispered something she couldn't quite hear. She looked up and melted into a kiss as sweet as she had ever known.

~ Nineteen ~

And I wonder where you are
and if the pain ends when you die
And I wonder if there was
some better way to say goodbye.

—Martina McBride
"Goodbye"

"Hi there, Emma. Sorry to bother you so early, but it's time for a wake-up call from reality!"

Emma should have known better than to leave her cell powered on overnight, but she thought if there was even the *slightest* chance that Christina or Samantha might call during the night, she didn't want to miss that.

"Hi, Lara," Emma answered, wanting the phone call as much as a toothache.

"Sounds like somebody had a late night."

Emma pulled the covers over her head, barely holding the phone against her ear. She wasn't tired from lack of sleep; she was just tiring of the constant intrusion of one world into another. Her work life was once again tapping for her attention like a door-to-door salesman who won't take no for an answer.

"Listen, Robert wanted me to call you. You'll be glad to know he's purchased a seat for you on a chartered jet leaving out of Columbia tomorrow morning at six forty-five a.m.," Lara said, imitating the sound of a travel agent going over the flight itinerary with a client. "He's also arranged ground transportation. Don't get your hopes up for a limo though; I think it's just a town car. Apparently he's not taking any chances of you not getting here in time for the meeting."

"What meeting?"

"Well, as luck would have it, Northeast Federal got hit with another lawsuit late yesterday afternoon, and they were on the phone with Robert immediately afterward requesting a meeting with the firm tomorrow. That's scheduled for eleven thirty a.m. Wednesday," Lara said. "Robert thinks they're ours to lose at this point, but he's not about to take chances on you not being here. So, yada yada, you get the star treatment. But if I were you, I'd plan on Wednesday being a very long day at the office. He's ordering lunch and dinner in."

"Right," Emma said. "Well, tell him I'll be there."

Lara scoffed. "Of course you will be. I'll send the flight information to your phone. *Welcome back!*"

Emma clicked off the phone and curled up under the blankets, hoping to stave off the encroaching realities of her departure at least a little while longer. *You get used to a place when you stay there for ten days. Especially when that place is called "home" and you haven't set foot there in years.*

She smelled the aroma of fresh paint wafting up from the main floor, and heard Michael and her father talking. Emma got up, dressed, and headed downstairs. She wasn't about to spend her last day in Juneberry in bed.

"Can't a lady get any sleep around here?"

Emma smiled at Will as she met him downstairs. He carefully painted the trim around the doorway inside the office.

"Sorry if we woke you, hon. Come on down and take a look."

Emma walked into the office. The new, larger windows were in, and they flooded the room with October morning sunlight. At the other end of the room where the kitchen pantry used to be, Michael guided a roller brush, laying the first coat of a lively yellow that reminded Emma of the Oval Office in the White House.

"Honey, we're going to have the new office completely finished by lunchtime. I can't believe how quickly everything's been made over."

"Me, neither."

"Once we've got two coats down, the last thing to do is buff this floor. We're going to clean the original hardwoods first and then seal it."

"Is the wood in good-enough condition?" Emma asked.

"See for yourself."

Will pulled up a section of the lavender drop cloth. Beneath it was a rich cherry hardwood. It looked amazing.

"Some of the imperfections will be visible, but this house has been here a long time. I see no reason to cover up the dings and scars. We've all got 'em."

Emma watched her father as he spoke with excitement about the new office. She wanted to freeze this moment in her memory for the inevitable time, just a day away, when she would have to fold him up and store him away until the next time they could spend time together. She put her arms around him and hugged him.

"Hey, what's that for?"

"It's for saying good morning," she said.

If this week had taught her nothing else, it taught Emma how precious life was—that life could be taken away when you least expected it. In less than twenty-four hours, Juneberry would be taken away from her. Emma felt like she was living the answer to one of those "if you only had one day to live, what day would you choose?" questions.

She walked to the other end of the office where Michael was

standing, eyeing the revitalized space, imagining where the furniture would go.

"You've done wonders with this space, Michael. I can't believe it was a cramped bedroom when we started."

"Do you want to go with me to pick out office furniture later, Emma?" Will asked from the other end of the room. "I'd like you to be there to help me pick it out."

"Sure. We can go after lunch."

Samantha held her newborn son, Jimmy, while an RN met with her, asking if she had any questions about the care and feeding of a newborn baby. This was standard procedure, but certainly not necessary since Samantha had plenty of experience.

In the speedy modern world of hospital birthing, the bill had already been dropped off in her room, slid under her door like at a hotel, before Samantha woke up. Doctors signed her release time for just before noon.

In another room at Wellman, Christina awoke in a small baby blue recliner she and one of the night shift nurses had dragged from the lounge into Bo's room around midnight. She'd dozed on and off through the night, getting up to check on her beloved, who'd transitioned from anesthesia to the deep sleep of recovery without ever waking.

Other than some stiffness in her petite frame, Christina felt reborn. She'd spent what were for her precious moments watching him sleep through the night, lightly touching his hand or his forehead, careful not to wake him, and praying over and over again her thankfulness to God.

In the early morning, when the sun rose again and light commuter traffic moved past their window, Christina realized she had all she wanted. Bo was alive, sleeping safely in a bed next to her, the very thing she'd prayed for. Words could never adequately express the gratitude she felt. Christina only knew she'd never be the same.

Bo's eyelids twitched once, then slowly opened. He gazed around the room. The early-morning sunlight was just bright enough for him to find the one object in the room he recognized, the woman he most wanted to see.

"Have you been here all night?" Bo asked, trying to sit up.

"Honey, don't move. Just lie still," Christina took his hand, stood at the side of his bed.

"What time is it?"

"About seven thirty. How do you feel?"

Bo looked at the cast on his leg and felt its cool roughness with his fingers. He wiggled his toes sticking out at the other end.

"Like I just fell off a house."

"Not funny."

Bo rallied himself from sleep, slowly raising his hands to his face, scratching the end of his nose. He looked rough and unshaven. There were creases in his skin, bruises from the fall, redness from the long sleep.

"I feel like I've been sleeping a million years."

Christina sat on the edge of his bed, smoothing rogue curls in his hair.

"Yesterday was an exceptionally long day," she told him, her voice languid and peaceful.

"What? Why are you looking at me like that?"

Christina smiled.

"It's too early for talk, but I'm so glad we're together right now."

"I scared you a bit, didn't I?"

"Yes, but I don't want to talk about it right now."

He cleared his throat. "How bad am I?"

"Broken bones, you lost some blood. The doctor says you'll recover, you'll just need time to mend and get your strength back."

"My appetite's already back."

"That's a good sign," Christina laughed. "I heard one of the nurses asking when the breakfast trays would be delivered. It shouldn't be too long."

Bo reached up with his right hand and touched Christina's face, lightly rubbing her cheek with the back of his fingers.

She held his hand in hers against her face.

"Listen, something happened to me yesterday," he said. "It's the kind of thing I think you'll appreciate."

"Don't tell me … you fell for me …?"

Bo started to laugh, then winced. "Now who's being funny?" he said through gritted teeth.

"I'm sorry, Bo. I just wanted you to smile …"

He smiled.

"So … tell me. What happened to you yesterday, besides the obvious, I mean?" she said.

"I was talking to Mike on the roof just before I fell. I told him he needed to watch out for Emma, and the minute I said that, I felt convicted. Like, even though I believed what I was saying, it still wasn't right for me to say it. During the next few hours I kept thinking about it, and I got angry … with myself. Then the storm blew in, and that made me even more upset. I finished the last shingle just as the rain started to come down. I stood up, and when I did, I felt this wall of air hit me in the chest. I lost my footing, but I thought I could adjust my weight. The next thing I knew there was nothing behind to catch me."

Bo stared into Christina's eyes.

"Have you ever felt like time just stopped or slowed down for you?"

Christina nodded her head.

"In an instant, I felt the front half of my left foot gripping the shingles, and the heel of my boot hovering in thin air. My right foot was already off the roof. As I fell, I could see Michael. He had this look of horror on his face, and I just had this inexplicable sense of clarity. I thought, 'I've just figured out the meaning of life, and I'm about to fall off the roof and die before I get the chance to tell anybody!'" Bo laughed, wincing again. Christina gripped his hand tighter.

"I was sorry I said those things to Michael," he continued. "I'm going to tell him that the next time I see him. Life's too short to play it safe sometimes. If he feels something special about Emma, he should go for it."

Bo shook his head like he couldn't believe he'd ever thought otherwise.

"I forgave my ex for everything she did, right at that moment, and I believed it was possible for everything to work out, I mean, to be all right." Bo's eyes began to squint shut. He paused, offering an expression of deep reflection. "I thought about what it would be like if I never saw your face again."

Bo looked into Christina's eyes, a look of repentance sculpting his wounded face. "Christina, will you forgive me?"

"Yes."

She'd waited so long for him to come around. Prayed and waited.

"And I can't—wait another minute to ask you this," he said, entwining his fingers with hers. "Will you do me the distinct honor of marrying me?"

Will scrubbed new yellow paint from his hands in the upstairs bath-room. Emma sat at the vanity in her bedroom across the hall, getting ready for their shopping excursion.

"Honey, it's your last day," Will called to her. "Anything you'd especially like to do?"

Emma ran a brush through her straight shoulder-length hair.

"I just heard from Jim that Samantha and the new baby are com-ing home around lunchtime. I'd like to stop by for a visit. I also promised to stop by and see Janette Kerr before I left town. I really don't know how I'll have time, but I said I would."

"How do you know Janette?" he said, peering around the corner, drying his hands on a towel.

"I met her at Samantha's party. Didn't I tell you? She's a friend of hers. I'm surprised you don't know her."

"I know Janette, just didn't know that you did. Have you ever seen any of her movies?"

"I don't think so. From the sound of it, she was kind of a small-time actress in the '50s and '60s."

Will stepped over to Emma's doorway, tossing the towels over his right shoulder. "That's not how I would describe her. When are you going over there?"

"This afternoon. Whenever I can fit it in."

"Well, we'd better get moving if you're going to get in all these stops."

An hour later, they were in Columbia shopping for furniture. At Will's request, she picked out a traditional-looking cherry wood desk with ornamental drawers and brass pulls at an upscale antique shop. A modern office supply store sold them a new computer, desk light, a comfortable cloth swivel chair, and a cordless telephone.

By this time, they were hungry and decided to walk somewhere for lunch. It was light fare, chicken salad at a local restaurant in Columbia a block from Will's law office.

"Emma, I don't mean to sound pushy or anything … but do you have any idea when you'll come home again?" he asked, sipping from his iced-tea glass, then setting it back on the table.

"I'll have some time around Christmas. That's probably the soonest I could come back. The firm has been more than generous, giving me all this time. But I'm going back to a madhouse. Our senior partner has a new corporate client and we're already preparing to respond to a major lawsuit. We usually serve litigation this large in teams, but we'll be up to our ears in it before long."

Will frowned, an expression Emma had rarely seen on her father's face.

"I'm just gonna shoot honestly with you, Emma. You've really come alive this week. Are you sure you're ready to charge back into the fray? I'll admit I don't know much about your Boston life and I'm sure it's wonderful. But what I've seen? You fit so perfectly here in Juneberry."

Emma wiped her face with a paper napkin, crinkling it in her palm before setting it on her plate. "I don't think anyone is ever ready to go back to work, but I feel like I've accomplished all I came here to do. It's been an amazing visit, Dad, but it shouldn't take long for me to get back into the swing of things back home …" The moment she said "home" she regretted it. Not because Boston hadn't been a good home for her all these years, but because it didn't quite sound right to speak of Boston as home while she was in South Carolina, while she was sitting across the table from her father. "But I won't stay away so long this time," she promised, hoping these words might distract him from her uncertainty.

Will dropped his napkin across his plate and leaned back in his chair. "One of the hardest things a parent is ever asked to do, Emma, is to let go. I'd like to ask you to do something that's probably going to be an even bigger challenge for you. When your career gets busy again, and your free time seems to evaporate—and it will. Hey, I'm an attorney too, and I know the value of an hour. But when that happens, I want you to stop for a second and remember where you came from, and hang onto it. And, honey … I want you to know, Juneberry will always be your home too."

~ TWENTY ~

When I give my heart, it will be completely.

—THE LETTERMAN
"When I Fall in Love"

In 1958, Janette Kerr left Juneberry, South Carolina, to chase her Hollywood dreams. The eighteen-year-old had starred in enough high school musicals, lived the drama of being chosen homecoming queen, and been asked to walk the runway in a chamber of commerce charity fashion show, to be certain she would be a huge star if just given the opportunity. She even won a statewide beauty contest in Columbia and was awarded a grand prize of three hundred dollars. Against her mother's wishes, Janette used her prize money to buy a one-way Greyhound bus ticket and rent a studio apartment in West Hollywood.

Fourteen years later, she packed up her belongings, climbed into her powder blue Cadillac convertible, and left Hollywood for good.

She'd seen the studio system up close as a contract actress at Paramount Pictures. She'd played the nightclub cigarette girl, a passenger on a train, and a chorus-line dancer. She'd even acted opposite Clark Gable in *Some Go East*, taking his money on-screen at a sound-stage newspaper stand and delivering her one line "Don't forget your change, sir!" right on cue.

"Oh, I may have never become a star, Emma, but I tasted lots of success. I'll bet you've never seen this."

Janette handed her an issue of *LIFE Magazine* from 1961. A beautiful, younger Janette Kerr graced the oversized cover. The twenty-two-year-old beauty, a Paramount contract actress, cover girl, and aspiring movie starlet.

"You look beautiful," Emma said.

"That was when the publicity department at Paramount was trying to break new stars by getting us different kinds of exposure. They wanted to find the next big thing, but it turned out *not* to be me."

"Still, it's an amazing accomplishment," Emma said, setting the magazine back on the coffee table.

"I don't know what I accomplished. I think God just gives us little tastes of something so we know what it is. That was my little moment of fame."

Janette sipped her tea. In honor of Emma's visit, she'd gotten out her best tea service, a white porcelain set with colorful, hand-painted daffodils on the teapot, cups, and sugar bowl. She and Emma sat in Janette's living room at her mobile home by the lake. It was clean and comfortable, the perfect living space for Janette and her sister Claudia.

"I danced with Cary Grant once at a birthday party for a Paramount Studios VP," she said, delighted with the memory. "He was so charming and witty. Those were the kinds of experiences I'd hoped for when I went out to Hollywood, and I had many."

"You must have wanted success as an actress, too?" Emma said.

"Yes, but like I told Beth, success is something you can't hang onto. You might have that spotlight shining its bright round beam on you for a moment, but the next minute it's gone. Oh, I'm not going to pretend it wasn't great fun to have that spotlight on me, but you can't keep it, and chasing after that light can make a person crazy."

"I can tell by your smile, you must have had some good times."

"I made seventeen pictures, appeared on television shows, *Gunsmoke, Dr. Kildare, Perry Mason, Star Trek.* I did lots of things like that."

"But you came back?"

"I came back *home,* Emma. I came back to people who really knew and cared about me. There's no other place like Juneberry in the world. Did you know that? Have you ever really thought about just how special this place is? To me it's the most precious place in the world, and do you know why?"

Emma shook her head.

"Because it's where I'm from. It's where my roots are. Everyone knows me here, and I've known them for a lifetime. When I was in pictures, nobody really knew me. Sure, I worked with the other actors, and was friendly with everyone, but it was just a group of people going 'round and 'round on a carousel. Everyone doing their best to enjoy the ride all by themselves."

"Is that why you came back?"

"Something like that. Both my mother and sister were living at the time and we had such fun together. I was the adventurer—always the one to take a risk. You're that way too, aren't you?"

Emma smiled. "I think so."

"Emma, I wanted to see you, not to change your mind about anything, that's not my place, but just to tell you something it took me years to learn."

Emma set her teacup back on the saucer and leaned forward to listen.

"The lights are definitely brighter beyond the horizon of the place you grow up. I suspect they are for everyone. But bright lights can't love you, Emma, and eventually they burn out."

"Is that what you wanted to tell me?"

"Yes, and this. I almost missed the last years of my mother's life. And do you know what I nearly traded those years for?"

"What?"

"A game show. I was offered a spot on a daytime game show and I struggled at the time about whether or not to take it. Now can you imagine how I'd feel today if I would have lost those last few years with my mother, in exchange for a silly game show?"

Emma had liked Janette instantly when she met her at Samantha's party, and was liking her even more with every moment they spent together.

"Emma, there will always be a pretty bauble out there somewhere tempting us to chase after it. My prayer for you is that you'll find what God wants for you. If that's in Boston, fine, but if it's somewhere else, like Juneberry, make sure you don't miss it."

Janette emptied the teapot into Emma's cup.

"That's what I wanted to tell you, Emma."

On her way back from Janette's, Emma drove down Main Street one last time, the AM radio tuned to a country station out of Columbia. Coming through the truck's small speaker, the music sounded tinny and popped with static. All the songs with fiddles reminded her of Michael.

She drove all the familiar streets, Armstrong, Carney, Hope—street names that reminded her of some of the twentieth century's greatest entertainers, on her way to Samantha's house.

At the last traffic light on Main, it dawned on Emma that she'd switched into good-bye mode. For the rest of the day, she'd be saying good-bye to whoever she saw—Jim, Samantha, Christina, Michael.

Good-bye. The word caught in her throat.

Before the light turned green on the corner of Main and Durham, Emma glanced in the rearview mirror and saw a familiar white truck. Michael waved. She looked at his reflection, noticed his dark hair falling across his forehead, stubble casting a shadow on his face. She gestured for him to follow her.

Durham Street was quiet, infrequently traveled. Emma parked Old Red along the curb, and Michael pulled up behind her. She left the truck running, exited, and walked to his driver's-side window.

"I thought that was you," she said, her smile appearing out of some deep place she didn't quite understand.

"Your dad's office is finished," he said. "I'm out running a few errands I haven't had time to take care of. How'd furniture shopping go?"

"Good. We found everything. Dad's excited, and I'm just delighted with how everything worked out."

"Hey, you haven't even seen it completely done yet."

"I know. But it was almost done before and it looked great then. Thank you, Michael. You've really done a lot for my dad and me this week."

"It's my pleasure," he said. Emma brushed Michael's hair from his forehead. She placed her hands on his arm.

"Listen, I'm in between visits today. I'm on my way over to see Samantha and the new baby. I was wondering if you had some time tonight when we could get together?"

"I think that can be arranged."

Emma smiled. "Good. I'll be home after awhile. I'll give you a call and we can decide what we want to do."

He signaled that was fine with a nod of his head. Emma told Michael good-bye, backing up a step before heading back to the warmth of Old Red, still parked and chugging on Durham Street.

Michael watched her shift the truck into gear and drive off for Samantha's. He was truly glad he'd been able to help Will and Emma. It was only when Michael peered into the future that he got a sickening feeling about the week. It felt like the past was repeating itself, though he somehow hoped he was wrong. He thought of the effortless friendship they'd rediscovered that so easily and comfortably tilted its head to meet in a kiss. And he allowed the thought that hurt most to meander into his mind again—that Emma was his soul mate.

Somehow, she'd been able to walk away once upon a different perfect season. Michael couldn't avoid the choking, bitter conclusion that Emma was about to do the same thing all over again.

"I choose who I love," he reminded himself. "It's not up to me whether they love me back."

There was only one problem with Michael's theory of love: He could choose whom he loved, but he couldn't seem to unchoose her.

※ ※ ※

Samantha handed baby James to Emma, wrapped up in his blue hospital blanket, wearing a cute little pair of footie jammies with a zipper running up the front.

"He's so little," Emma said, taking the baby into her arms as if she were carrying a stack of wrapped gifts from Macy's. "I'm afraid I might drop him."

"You won't drop him."

Emma sat in the middle of the Connors' long green living-room sofa. Samantha took a seat next to her and Jim settled into the chair that knew him best during football season.

Noel chuckled at the sight of Emma Madison holding a newborn baby. It was obvious to everyone that Emma was one of those women who had never actually held a baby before.

"He's just had his afternoon feeding, so he's going to be taking a nap very soon," Samantha said, clearly delighted to watch Emma holding their new baby.

"Oh, he's blinking his eyes. He looks so sleepy."

"I'm going to put him in his bassinet and see if he'll go down to sleep."

Emma handed the baby back to Samantha, and she tucked his blanket around him in the bassinet.

"What time do you leave tomorrow?" Samantha asked, returning to her seat next to Emma.

"Six forty-five, but I'll need to be at the airport by no later than six a.m."

"Do you need someone to take you?" Noel asked, sitting straight-legged on the living room floor like it was just as comfortable as a chair. "That's one trip I think I know by heart."

"You know, I may take you up on that. My dad's offered to take me, but he's really not supposed to drive yet. I'd really appreciate that."

"No problem. I'll be there around five?"

Emma made a face like reality was really sinking in. "Yeah, I guess so."

"Gosh, that's sounds really early." Samantha said. "How many more stops do you have to make tonight?"

"I want to stop out at Christina's, and then spend a little time with Michael. I'm hoping to make it an early evening."

"Well, good luck with that."

After a moment of laughter came an extended moment of silence, the kind that signals there's nothing left to say. Emma stood and straightened her clothing.

"Well, I'd better be getting on my way," she said.

"This week has gone by so fast." Samantha held Emma in a warm hug. "I can't believe it's already over. I'm so glad you came. Of course the reason for the visit wasn't all that fun, but I know your dad is doing great and we'll all continue to keep our eye on him."

Samantha let go of her favorite cousin.

"Thanks for everything, Samantha. You made this week wonderful for everyone."

Samantha smiled. Emma gave hugs to Jim and Beth, received their well wishes for safe travel and hopes for a speedy return. Emma waved at Noel.

"I'll see you tomorrow," she said, then headed out the door, down the front stairs, and across the yard through the fallen leaves. She felt certain that if she turned around, she'd see Samantha still standing in the doorway, watching her leave. She didn't turn around for fear that she might start to cry. Instead, she stared at the ankle-deep leaves as she kicked through them on her way back to Old Red. When she reached the truck, she couldn't help herself. Emma turned. But Samantha had already disappeared into the house. A small glowing lamp in the picture window was all that greeted her, and quiet melancholy rose inside Emma. Samantha was surrounded by her family, warm and safe in her home. But she was now alone.

Emma checked her phone messages as she sat in the idling truck. There were two, one from her dad, and the other from Christina.

Emma glanced up the street. A mint green Z28 sports car with two wide racing stripes across the hood passed by. The car was stuffed with laughing teenagers. It turned left on Ruth Street and continued up the hill. As the taillights faded into the distance, she wondered what sort of life those kids had ahead of them. Would they long to leave Juneberry someday as she had?

Emma clicked the message button on her cell phone.

"Hi, honey, it's your dad. Christina just called. She said she'd tried to reach you on your cell, but couldn't get through so she called here. She wanted to tell you she's not going to be able to say good-bye to you tonight. She's headed back to the hospital. I guess Bo's in a lot of pain, so she wanted to get over there, but she said you can call her if you like."

Emma pulled out the black knob on the dash, bringing Old Red's headlights to life. Juneberry looked so pretty with the leaves blowing in the wind. She pulled away from the curb and drove off into the evening. She glanced down at her cell phone and dialed Christina's number with practiced ease.

"Hi, this is Christina."

"It's me. How's Bo doing?"

"Well, he's been in a lot of pain. They just gave him something and it's starting to kick in."

"Oh, poor guy. It doesn't sound fun."

"No, but at least he's comfortable now. His eyes are closed. I think he's down for the night."

"I heard we won't be able to get together tonight. I'm sorry to hear that. I was looking forward to it," Emma said.

"Me, too, but if you have a minute we can talk right now if you like."

"Sure," Emma said, taking the wide turn at Mill Road. The sunset streaked faded purple lines in the western horizon. The sky's good night reminded Emma that her time in Juneberry had come to a close.

"Earlier today I was thinking about all that happened this week," said Christina. "I know it was your dad's health crisis that brought you down here, but then Bo had his accident, and Samantha had her baby ... and ... well, I just think it's more than coincidence. I'm glad you were here for all of these things. Even though you've been away for a long time, you're still my friend. It's good when friends are here for our times of need, you know? We all needed each other big-time this week, and God worked it out so that we were all together."

"I hadn't thought of it like that."

"If you hadn't been here, Bo still would have fallen off the roof, Samantha would still have had her baby, but I would have been in that waiting room all alone." Christina sniffled. "I'll never be able to thank you enough for staying with me."

"It's been a hard week, but a good week. It's going to be hard to go back."

"I know what you mean. I'll admit this isn't the way I'd like it to be, but I think everyone understands you've got a life outside of Juneberry. I know I can speak for Samantha too, we just really want you to come back soon."

"I will. I promise."

"Well, good. So do you want to hear the big news or what?"

"Big news? You mean there's more big news?"

"Yes! Bo's asked me to marry him."

"Christina, that's fantastic! He asked you at the hospital?"

"Uh-huh. There are so many details to work through, of course, but it's official."

"You said yes, then, right?"

"Duh, yes, obviously. We'll need to get through this crisis first before we plan a wedding date, but I think it will be sometime this year."

"I won't miss it, Christina."

"You better not. I love you, Emma."

Emma pulled into the driveway and parked Old Red underneath the sheltering arms of the three weeping willows. Her father's house, and hers, too. The lights were on inside, warm and inviting, and she could see Will cooking in the kitchen.

"I love you, too," Emma said. "I'll talk to you soon. Bye."

~ TWENTY-ONE ~

Baby, baby,
when first we met
I knew in this heart of mine
That you were someone I couldn't forget.
I said right,
and abide my time.

—ALISON KRAUSS
"Baby, Now That I've Found You"

Michael heard three knocks at his front door. He reached for the remote that controlled the stereo, turning down the volume on the Alison Krauss song as he walked through the living room.

Emma smiled at him when he opened the door.

She was beautiful. He wondered how many times he'd dreamed of moments like this. Her smile softened, her eyes connected with his like an answer to a prayer, and a slight breeze caught her hair, sweeping strands across her face.

"Emma … you look …"

"Cold?"

"I'm sorry … I was a little distracted there for a moment. Yes, come in, please."

Emma stepped onto the entryway rug. A pair of Michael's work boots toppled over as he shut the door.

"Have you decided what you want to eat?" he asked.

"Yes," Emma said. "Anything edible ... and portable. Let's just grab something and come back here, if that's okay. I really don't want to face a crowd."

After an awkward pause, Michael stepped toward Emma. He opened his mouth as if to speak, then stopped and instead wrapped his strong arms around her like he couldn't last another minute without her. It felt good to hold her again. She brushed her cheek against his, and the moment blurred into a kiss. *Her* kiss. He was lost in a spell of dizzying perfection. The kiss ended, the spell was broken, but Michael continued holding her.

"What was that?" he asked, hoping she felt the powerful electrical current that had just passed through them like lightning.

"I don't know," she said, setting her forehead against Michael's shoulder. "I don't have words."

Michael let her go and they both took a step back.

"I guess I was hungrier than I thought," she said with a smile— the sweetest Michael had seen from Emma all week.

"Um ... I think this would be a good time to go get some food then," he said, collecting his truck keys from off the entryway table, and lifting his coat from a wooden peg next to the front door. He held the door for Emma, and she waited for him in the porch light until he'd locked up the house.

"So you really don't have any specific thoughts about food?" Michael asked, once they'd climbed into the truck.

"Well ... those shrimp we had the other night were pretty good. Where did you say you'd gotten those?"

"Allen's Place. Seafood is a great idea," he said, fishing his cell phone off a storage ledge on the dash.

"Then Allen's Place it is."

Michael pushed a button on his cell while he backed the truck down the slanted driveway.

"Hey, Jennifer, it's Mike. Do you think I can get a to-go order for a dozen grilled shrimp ..."

"You have their number programmed?" Emma teased. He nodded.

"... rice and hush puppies."

"Can you ask if they have stuffed crab?"

"... an order of stuffed crab, and how about a pound of crab legs too ... yes, to go ... all right, Jennifer. Thanks, we'll see you in a few minutes."

Michael set the phone back on the dash, next to a package of peppermint gum. "About fifteen, twenty minutes."

"That's fast," Emma said. "But what's with the 'Mike' ... and who's Jennifer?"

"Jennifer? She's my girlfriend, of course. I thought maybe you two should meet." She punched his arm teasingly.

"So where is Allen's Place? Or should I say Jennifer's place? Is it off Main? I think I've seen it."

"Yeah, it's not too far from where we ran into each other a week ago today. We ran past it on our way to Meredith's Bakery. It's just down the street. If you like their shrimp, you'll like the rest of their menu too. Allen's is one of those places that manages to get everything right." Michael turned on the radio.

"Mmm, I love this song," Emma said, reaching over to turn up the volume. They had twenty minutes or so to kill before dinner would be ready. Michael just cruised around downtown. Shop signs on Main Street were lit in radiant neon cursive letters spelling out the names of the businesses. Emma hummed along with the song.

"You sound happy tonight," said Michael.

"I am. And if I had to come up with a reason, I'd stumble. There are too many to count," she said, still humming along with the sweet country tune.

"Hey, you'll get no cross-examination from me, counselor. If you're happy in more ways than one, I'm good with that."

Michael turned the truck around in the town square; kids were hanging out near their cars, laughing and teasing one another. The officer in a nearby police car gave Michael a friendly wave as they drove past.

"You know everybody in Juneberry, don't you?"

"Most, I guess," he said, keeping his eyes on the road.

Emma turned to face Michael. "Is it just me or does this feel like a perfect night to take a stroll?"

Michael didn't answer; he just slowed the truck and parked it underneath a gas street lamp on Main about two blocks from Allen's. It was still early, though the town wore the look of a much later hour. Only a few people walked this part of Main Street.

"I feel like Christina. I just want to shout and say hi to everybody we meet!" Emma said, jumping down the sidewalk.

"Go crazy," Michael said. "Don't let me stop you."

They strolled along Main Street, window shopping, though many of the stores were already closed. Emma threaded her arm through Michael's.

"What is it about this place, Michael? It's so far removed from the rest of the world. Things seem so simple, it's almost perfect here."

"I think it is perfect," Michael said. "Well, not perfect, but people work hard and treat each other with respect here. That makes more of a difference than you might think."

They walked beyond the awnings, past the St. Charles Pub.

"I'll miss it," she said.

"Really?" he said. "That surprises me a little."

"Surprises you?" She tried looking into Michael's eyes as they walked. "Why?"

"Because it's a big change. I mean, you've obviously been through a lot this week, we all have. I would have thought you'd be missing Boston right about now."

"I do miss Boston. I really like it there. But this is so peaceful, you know? Well, of course you know. Dad says that sometimes after church, when it's been especially meaningful, he experiences a time of reflection he calls the afterglow. I love that word. That's exactly what I feel like now. It's almost as if the whole week's been a church service and this is my afterglow." Emma looked up at the stars, pinpoint specks of pure energy. "I think I'd classify it as a spiritual thing. I can't really tell. I just know I feel it going through every part of me."

Michael squeezed Emma's hand. "We're almost there."

He meant "almost to Allen's Place," but another thought crossed his mind after the words spilled out. Almost.

What sort of "almost" would tomorrow bring?

Michael took Emma by the hand and they headed across the street. A single car's headlights appeared, its loud muffler rumbling as it drove toward them. Michael pulled Emma as they ran between the white lines of the crosswalk. A blinking sign, an orangey-pink and white, instructed them: "Don't Walk."

"Michael, we're not suppose to walk," Emma laughed.

"We're not walking, we're running."

On the other side of the avenue, they crossed one more street and walked downstairs into Allen's. A three-hundred-gallon aquarium stretched the length of the rear wall, filled with exotic tropical fish swimming between underground ferns and treasure chests. The smell of butter and garlic filled the air.

Michael approached the hostess, a smiling woman who looked to be in her late sixties. She smiled broadly when she saw Michael.

"Mike, you're right on time. I'll get your order."

The woman disappeared into the kitchen.

"Jennifer?" asked Emma.

"Yup. I did some work here a couple years back. She kept calling me Mike even though I told her my name was Michael. After awhile I just gave in. I mean … with food as good as this, she could call me Stan for all I care."

"You're crazy, you know that?"

"Yes, I do." *Crazy for you, Em.* "You know, it might have been fun to just get a table," he said.

"I was thinking the same thing, but let's just take the food home. I'd love to have dinner by the fire."

Jennifer returned with two paper grocery sacks filled and rolled closed at the top.

"Wow, did we really order that much food?" Emma said.

"It's probably the crab legs," Michael said.

"How many legs does a crab have?"

Michael shot a smile to Emma and gave the hostess two twenty-dollar bills.

"Well, aren't you going to introduce me, Mike? Wait … you're Emma. Am I right?"

"Jennifer, meet Emma. Emma, Jennifer. It may be called Allen's Place on the sign, but Jennifer is the brains behind the operation."

"Good to meet you," Emma said. "I really like this place. And the food …"

"That's Allen's department," she said. "But I don't mean to keep you, the night is young."

"Be sure and tell Allen I said hey," Michael said.

"I will," Jennifer said, smiling. "You two have a good night now."

They stepped out into the night and nearly ran back to the truck.

Emma was right, Michael thought. A real wood fire was exactly what they needed to chase away the chill from their bones.

"Gosh, it's turned cold," Emma said, sliding into her seat and rubbing her hands together for warmth.

"Let's get this truck started."

Michael's house wasn't five minutes away. He turned right at the stoplight, which had switched over to a blinking red. A few more side streets, each shorter than the last, and they were once again parked in Michael's lighted drive.

They let themselves in through the front door, shutting the cold behind them. A simple lamp on an end table by the sofa welcomed them with a golden glow. Emma grabbed the bags of food like a relay race baton and took them into the kitchen. Michael collected a handful of kindling and paper, and soon a growing flame burned.

Michael took a thick flannel blanket out of the cedar chest in the guest room and pitched it open on the floor in front of the fire. He added another, larger split of wood to the flames and moved the mesh screen back in place.

Emma appeared from the kitchen carrying their dinners on a large cookie sheet she'd covered with a patterned kitchen towel. She set the do-it-yourself tray on the hearth of the fireplace, already warm from the fire.

"This is perfect," she said, sitting down on the soft blanket next to him. "The fire's wonderful, Michael."

Michael clasped his hands together, entwining his fingers to offer the sign-language symbol for prayer.

"Say grace?" he asked.

"Yes."

Emma closed her eyes and breathed deeply, letting her breath pour out like a comma, a pause between whatever had happened before and what was about to happen now. She felt the crackling fire caress her face with its warming fingers.

Michael offered thanks for the meal.

"What else can I do to make this, your final night in Juneberry, perfect?" Michael asked, tasting a bite of stuffed crab.

"You don't have to do anything," she smiled. "It already is."

"So are you still in the afterglow?" he asked, leaning against the leather ottoman behind him.

"I must be," she said. "I have this feeling like everything is just as it ought to be."

"That sounds like a very good feeling."

"It is," Emma said. "It dawned on me at some point this week how special this whole experience has been."

"Give me an example."

"Well, the way I ran into you, for example, that felt special. And how Samantha happened to visit my dad the day he had his heart attack. I'm not sure that was mere coincidence, you know?"

Emma brushed her hair away from her face. "So much of life is all about the ordinary, and then suddenly—whoosh! You find yourself in the middle of a week where *nothing* is ordinary. I feel a kind of peace I've never felt before, Michael. It can't be put into words."

Michael scratched at his ear in the crackling light of the fire.

"Do you mind if I ask you something … about us?"

"Yes, I mind," Emma said, wiggling a grilled prawn from its skewer. Then she laughed. "I mean, you can, but I can't promise a clear answer on that subject."

Michael shrugged. "Okay, I won't ask then." The fire seemed suddenly dimmer.

"No, don't do that. I didn't mean to …" Emma set down her plate. "Ask me anything, Michael. I'll answer best as I can."

"Have you noticed how much this week has felt like that summer before you left for law school?"

"I have noticed some similarities."

"Well, I've really enjoyed every minute we've shared and … I guess I've been wondering if you're feeling the same way I am, which is to say, I think I'm falling in love with you …"

Emma looked into the fireplace, then back at Michael.

"Michael …" she began.

"Yeah."

"You already know how much I've enjoyed our time together, but I'm still processing everything." Emma sat upright. "There is one thing I know I need to do before I go, one thing I need to say."

Michael listened intently, the room a perfect glow from the fire.

"I didn't get it right last time, and I'm sorry. I've always regretted my decision."

A prickling sensation rose up the side of his neck.

"What decision?" he asked, waiting on the next words that would come from her mouth.

"I left without saying good-bye," Emma said. "This time, I'm not going to sneak away. I'm going to do right by us."

Michael nodded in short, quick motions.

"And doing right means … saying good-bye to me, in person?" he asked. He wanted Emma to hear how it sounded in plain English.

"Yes," she said. "I want us to stand face-to-face and be able to say 'good-bye.' I want to do my best this time."

"I have to be honest with you, Emma," he said, sounding like a cowboy who's slept more nights under clouds than under the stars. "Your best could still use some work."

Earlier that evening at a popular watering hole in Boston frequented by lawyers, politicians, and others who plied the legal trade, Lara Gilmor spotted Colin ordering a drink at the bar. In his charcoal suit and tie, he looked like he'd just left court. To Lara, Colin always looked like he was on the verge of claiming the city as his own.

She'd spoken to him when he'd visited Adler, McCormick & Madison, only about business, but she'd hoped for a casual conversation some day, or night, in a less formal setting. Lara approached him from behind.

"Colin?" she said, like she had just noticed him.

Colin turned around to discover the 5'4" blonde standing at his elbow in the crowded, noisy bar.

"Hi, it's me, Lara Gilmor. I'm an attorney at Adler, McCormick & Madison. I saw you standing here by yourself, so I thought I'd come over and say hi."

"Yes, Lara, right. I think I remember you. Didn't we talk about the Jackson case? Or was it about the latest episode of *Boston Legal*?"

"The Jackson case. I work with Emma—we're really good friends. We talk on the phone all the time."

"Oh, right, right. Sorry, it's just hard to place someone out of familiar context," he said, taking a seat on a tall, trendy bar stool. He gestured for Lara to take the other open seat. "So what do you hear from Emma?"

"I just spoke to her not long ago, and she's doing fine. You know she's coming back soon."

"Tomorrow."

"Yes, tomorrow. Everyone will be thrilled to get her back in the office. You know, losing a partner unexpectedly really throws everything into a spin."

"I can imagine."

"I'm sure her friends and family won't be as excited about her going home as we'll be about getting her back."

Lara took a sip of her drink.

"Well, she is fun to have around. I can imagine they'll miss her," Colin said.

"I think it's more than that."

"What do you mean?"

"Well, she hasn't come right out and said anything, but I think she's sorta conflicted about coming back," Lara said, raising her eyebrows.

"What do you mean?" Colin asked.

"I could be wrong, but I think she's hesitant to come back because she's found a boyfriend. I mean, why else would she drag her feet about coming back all this time?"

Working her eyebrows again, Lara gave Colin the cue that it was time for him to read between the lines. He set his drink down on the bar.

"Well, maybe she's just enjoying reconnecting with old friends."

"Hmm … could be, if by 'old friends' you mean an old boyfriend …"

Colin stared at his drink, then looked into Lara's eyes. "Did you ask her directly about this?" He sounded like an attorney questioning a witness.

"No, I don't like to meddle in someone's private affairs," Lara said. "Still, it's not hard putting two and two together."

Colin stood, traces of jealousy pinching his face. He removed his billfold from his front suit-coat pocket, and tossed a few bills on the counter.

"Thanks, Lara. I'll see you later," he said, and excited the bar.

Lara sipped again from her candy-striped straw before returning to her friend's booth along the wall. She was very pleased with herself.

The embers glowed orange in the still, dim room. Emma was lying on her back, traces of firelight softening her skin. Michael was next to her on his stomach; balanced on his elbows, chin resting on his hands. She looked at him, half marveling, half curious. Their faces were mere inches apart, but there was a greater distance between them she couldn't quite grasp.

"Please, I want to know," said Emma, continuing a conversation that had been left incomplete at least ten minutes earlier.

"Isn't it obvious?"

"Nothing's obvious to me these days."

Michael leaned over and kissed Emma on the forehead, then the bridge of her nose, finally, on her lips.

Emma closed her eyes. When she opened them, Michael had returned to his relaxed posture. He was looking into her eyes.

"I love you, Emma. How much more obvious can I be?" he said.

"Michael …"

"I can love whoever I want, Emma, but I can't make someone love me back," he said. "That's how it feels to be in love with you."

"Michael, I *do* love you … it's just that …"

"You don't love me, Emma. You just love the *idea* of love." Michael stood and turned on an overhead light.

"I know it's been an emotional week for me—okay, that's an understatement, but we have a certain connection. If it's not love, what is it?" she asked.

"Emma, you don't leave someone you love. When you can't live without somebody, that's when you know you really love them."

"When you can't live without someone …" Emma repeated, then suddenly sat up. "Wait … are you saying you can't live without me?"

"Not this week," he answered. "You didn't say good-bye last time, Emma, but you're saying it tonight. There's something I should have said last time, too. Something that I've regretted all these years."

Somehow, Emma knew the word he was going to say before it left his lips.

"Stay."

~ TWENTY-TWO ~

Oh, won't you stay
Just a little bit longer?
Please let me hear
You say that you will
Say you will.

—MAURICE WILLIAMS & THE ZODIACS
"Stay"

At five a.m., Noel pulled his truck into the Madisons' drive, leaving his headlights on and the engine running. It was cold outside, the overnight temperature falling a notch closer to winter.

The lights were on inside and Noel could see Emma and her dad moving around inside the kitchen, straightening up the breakfast table, carrying her bags to the door.

Noel got out of his truck and crossed the yard, coming nearer to the porch, but stopped short. Mr. Madison was holding his daughter, embracing her in a good-bye hug that Noel didn't want to interrupt. Mr. Madison pulled back just slightly and spoke to Emma. It was like watching a silent picture show, images without words. She listened, nodded her head as he spoke. Noel turned his back to give them privacy. Then the door opened and Emma greeted Noel.

"Hey, good morning," she said, in a mood that seemed positive and upbeat. She was wearing her lawyer clothes, the suit she'd been wearing when he'd picked her up the first time. It looked like it'd been pressed at the dry cleaners.

"Good morning," Noel said. "Let me help you with your bags."

Will Madison picked up the lighter of the two and carried it outside.

"Noel can get those, Dad."

"I got it," he said. "Good morning, Noel."

"Morning."

"I wish there were more days in October," Will said. They all walked across the grass, which was still wet in places from all the rain.

"What's that supposed to mean?" Emma asked.

"Fall is such a beautiful season, but time seems to fly by so fast. Just like seeing you."

Emma embraced her dad one more time. "I love you very much, Dad."

"I love you, too, Emma," he said, kissing her on the cheek.

In a reversal of Emma's arrival ten days before, Noel packed her suitcases into the back of his truck and closed the tailgate. He climbed into the driver's seat. Emma climbed in the passenger side door.

"Call me when you're safely back in Boston," Will said.

"I will, Dad."

Will slammed the heavy door shut. Noel waved to Will through a fogged windshield before backing out of the drive. Out of the corner of his eye, Noel noticed Emma kept her eyes forward, watching her father's image fade as the truck's headlights dimmed.

Noel turned the wheel, shifted into drive, and sped the truck away in the early morning darkness.

"Thanks for taking me to the airport, Noel. It's a cold, yucky morning, so I really appreciate it."

"No problem. I get to be the first and last one to see you." Noel smiled. He turned the blower on high, blasting hot air through the defrost vents and onto their feet.

Emma thought about her day and how, from here on out, it would become increasingly more complicated. From pickup truck, to private corporate jet, to ground transportation, to corporate boardroom and an all-day meeting with Northeast Federal.

She would have to find a way to quickly adjust to the rigors of her legal profession. She'd be meeting new clients from NF. She still had to read through, and be ready to discuss, the lawsuit they'd been served. Lara already warned her that it was going to be a long day. She'd be stuck at the office until at least nine or ten, sitting in strategy sessions with Robert and the other attorneys.

"You're sweet, Noel. You've got a bright future ahead of you."

"Thanks. Coming from you, that means a lot," he said, the two riding along in the dark. Few cars were on the road. "Did you accomplish everything you'd hoped to while you were in Juneberry?"

"That's a difficult question to answer," Emma said. "I don't know. I wish some things could be simpler."

She looked over at Noel. His face was lit by the pale white lights of the old truck.

"You're at such a great age, Noel. I envy you. Your life doesn't have many fingerprints on it yet. The more you live, and the more choices you have to make, the more smudges you get. Things aren't as simple the older you get. I mean, we make decisions the best we can, but the world only grows more complicated, until one day you wake up and you've lost faith in your ability to be innocent."

"Do you believe innocence can be redeemed?" he asked.

"No, I don't think so. Not unless you were to die and fall into a beautiful water, and be washed clean again. I guess that's the literal interpretation of that 'clean slate' idea." Emma closed her eyes and leaned her head back the seat. She wasn't ready to think about Boston, or forget Juneberry.

"I think life is about being redeemed," Noel said. "I think it *is* possible, and when we decide we want that more than anything else, that's when it can happen."

She opened her eyes to look at Noel. "I don't follow you."

"Faith. It's by faith we find redemption. That's how we get the smudges washed off, fall into that beautiful water, and regain our innocence."

"I'm not really a religious person, Noel."

"Few people are anymore, Emma, but redemption is still offered through Christ just the same. Anyone can believe in Him, anyone can ask for it."

As the sun rose that morning, highway traffic became brisk and heavy. Noel and Emma talked about his faith in Jesus, his seminary plans, and new beginnings. Emma listened, asked questions, and didn't feel put-upon or accosted by Noel's words at all. This surprised her. Perhaps it was because she liked him already, because she trusted him.

"You'll want to follow the signs to where it says Air Cargo. I'm supposed to board somewhere nearby."

Noel pulled through the gate into the parking area surrounded by a chain-link fence. The business-jet office was small, but airline personnel were going about their business as if it were just as busy as the main terminal. A Cessna 560 waited just outside on the tarmac.

"Noel, I don't want you to have to wait again. I'll just get out here and go into the office. You go on back to Juneberry."

She leaned across the front seat of the truck and gave him a hug. He said, "All right," and told Emma that he'd be praying for her.

Remembering his prayers for Christina, she thanked him. They unloaded her bags and he climbed back into his truck.

She said good-bye to Noel, the last familiar face from her hometown, with a silent wave through the window. Noel gave her his friendly smile, turned the truck around, paused at a stop sign to let a rent-a-car shuttle whiz past, then drove back through the gate. A moment later, he was gone.

Emma rolled her luggage into the office. She checked in with the woman behind the desk.

"Good morning," she greeted Emma.

"Good morning. My name is Emma Madison. There should be a ticket here for me."

The woman looked down at her computer screen, punching keys in rapid succession. "Emma Madison." She smiled, peering up from the screen. "I've got you right here. Two pieces of luggage?"

She glanced over the counter, then resumed clicking away on her keyboard.

"Okay, you're all checked in. The jet should be boarding in just a few minutes."

Three men in business suits and a woman wearing a suit not unlike Emma's sat in the small waiting area reading newspapers, drinking coffee, and tapping away at laptop computers.

Emma took a seat in a black plastic chair along the windowed wall overlooking the airfield, folding her skirt underneath her as she sat. She'd only brought one professional outfit with her to South Carolina, the silver tweed suit with a straight skirt, white blouse, and black pumps. It felt like a costume. She closed her eyes and breathed. *Time to transform myself back into being a lawyer*, she thought.

Her cell phone rang, disturbing the mutual silence observed by the regular corporate business travelers. Emma stood up from her seat, taking the call outside.

"Emma?"

"Yes?"

"It's Colin. Have they begun boarding yet?" he asked.

"No, not for a few more minutes. Why? How did you know I was at the airport?"

"I've volunteered to be your ground transport. Robert asked me if I would. I thought I'd better call and make sure you're still scheduled to depart on time."

"Colin, that's nice of you to pick me up, but you didn't have to volunteer. They could have called for a service or I could have just taken a taxi. Your time's far too important to be spent as my driver."

"I don't mind, Emma. You've been gone a long time and I'm looking forward to seeing you. I'll be at the business gate waiting for you when you land. Just keep your cell phone on and we'll connect one way or another."

On the other side of the waist-high chain-link fence, Emma watched the pilot open the door. It folded down, transforming into stairs.

"The captain has signaled that at this time passengers are welcome to begin boarding," came a voice over the loudspeaker. "Please make your way out to the jet and enjoy your flight today."

"That's my cue, Colin. They're boarding our jet now. I guess I should just say thanks for volunteering to pick me up."

"It's no problem. I'll see you in Boston in a couple of hours."

At thirty thousand feet, Emma closed her eyes and tilted her head back into the white leather chair. This was the last moment of personal respite before surrendering her life back to Adler, McCormick & Madison. Emma sipped a glass of orange juice and thought of what her father had said in the kitchen before she left—that he loved her, that he prayed for her daily, and that it had been the fulfillment of his greatest desire to see her return home.

She wondered how her father could dream of something so simple. He hadn't tried to guilt her into returning home as soon as possible; that wasn't his style. He hadn't even asked her to commit to a next visit. He'd just been content with the time God had given him, thankful to see his only daughter, and just leave it at that.

The skies above Logan appeared cloudy and cheerless. It looked like someone had pulled shut a lid on a gloomy silver dome. Emma called Colin's cell as she deboarded, and found him waiting in his BMW on the other side of the gate.

The corporate jet indeed allowed Emma to bypass the crowds of people hustling around inside the terminals, just as Robert had promised, but there was no avoiding the horrendous traffic and construction delays plaguing the city. They sat bumper to bumper in gridlock, inching their way out of the south tunnel.

"Welcome back to the big city, Emma," Colin joked, frustrated that his powerful BMW couldn't emancipate them from the tedious commuter crawl. "This is the big day, right? You start work with Northeast Federal?"

"How did you know about that?" she asked.

"Robert told me. We played tennis at the club on Saturday. That's when he tapped me for chauffeur duties."

"You've known about this since Saturday?" Emma asked.

"It's no big deal. He just wanted to make sure you got back when you needed to. That's when we discussed the corporate jet and my picking you up. It's an extravagant perk, Emma."

Emma gave Colin a doubtful glare.

"When you and Robert plan details of my life without consulting me, it makes me feel like a commodity."

"Emma, Robert's been doing you a favor these past ten days. Premier travel treatment to get you back home for an important meeting isn't about planning your life—it's only about business."

Traffic cleared up once Colin navigated past a two-car fender bender. The whirling blue lights from the police cruiser flashed in the right lane. Emma recalled the last police cruiser she'd seen in Juneberry. No lights were flashing. The policeman smiled at her. He was a friend of Michael's.

Emma and Colin drove into downtown Boston in silence.

Colin pulled the BMW in front of a corporate high rise on Federal Street. "Robert asked me to deliver you, and I've done that. I'm sorry if you feel manipulated by this…. I assure you that wasn't our intent."

Emma turned to Colin. "I'm sorry if I bit your head off. I know you meant well. It's just that this shift back into the fast pace feels a bit like whiplash."

"Well, I'm glad you're back. I'm sure your office is, too. You'll find your groove soon enough."

"Thanks," she said. Emma got out of Colin's car. A bitterly cold breeze cut through her like a razor. Colin pulled her bags out of the jammed trunk space.

"Robert wanted you to meet him right away in his office. I'll call you later, okay?" he said.

"Okay."

Emma hoisted her carry-on over her shoulder, rolling the larger bag behind her. She managed the rotating front doors and got into the east elevators that went all the way up to twenty-sixth floor. When they opened, she made her way down the wide hall with the bright fluorescent tube lighting and entered the reception area of Adler, McCormick & Madison.

"And here she is," the firm's receptionist greeted Emma.

"Hi, Susan. It's nice to see a friendly face. How are you?"

"I'm fine, but things haven't been the same around here without you, Emma. We've missed you. Robert's in his office. He wants you to see him right away."

"Thanks."

Emma ferried her luggage around one more corner and into her office. Everything was just as she'd left it: the large mahogany desk in the center that Robert ordered for all the partners, the Asian rug laid out underneath it. Her soft leather couch along the short wall next to the door. Her phone, computer, bright orange coffee mug filled with pens, and a copy of the latest Sue Grafton book all sat on her desk, untouched and yet dust free. Someone had even been kind enough to water her philodendron and the mini rosebush on the windowsill. She'd have to thank Susan later.

A memo board on the wall next to the door caught Emma's attention. On it, she'd pinned ticket stubs from *Les Miserables*. Next to the stubs, hung a hunky photo of Hollywood heartthrob Ricky Costell that Lara had pinned up and personalized for her in her best impersonation of heartthrob handwriting, "I love you, Em." There were half a dozen business cards from people she'd run into at soirees as well as from potential clients and the menu from a Chinese place that delivered. It struck Emma that there were no photographs of close friends, family, or siblings on her wallboard.

She stowed her luggage in the corner behind her desk and set out to freshen up before meeting with Robert. No sooner had she crossed the threshold of her office door when she heard Robert's voice.

"Emma!"

She looked and saw Robert standing just outside his office.

He waved her over and simultaneously disappeared inside. Emma zigzagged through the support staff cubicles, waving hi to a few as she made her way to his grand corner office.

"You just get in?" he asked, standing in front of the compressed glass window with the shade completely open. Outside, the dark clouds had taken the sky hostage.

"Yes, just a few minutes ago."

"Sit down, I'd like to talk to you for a moment."

Emma took a seat in one of the two thousand-dollar leather chairs Robert provided for clients. He was wearing a navy business suit and striped tie and suspenders to dress up a more conservative look. His jacket hung on an antique coat rack near the door.

"First of all, welcome back."

"Thank you," Emma said.

"I don't think any of us knew when we heard about your father's heart attack it would mean losing one of the firm's key partners for the next ten days. But we endured. Before I tell you what's on the agenda for the day, I need to see if you're ready for Northeast Federal."

"I'll fall into gear quickly, Robert. Don't worry about me."

"Good. I need to say something about this trip of yours, Emma. Look, I'm the first one to say if you have an emergency you should take time off to attend to things. But to stretch two days into ten? A planned vacation is one thing, but we're in a critical time here, and we needed you in the office as soon as possible. How soon was it that your father got out of the hospital, the second day? This sort of thing sends a message to everyone that we're an unbridled firm, that our leadership is ungovernable. I don't need to hear any explanations about why your trip was extended. What I want is your word that you're 100 percent here, invested in the longevity and success of this firm, and a bright career that's right in front of you."

"I'm back, Robert. Ready to work."

"Good, now that that's behind us, let's get you up to speed on our meeting this morning with Northeast Federal."

TWENTY-THREE

I would not have chosen
The road you have taken
It has left us miles apart.
But I think I can still find
The will to keep goin'
Somewhere in my broken heart.

—BILLY DEAN
"Somewhere in My Broken Heart"

The meeting with Northeast Federal started promptly at eleven thirty a.m. It paused briefly at one thirty so people could take a bathroom break and the caterer could sneak deli sandwiches into the board-room. In attendance from Northeast Federal was an attorney from their in-house general counsel, the senior VP of corporate relations, the VP of product operations, and a woman who took notes in short-hand and with a tape recorder. Representing the firm were Robert, Emma, and two associate attorneys.

At five thirty, the meeting dispersed and Adler, McCormick & Madison had successfully added a new corporate client to their active roster. Northeast Federal wouldn't sign the contract until they were confident in the attorney chosen to represent them as lead counsel in court. Robert assured them it would be Emma.

"Emma, let's you and I plan to have dinner in my office," Robert told her after the clients left. "Let's take a twenty-minute break. I'll have Sue order in dinner from that Italian place over on Hanover Street."

Emma returned to her office, closed the door, and crashed on the sofa. The meeting had been grueling. She'd been in countless long meetings before, it was practically her life, but this one had seemed interminable. Maybe her stamina for long, intense exchanges had atrophied over the previous ten days.

She missed her friends in Juneberry. She wanted to know how they were doing. Samantha and Jim with their newborn baby. Christina and Bo and when he'd be released from the hospital. Michael—their last conversation hadn't resolved anything. Her father—spending his first day alone in the house. She hoped he wasn't moving the new office furniture around by himself, trying to decide where it all should go.

Emma got up from the leather sofa and pulled herself to her desk. She wanted to hear a voice from home more than she needed a twenty-minute nap.

"Hi, Christina."

"Well, how nice. A phone call from my old friend, Emma Madison. What are you up to, girl?"

"I'm sitting in my office on the twenty-sixth floor looking out at a very dreary Boston skyline."

"Sounds cold. Hey, did you make it back okay?"

"Yes, unfortunately," Emma joked. "I'm only half kidding. It's been a long day and I'm missing all of you terribly."

"Aww …"

"Last week was incredible, Christina."

"I know. Samantha and I were just talking about it. We tried to put it into words, but there's no way."

"How's Bo doing?"

"He's doing pretty good. He was released this afternoon and I've got him staying in my guest room so I can keep an eye on him." Christina laughed. "Poor guy. He doesn't know what to do with all this attention."

Emma smiled. "So you got everything you wanted?"

"Well, officially, people aren't supposed to say things like that out loud, but yes, yes I did.

"Have you guys set a date yet?"

"November 17. The week before Thanksgiving."

Emma marveled at what she'd witnessed with her own eyes. Christina was such an amazing woman. She'd longed to marry the love of her life, and then suddenly found herself longing just for him to live. She got both.

"You have the perfect life, Christina. I envy you."

"Don't envy me, Emma. You could have it too."

Emma turned in her chair and looked out through the narrow glass window that ran the length of her office door. Robert returned from the break room carrying a mug of coffee. His reading glasses were still on his face. He paused to look through her door window— the lights were off—then checked his watch before going back into his office.

"Just tell me where to sign up," Emma said.

"Emma, you can live your life any way you want, but don't make choices and then play the role of suffering martyr," she said. "Hey, do you have a second that I can tell you something?"

"Sure, go ahead."

"On the subject of having a perfect life, I'm compelled to tell you it's faith that's given mine all its meaning and worth. We didn't really talk about it much while you were here, but I believe my faith in Jesus Christ is the reason for *everything* good that's happened in my life. It's something I grew up with in a Christian home, but it's also something I tested in college and for some time after. Faith in Christ is wonderful, Emma, and it's something I want for you."

"You're the second person who's told me that today," she said.

"Noel?"

"Yes, he's really something," Emma said, remembering their conversation in the truck that morning. "Well, I'm just trying to get through today right now. I've got to run to another meeting, but if you talk to Sam tonight, will you tell her I'm thinking about her?"

"Sure. I love you, Emma."

"I love you, too."

Emma hung up the phone and glanced at the clock on the wall. She walked into the office gallery. Susan turned the corner on her way to Robert's office.

"Oh, Emma. There you are. Would you tell Robert that dinner will be delivered in about forty-five minutes? They know to ring the outside door when they get here."

"Are you heading home?" Emma asked.

"Uh-huh. Nine to six, that's my day. I think some of the associates are working late tonight, but I've got to drive home to Peabody before the snow, then my husband's taking me to dinner. It's our anniversary."

"Oh, congratulations. That's wonderful."

"Twenty-four years and still going strong," Susan said, crossing her fingers, and making her way to the front door a few steps at a time.

"Have a great night."

"Thanks, you do the same."

"Did you say 'snow'?" Emma called out to Susan, just before she passed through the glass doors.

"That's what they're calling for."

Emma entered Robert's office rubbing her forehead. Both her mind and body ached. He was sitting at his desk with notes from the NF meeting opened in front of him.

"Dinner should be here in forty minutes or so," she said.

"That sounds fine. Come on in, sit down."

Emma took the same seat she had hours earlier, though the mood in the office was different. This morning Robert had been the senior partner, the competitive bulldog who would fight anybody who challenged the firm he'd established nearly forty years before. The NF meeting had gone well, and that mellowed him a bit. He looked reflective, relaxed, and, Emma thought, a little fatherly.

"You were great today, Emma. That's what I mean by teamwork," he said, leaning back in his chair. "You can do what no one else in this firm can do, and that's connect with people and build trust. I intuitively felt that from you the first day I interviewed you as an associate. You scored big with the Interscope win, and you helped land what might become the largest billable client in the firm's history."

"It's been a good day for the firm," she said.

"And a good year for the firm and a good year for you. Would you like to try and guess what your bonus will look like in December?"

Emma just smiled and shook her head. "As funny as this may sound, I haven't really thought about that yet."

"Well, I have," Robert said, closing the NF file and reaching for a plain manila folder, much thinner, sitting on a tall stack of legal papers in the corner of his desk. He opened it with grace and flair, watching for her reaction.

"How does $400,000 sound? Not salary," he said. "Bonus."

Emma's jaw dropped as she responded with total shock. "That's unbelievable, Robert."

"No, it's not unbelievable, Emma. And it's not just your bonus. It's also a glimpse into your future."

Emma looked confused. "I'm not following you."

"How long has it been since you made partner, five years? It's time you and I talk seriously about your next promotion. Perhaps I haven't given due diligence to what your professional aspirations might be. Have you given any thought to how high you'd like to go, Emma?"

She wrinkled her face, adjusting to the strange turn the conversation was taking.

"Robert, I'm having a hard time thinking about long-range planning right now, but I've thought about being a good lawyer, about helping clients win cases. I don't have long-term goals."

Robert chuckled.

"That's the difference between you and me, and Colin too. I calculate everything that happens in the business world. One victory paves the way for another door of opportunity. One star player on a team might mean a trip to the championship. Do you follow?"

"Honestly, Robert, not at all."

"Let me tell you about my vision," he said, coming around to sit on the front of his desk. "Word is spreading about your big win in the Interscope case. You don't see it, but you're gaining a reputation as the go-to attorney specializing in insurance lawsuits. With health-care cases on the rise, Emma, we've struck a vein of gold. This firm has the potential to double its size in attorneys, and triple in terms of earnings. If you're not a millionaire already, you will be by this time next year. But that's not all, Emma. Far from it."

Emma listened to Robert spill his vision for the world of tomorrow, an ever-growing legal firm with a national reputation for winning health-care and insurance cases. It all lined up for Robert. He saw his vision as if it were a certainty.

"That's why you should give careful consideration to what you want." He chuckled again, louder this time. "I have to tell you honestly, there was a part of me that wasn't sure you were coming back at all."

"Is that what this is, Robert? A big check to make sure I stay with the firm?"

"I'll make it even simpler than that, Emma. It's an informal evaluation of where I think you are in your career, and what likely scenarios there are for your future, depending on the decisions you make today. We've touched on what the next year will look like in your professional life. Do you want to see into the not-so-distant future?"

"I'm listening."

A greedy smile appeared on Robert's face, the same one he'd worn at the courthouse after Emma's victory against Kenneth Blackman.

"There's talk about you in political circles. Emma, you may not realize it, but you're in a grooming town. Boston has a two-hundred-year history of politics and a robust political party system. You're a successful lawyer, young and beautiful, and developing quite a name for yourself as a champion of health-care reform. There are people who see you going further than just a partner in this firm."

"What do you mean, Robert?"

"I play golf with Darrell Brown; he's the dean of Massachusetts state politics. He's, among other things, a political talent scout, and you're in his purview. If he sets a political career in motion, things mysteriously fall into place."

"You've got to be joking."

"Hardly. An appointment as United States attorney for our district is within easy reach. Then, if you wanted to run for attorney general on issues like health care and consumer protection, you'd be a shoe-in."

"I don't believe you. You're telling me I could run for public office in Massachusetts?"

"I'm telling you that you could *win*, Emma. I want to keep you here another year or two, but Brown is pushing to assist your appointment to U.S. attorney. After that, the sky's the limit. Congresswoman, senator, governor."

"And you'd be okay with losing me as partner if I presumably entered politics?"

Robert smiled, the old competitive spirit heating up in his bones.

"Let's just say if you were to climb up the ranks to political office, you'd still be in a position to help your friends who helped get you there."

Emma couldn't believe what she was hearing.

"Go home, Emma. It's been a long day. You don't have to decide your destiny tonight, but remember, every decision you make affects your future."

Robert took a box of matches out his vest pocket and walked back behind his desk. He removed a cigar from a box and stuck one end in his mouth. "See you in the morning, Emma. Bright and early."

He lit the other end of his cigar, sending a swirl of ashen smoke above him in a cloud. Emma got up from her seat and left Robert at his window overlooking the city.

Emma called for a cab and hauled her luggage, which by now was feeling like a heavy, unwelcome shadow, back down to the street below. The temperature had dropped considerably, and although the taxicab arrived in less than five minutes, Emma was utterly numb by the time she slid inside.

"Back Bay," she told the driver, closing her eyes and languishing in a cab that was not just warm, but exquisitely warm. The driver whisked her away down Federal Street. The lights in the city shone bright like Christmas lights. It was almost seven o'clock, fourteen hours since she'd left her father's house. She realized she'd been sent home before dinner arrived at the office and Emma felt completely drained. The driver had some kind of talk radio playing but pushed in another preset on the radio as he turned up Essex Street. A country song started playing. Emma couldn't make it out.

"Excuse me. Could you turn the radio up just a little?"

"Sure," he said with a heavy accent.

The driver turned up the radio and Emma rested her head again listening to the words.

If you ever have forever in mind
I'll be here and easy to find

The taxi coursed down Boylston Street. Emma told him the address and the driver relayed it to the dispatcher.

A minute later, the taxi pulled up to Emma's townhouse, and she paid him through the plastic divider between the front and backseat.

She turned the key in the front door, and pushed it open with her foot, dragging her bags inside. The house was completely dark, so she switched on the hall lights and turned off the alarm system, locking the door behind her.

After emptying her bags and starting a load of laundry, Emma drew a hot bath. She desperately needed to soak awhile and allow the day to unwind before going downstairs to the kitchen to make a bite of dinner. As she soaked in the hot, soapy water, only one thought registered in her mind: Her world had been flipped upside down like a car on the Zipper ride at the county fair.

Emma couldn't come up with one detail in her work or personal life that was the same as when she'd woke up that Monday of the trial ten days earlier. She couldn't begin to unravel and make sense of it all. Somehow her predictable ticktock world had gone haywire.

She finished her bath, pulled the stopper out of the drain, and made her way to the kitchen wearing warm pajamas, her bathrobe, and slippers. Her hair was wrapped in a towel on top of her head.

Ten days out of town left few choices for dinner. All the lettuce and fresh produce in the refrigerator had gone bad. Emma opened a jar of spaghetti sauce, lit the gas stove, and set a saucepan half filled with water to boil for pasta.

Even more than the bombshell meeting with Robert, thoughts of Juneberry continuously played on a movie screen in her mind. She lifted the cordless phone in the kitchen and called the one person she wanted to speak to most.

"Hi, Dad, it's me. Sorry I didn't call you earlier," Emma said.

"I knew you'd call when you got a chance," he said. "So how was your first day back?"

Emma covered the saucepan with a lid. "From one lawyer to another—it was a long day. It started with a trip to the woodshed this morning when our senior partner reprimanded me for being away longer than is allowed."

"That's always a lot of fun."

"Yes, then I spent five hours listening to a new client confessing their sins and their troubles, and asking us how we planned to get them out of it."

The audacity of it made Emma laugh rather than cry. She covered her eyes for a moment with her open hand.

"It's clients like those that make you glad you became a lawyer," he said in jest.

"At the end of the day, our senior partner brought me back into his office, dangled a whole lot of dough in front of me, and intimated a powerful career in state politics could be mine if I had the ambition to chase after it."

"So he tempted you with money, power, and fame. What do you think he wants from you?"

"That's a good question. I'm not sure I know. But it wasn't a good day for bribes, not coming off all that happened in Juneberry," Emma said, breaking angel hair pasta and letting it fall into the boiling water.

"Something happened to you down here, didn't it?"

She took a seat at the marble island in the middle of her small kitchen. "Yes, something did happen to me, but I don't know what to do with it. It's like there are five masked strangers, but I know they're good. And they're helping me in five different ways, but I don't understand what they're doing."

"But you trust them and believe in them?"

"It was something that came to mind on the flight this morning. I thought about the image again in the taxi, but like so much else, I'm not sure what it means."

Emma got up from the island to stir the pasta. She unscrewed the cap from the jar of spaghetti sauce and poured half of it into another saucepan.

"Honey, it sounds like you've had an exceptionally eventful day. Are you ready to hear a little feedback?"

"Please," she switched the phone to her other ear while she stirred the sauce.

"Well, first, I think your senior partner is afraid of losing you. His first instinct was to lash out, but after he saw you back at work doing your job, well, he got to thinking you can attract more bees with honey, so he went to his checkbook."

"Yeah, I thought of that too," she said. Her dad's voice sounded comforting and wise.

"Point two, I've had clients like the ones you've described. They'll pay well, Emma, but let me tell you if you don't know already, they'll exact a pound of flesh from you along the way. Last, but not least, I'm intrigued by this image of five helpful strangers. It sounds like a dream to me. You weren't dozing off were you?"

"Maybe."

"And you don't know who they are?"

"Christina, Samantha, Noel, Michael, and you."

"What made you say that? I thought you didn't know who they were?"

"I don't know, I just thought of it, but it makes sense." Emma lowered the heat on the spaghetti sauce. "I don't know if it means anything, but you've all helped me in some way this week. Maybe it did come to me like a dream."

"I know this week has meant a lot to you, Emma," Will said. "It's meant a lot to me, too. Why don't you get some rest tonight and maybe things will make more sense in the morning."

The pasta boiled inside the stainless steel pan. Emma shut off the burner, letting it sit.

"I'm just going to have dinner and go to bed. You're right, things will make sense in the morning."

"They always do," Will told her. "And, Emma?"

"Yeah, Dad?"

"I love you. Good night."

Emma drained the pasta and moved it to a plain white dinner plate. She added the sauce and parmesan cheese, and took her dinner to the small table in her kitchen. It was the first time she'd eaten by herself since the breakfast before the trial.

"The trial," Emma thought to herself. It seemed to her in a weird way that her entire day, week, and life had been a kind of trial. She twirled her pasta around a tablespoon with her dinner fork while she twirled thoughts around in her head. *All trials eventually go to the jury for a verdict*, she thought. *Even if nothing else in my life makes any sense, there's going to be a verdict.* She started thinking about handing her life over to a jury and what kind of a verdict they'd bring back. She didn't like the answer.

TWENTY-FOUR

Yes, I admit
I've got a thinking problem
She's always on my mind

—DAVID BALL
"Thinking Problem"

The following morning, Samantha placed a kindness call to Will Madison. Samantha's personality tilted toward melancholy, and she sensed in her spirit that if Emma's absence had left a gap in her life, there was an even larger hole in Will's.

"I'm doing fine, Samantha, though I appreciate your call. Emma and I spoke last night. She's home now, safe and sound, and I'm told my new office furnishings will be delivered sometime between the hours of 9:00 and 5:00 p.m. today, so I have plenty to keep my eye on around here."

"I'm glad to hear it, Will. It's just so different not having her around this week. We all went so long without seeing her, and then she was here every day, and now she's gone again. It takes some adjusting."

"You know she'd probably love for you to call her, Samantha. Just to talk, check in on her. I think the last week and a half meant a lot to Emma, and she's just beginning to figure that out."

"Having her gone just feels strange to me and I can't put my finger on why."

"You know she appreciates you, don't you, Samantha? Just call her. She'd really enjoy that."

Samantha said good-bye, offering her usual help if there was anything he needed. She hung up the phone and listened to the sounds of her house. Jimmy was sleeping—everything seemed as it should.

Except for one thing. She missed Emma.

Michael finished the last of the work on the Macintosh house while Bo was laid up at Christina's place. It was his first trip back to the scene where his best friend had almost died.

There wasn't much to do. Michael leaned the ladder against the side of the house, scaling to the rooftop again. He collected tools, nail clips, and scraps, tossing them safely to the earth below. In the yard where Bo had fallen, Michael found the nail gun he'd been holding, hidden in the tall grass. He loaded everything into the truck and headed back to town.

Michael hadn't planned any visits that morning. He was as surprised as Samantha was when he found himself knocking at the Connors' door around eleven thirty. Before the door opened, he looked down at his work clothes, checking to see if he was presentable.

"Michael?" Samantha said, opening the door. Upstairs, Noel moved the shade from his bedroom window and saw Michael's truck parked out front.

"Hi, I ran into Jim at the Mobil station and asked if he thought it'd be okay for me to pay you a visit."

"Sure, it's fine, Michael. Come on in."

Samantha swung the door open wide and he stepped into the Connors' house.

"Thanks," he said, wiping his boots on the doormat. "I can't remember the last time you and I got the chance to talk, just the two of us."

"I can't believe I remember this, but I do. It was at the high school football game," Samantha said. "Probably twelve years ago."

"Good memory. That sounds about right."

"Well, do you want to come into the kitchen? You probably don't drink tea, do you?" she asked. "I've just baked banana bread, and there's a fresh loaf cooling on the kitchen counter."

"Ah, sure. Tea would be great," he said, as they walked together through the living room.

"You know, Michael, I kind of hoped we'd get a chance to talk at some point. Have you spoken to Emma since she's gone back to Boston?"

"No."

Samantha went about her business of serving tea and bread.

"Here you go," Samantha said, handing Michael a cup of tea on a saucer. She set down a plate and napkins on the table between them. "The baby's just gone down for a nap, so we should have a little time before he needs attention."

Michael sipped the hot tea, burning his lip and scalding the roof of his mouth. He set the cup back on the saucer.

"I just wanted to talk to you about something," he said. "It's been on my mind yesterday and today."

Samantha gave him her complete attention.

"Are you still keeping it?" he asked.

"Yeah," she said. "How about you?"

"Yeah, me, too," he said, suddenly looking disappointed and frustrated. "I really thought something was going to happen this time. It had been so long, I just expected some different outcome."

A silent tear fell from Samantha's eyes. She wiped it away quickly.

"I just feel like maybe there was more we could have done, I just don't know what it is," she said.

"Does Christina know?"

"I've never told her. What about Bo?" she asked. "Have you ever said anything to him?"

"No."

Samantha shook her head.

"It's the only secret I've ever kept from Jim in all the years we've been married. I guess he probably suspects something, but he's never asked me."

Samantha looked away. "We were so young, but I really feel like it had meaning. Like it was a calling. I just never imagined it would go on for this long."

"I think I would like a slice of the bread," Michael said.

"Help yourself."

Michael carefully unfolded the neatly wrapped foil. The bread was still warm. He took out one slice and laid it on his napkin.

"The vow," he said.

"The vow," Samantha repeated. Michael noted how silly it sounded coming out of the mouths of adults. "When my mother asked me, 'Who's gonna take care of that little girl now?' I knew the answer. We made a promise that day to watch over Emma, and I know we've done our best. I haven't done it perfectly, but you do what you can."

"I can't believe how young we were when we did that. You were her cousin, so it made sense that you'd want to keep an eye on her, but I was just a guy who felt drawn to her. It was probably just a little grade school crush."

"Whatever it was, we kept our eyes on each other, and tried to make sure the people we loved were okay. I think maybe we knew we were supposed to do that. I don't think my mom would have called what she did a pledge, but she looked after so many people over the years, including Will and Emma. Surely that's where we got the idea. Or maybe we would have done this anyway. God does work in mysterious ways."

"So how do you think we're doing?" he asked.

"I don't know," Samantha said. "She's so wonderfully complicated. She's a mess!"

They laughed.

"What do you think drew you to love Emma so much?"

He tore at the soft bread.

"You know … I just *saw* her. From the very beginning I saw something in her that was … for lack of a better word, special. Then, at every turn, what I saw in her grew, changing into something bigger. We played softball when we were kids and I saw it. I noticed her standing at the high school dance without a partner and it wasn't loneliness that drew me to her—it was something more. Of course, it all culminated in that amazing summer when we laughed and loved and dreamed together. When she left so suddenly, I couldn't stop 'seeing' her. You know what I mean? I prayed for her for a dozen years, that she was well and that God would take care of her. I don't know, Samantha. Even though for a brief time I thought we were meant to be together—and maybe I still do—I guess I have to admit it's more likely that God just made me a shepherd. Calling it The Vow just gives all of this a name."

Michael leaned back in his chair and popped a piece of the banana bread into his mouth.

"You sound a lot like Noel."

"In what way?" Michael said, placing his hand on the cup of hot tea, then deciding to let it be.

"I think his only interest is being the right person at the right time. You must have a special calling on your life too. To love her, and live without her. I've watched it all my life."

"Sometimes I feel like a minor character in my own life. I fit in with everything going on in Juneberry, but there's this one piece in me that never feels quite right. I guess all I can do is watch and wait for God to restore that, and believe I'll see one day why He cast me in this role."

"Does she know how you feel?"

"Not really. At least I don't think so. I have a feeling all she sees is the romantic yearning ... and I'm not going to deny the truth of that. But the deeper love? The love that wants the best for her no matter what? I really don't know if she understands that kind of love."

"Did you ask her if she wanted to stay?"

Michael nodded his head. "Yeah, she wanted to go back. It's just something I have to come to terms with. We fit together so well, but I just don't think she sees it. I can't even assume she's had the same experience I've had then or now."

"Oh, I don't think that's true."

"You don't?" he said.

"No. You should have heard her talking about your relationship on Sunday. She described the two of you as soul mates. I think she really loves you, Michael. It's obvious to everyone but her. Or maybe you're right—maybe she just doesn't know yet what love really is."

Michael didn't speak; he just stood up at the table to leave.

"God's still at work, Michael. Who knows what will happen next. You've always done what you knew was right, so keep trusting God. We vowed to look after Emma, and He's vowed to look after us. For twelve years, that meant little more than daily prayer. Then we got to spend ten days with her. God might just be up to something with all that. All we can do is keep praying, keep listening. And wait."

⁂

Bo tried to get comfortable on the large floral sofa in Christina's sitting room. The couch was large enough with its extralong cushions, and a million and one pillows, yet with nothing but silence around to distract him, he was fidgety.

He'd read the morning newspaper and eaten eggs and toast for breakfast with a glass of orange juice. Christina had brewed a pot of coffee and lovingly checked on him every thirty minutes. But Bo was used to working hard every day, figuring out what needed to get done on the job site, and fixing whatever was broken. He just wasn't the kind of man who could lie around all day, even if it was his body that now was severely broken.

Christina came in the room around noon to check on him.

"Are you doing okay?" Christina asked, walking into the pretty white room.

"I'm ready to get this cast off. How long have I been wearing it?"

"Three days. You ask me that every time I come in here."

"Sorry, I'm not used to sitting still for very long."

Christina sat down on the couch with him, taking his hand in hers.

"It's too bad you're not a wedding planner. This would be a great time to write the invitations and make up a checklist of things we need to do."

Bo made an exaggerated frown.

"I'm just joking, Bo, but I do think we need to find something constructive that you can do. Is there anyone you want to talk to?"

Bo thought for a moment.

"Yeah, there is," he said. "Michael. I promised I'd call and I haven't done that yet."

"Well see, there you go. Let me get you the phone."

Christina left for the office, where she kept her portable phone. She returned in less than a minute and handed the receiver to Bo.

"I'm going to go write for another thirty minutes or so, then I'll come back out and fix us some lunch. How does tuna salad sound?"

Bo rolled his eyes.

"Okay, how about I carve up some of that roast beef from the other night and make sandwiches?"

"Christina?"

"Yes?"

"I love you."

Christina smiled and left the room. Bo dialed Michael's cell phone and he picked up on the first ring.

"Hey, you're not looking for a new hammer man, are you?"

"Next time we're going to nail your feet down," Michael said. "How you feeling?"

"Bored, but that's to be expected, I guess. Christina's taking real good care of me, so I can't complain. How about you?"

"Hanging in there."

"Hey listen, I've got two things I want to talk to you about. First of all, I've asked Christina to marry me in November and I want you to be my best man. Will you do it?"

"Of course. And you're going to be out of your cast by then, right?" he asked.

"If I have to rip it off with my own hands."

"That's great news, Bo. I'm happy for you, man."

"There's one other thing that's been on my mind since Monday.

I'll have to tell you the whole story sometime, but I want to apologize for what I said about Emma. I think I was just mixing up my ex with every other woman on earth, and she didn't deserve that."

"It's no problem. I understand."

"You need to go after her, Michael. It's time for you to tell her how you feel."

"Why do you say that?"

"Let's just say it came to me in a moment of clarity. You and Emma are meant to be together, and if I said anything to derail that, I'm sorry. I shouldn't have said anything 'cause I think … well, who cares what I think. You and Emma ought to be together and that's the bottom line."

TWENTY-FIVE

When I see you walking down the street
You're the kind of girl I'd like to meet
You're so pretty. Oh, so fine
I'm gonna make her mine all mine.

—THE SWINGING MEDALLIONS
"Hey Baby"

"So, was there any part of Boston you missed?" Colin asked Emma over lunch on Friday at Francesca's near the Commons. The elegant little Italian restaurant overlooked a rainy Beacon Street. He scratched at the fine linen tablecloth with his fingernail. The ice chips in their water glasses swayed with the rocking of the table.

"Yes, of course," she said. "But … you seem agitated. Did I do something to upset you?"

Colin stopped picking. "Sorry, I've had a lot on my mind recently."

The waiter came by and removed their salad plates without speaking. A moment later he refilled their water glasses.

Colin sat up straight and put his hands in his lap. "Continue," he said.

"There's not much to say. It's just that the fast pace here in Boston kept me from remembering my roots. It kept me out of touch with people who matter to me. It's a whole other side of who I am."

"I don't follow you," Colin said. "What whole other side?"

Emma wasn't sure just what she wanted to share with him or how much Colin could understand.

"As much as I like what I do—representing someone who needs help—I've realized sometimes I need help too."

Colin smiled, but Emma couldn't tell if it was a real smile or something to fill the space because he didn't know what she was talking about.

"Well, there's more to life than just work, Emma."

She laughed.

"Am I hearing right? Did Colin Douglas just say there's more to life than work?"

"I don't just work, Emma. There are a few things you aren't aware of," he said.

Emma tilted back her chair. "I'd love to hear about those things. What's something you truly care about?"

"Well, I care about lots of things. I exercise regularly at the gym, play tennis and racquetball. I have a social network there—people I like to visit with every week. Sometimes I play a game of cards with the guys at the club. They're retired lawyers who have a lot of great stories. I am a staunch supporter of the Sierra Club because I appreciate wildlife and the outdoors. I have a good opinion of which restaurants in Boston and Cambridge are the best and could probably write a review column for the *Boston Globe*."

Emma laughed.

"I like hearing those things about your personal life."

Colin smiled.

"And there's more … before the first of the year I'll probably buy a time-share on Martha's Vineyard because I really look good in shorts," he joked. "And I enjoy loafing around in netted hammocks. Oh, and dropping quarters into fortune-teller machines on deserted boardwalks. See? There's much more to me than just brilliant legal work, Emma."

She laughed.

"You've made a compelling case, counselor. But it's people that really matter most. Who are the people in your life you care most about?"

"I have a father in a nursing home an hour away from here, where my brother lives. I share in the responsibility of taking care of him."

"I'm sorry, Colin. I didn't know that," Emma said. "And your mother?"

"She passed away when I was young. I never knew her very well."

The waiter appeared with their entrées. "Chicken with lemon grass and red pepper." He set Colin's plate down in front of him. It was a culinary work of art.

"Curry eggplant with summer squash and asparagus." He presented Emma's plate, and offered them both fresh ground pepper, which they declined.

"Enjoy your meal."

"I think what's important for you to know, Emma, is that I have an eye for appreciating beauty. I can tell excellence when I see it in art, film, or food. It's a gift I employ in my work and in my personal life."

Emma took a bite of her meal. "Mmm ... based on the flavor of this curry eggplant, I would have to agree. You do have good taste in things, Colin."

"Not just things, Emma, people. Take you, for example. You have depth and intelligence, and a basic goodness about you. And most importantly, you're honest and caring. Do you realize how rare that is in the world?"

"In some places it's less rare."

"When something is rare, it has value. I'm not just a lawyer,

Emma. Law is just a means to an end. I'm someone who's going to succeed in life because I'm determined to win at things I want to win."

"I've never heard you speak so candidly."

"I think I've been derelict by not showing you the scope of my ambitions. We hold very unique positions in Boston law, Emma. The opportunities for us here are rich."

"You're the second person to tell me that in the last two days," Emma said.

"That just confirms that what I'm saying is true. I know what I want. What about you, Emma, do you know what you want?"

"I don't think I'm as ambitious as you are," she said.

"Why not? Robert thinks your future's extremely bright. He thinks you can write your own ticket. I happen to agree with him, with only one caveat."

"What's that?"

Colin put down his knife and fork. "You'll need a partner, and I don't mean at the law firm."

Emma had spent the last two days thinking about Robert's proposals and predictions, about her future at the firm and a possible political career. She had convinced herself it was primarily a ploy on Robert's part to keep her at the firm.

Now after hearing Colin speak, Emma had to rethink everything again. These men had the same look in their eyes, a look she could only describe as greed. They both behaved as if Solomon's gold were just beyond their fingertips, and Emma was the key to that treasure.

"Do you know what brought me to Boston, Colin?"

He shook his head.

"It's kind of funny. I came here to be a success too, but mostly I came here to find a place where I belonged, and would never have to worry again because I could protect myself from anything that threatened me."

"You've succeeded at what you set out to do," Colin said, smiling.

"No, Colin. I think I failed. I severed my roots, cut myself off from my lifeblood and the people who love me. I was such a fool. Why didn't I ever see it?" she said, shocked by the clarity of her vision. "Thank you, Colin, for clearing something up for me."

Emma stood up from the table, pushing back her chair.

"Good-bye, Colin."

"Good-bye? Emma, wait …"

She exited through the busy restaurant and out the front doors, and hailed a taxi in the rainy street. Colin followed her outside, but didn't try to stop her as she stepped off the curb, climbed into a yellow taxi, and was whisked away.

"Where to?" the driver asked her.

Emma gave her the address on Federal Street for Adler, McCormick & Madison. It was still early in the Friday lunch hour; there was a good chance Robert would be there. Emma needed to see him immediately. It all made sense now.

She rode the elevator to the twenty-sixth floor and strode through the office. Robert looked up from his desk when he heard the commotion. Emma saw that he had someone else in his office, but barged in anyway.

"Robert, I need to talk to you," she said, catching her breath, still wet from the rain.

"Emma—I was just talking with …"

"Robert, I quit. I'm sorry, but I can't wait another minute to say that. I'm sorry if it sounds abrupt. I know you've been incredible to me these past nine years, but I have to go and I have to go right now.

I finally figured it out. I'm in love with someone who's never used me or taken advantage of me, and I come from a place where people watch over each other, and I've been so blind for so long. I have to go back. So, effective this minute, I quit."

"Emma, if you'd let me get a word in edgewise …"

"Don't try to talk me out of it, Robert. My mind's made up. I've got to call my dad. I've got to put a call through to …"

The man sitting with his back to Emma in Robert's office chair turned around to face her. It was Michael. He stood up.

"Hi," he said. "I came to Boston because I needed to find out how you really felt about me. Now I think I know."

"That's what I was trying to tell you, Emma. We have a guest in the office," Robert said, pointing to Michael.

Emma rushed to Michael and held him for all she was worth. Tears came, and at that moment Robert shook his head slowly, a smile coming to his face despite the obvious truth that he had just lost his star lawyer.

"You really do love me," she said, tears forming in her eyes.

"I do," Michael said.

"Emma, why don't you show Michael your office?"

Emma lead Michael across the gallery floor to her office. All the associates in their cubicles stopped work to watch them, the Boston hotshot lawyer and the Juneberry cowboy. She closed the door behind them.

And kissed him.

"What made you come up here like this?" she asked.

"I had a long talk with Samantha and with Bo. I just felt like it was time to tell you how I feel, how I've felt about you my whole life," Michael said.

She shook her head in disbelief. "I just quit my job."

"I know. I was there."

"I'm moving back to Juneberry," she said, shocked by the sound of the words coming out of her mouth. "I'm going home."

"I was hoping you'd come back with me."

Emma threw her arms around Michael, feeling his embrace close in around her. It felt like a healing.

Outside in the lawyers' gallery, Emma heard a commotion. She opened her eyes to see Colin making his way to her office. Susan followed behind him.

"Mr. Douglas, you can't go back there without an appointment," she called after him.

"I just want to talk with her," Colin said, sounding only half reasonable.

Emma opened her office door, pulling it all the way to the wall and coming out in the gallery to meet him. Lara entered the room too, just back from her lunch.

"Colin, what's going on?" Emma asked him.

"Emma, you didn't give me a chance to finish our discussion. You ran off in such a hurry, I didn't have time to ..."

Michael stepped out from Emma's office.

"Is this him?" Colin asked, looking first at Emma, then to Lara.

"Is this who?" Emma said.

Robert stepped into the middle of the circus.

"What in blazes is going on out here? Colin, what are you doing?"

"I'm sorry, Robert. I came to talk to Emma."

"Go ahead, Colin. I'm listening," Emma said.

He saw Michael in the doorway. He ran his hand through his hair.

"Emma, I don't think you've given us a chance ... I mean the way I feel ..."

"Colin, I don't think you ..."

"Emma, please. Let me just say this. When I told you I don't just care about work, what I should have said was … I care about you."

"Oh, Colin, I'm sorry …"

"I should have said that to you months ago."

"Objection," Robert said. "I think that's a weak opening statement, counselor."

"What?" Colin said, taken aback by Robert's interruption.

"Colin, as long as I've known you, you've always acted with certainty. You've always known exactly what you've wanted and gone for it. I've never seen an ounce of indecision on your part."

"Colin's not on trial here, Robert," Emma said.

"You're right, he's not, but you should be, Emma. It seems your two worlds have collided. Care to give us a summary statement of where your heart stands?" Robert asked.

Emma turned so that she could speak to all three men at once.

"I feel as though I've been caught between those two worlds these last two weeks. I know that doesn't explain everything. Until now, I haven't been able to explain it to myself."

She looked to Michael for strength.

"I became reacquainted with friends and family I hadn't seen in years. I returned to a special place and to someone special I'd nearly forgotten."

"I see where this is headed," Colin said.

Emma approached him.

"Colin, you're a wonderful man, and a great attorney, but I think Robert's right. You don't love me, you just think you do. You have a brilliant future waiting for you here, but it's not any life for me."

Emma looked across the room to Michael again.

"I want something timeless. Something I can no longer live without. Oh, Michael, will you forgive me for taking so long to see?"

"I think I can do that."

Colin Douglas wasn't used to losing. He looked like a broken man.

"Well, I guess there's nothing left to say except good-bye. I wish you well."

Colin headed toward the front door. Lara caught up with him on his way out.

"Colin, I'm so sorry things turned out like this. You were so honest and direct in what you said to Emma. I just wanted you to know, I really admire that."

"Thanks, Lara," Colin said.

"If you need someone to talk to, I'm here," Lara said.

Back in the gallery, Robert approached Emma.

"I can't say I didn't see this coming," he smiled, giving her a hug and his blessing.

"Why don't you take the rest of the day off? We'll make your resignation official tomorrow. That way I can get in touch with accounting this afternoon and have them make out a check for this year's Christmas bonus. It's a little early, but I know you have plans to make."

Emma hugged Robert. He had changed her life, in his own way. Emma felt like she had his blessing for whatever she wanted to do in the future. For the first time in a long time, she knew just what that was.

"Thank you, Robert," she said.

Emma and Michael went back to her office. She looked at the memo board above her office sofa, scanning the business cards until she found the one she was looking for.

"Barbara Jones," Emma said. "Real-estate broker."

She turned around to face Michael, her expression as light and innocent as a senior graduating from high school.

"I feel like everything is ahead of us, Michael. I feel like I'm starting over again. Everything's come together so beautifully," she said.

"No, not quite yet," Michael said. He reached into jacket pocket and removed a dark blue jewelry box. He opened the lid and held out a diamond ring.

"Your dad helped me pick this out."

The sight of the ring made Emma speechless again.

"Emma, I've been committed to you all of my life. I've watched over you as best I could since the day I first met you. If you'll say yes, I'll be committed to you for the rest of my life. With happiness and joy, forever."

Emma kissed Michael.

"I know where I belong now. With you."

She kissed him again, then added just one more word.

"Yes."

~ TWENTY-SIX ~

She's gone country, look at them boots
She's gone country, back to her roots.

—ALAN JACKSON
"Gone Country"

On November 17, Juneberry was abuzz with the delight of a rare double wedding.

Pastor Brian Collins was preparing to perform the ceremony at Hope Community Church. Ladies from the church had decorated the front of the sanctuary with bouquets of fresh-cut roses. Noel Connor sat in the back room, tuning his guitar. "He sounds just like George Strait," Emma had told Michael when they were making plans for the wedding music.

"Isn't it wonderful, Will? Your daughter is getting married. And she's come back home," Beverly Williams was smiling, her words spilling out with a joy shared by many in the small town. "This has been the most wonderful fall."

Will escorted Beverly to her seat on the bride's side of the aisle. Emma had asked her father to wear a black tuxedo because she'd always wanted to see him in one. Will obliged.

Bo, fresh from a cast-removal procedure, wore exactly what Christina had asked: a black Pierre Cardin suit, white shirt, black bolo tie, and brand-new cowboy boots. His hair was slicked back like an actor from an '80s movie.

Michael asked Emma if she had any special requests for his wedding-day attire. She suggested a black designer suit like Bo's so everything would match, but with one addition: the white Stetson he had worn to the Whitfields' farm the night of the party. He was happy to comply.

A double wedding meant double the guests. The parking lot filled up half an hour before the ceremony was to begin. The sanctuary was packed. In the bridal room, Christina, Emma, and Samantha spent the morning getting their hair, makeup, and beautiful white dresses just perfect.

"This is going to be the most wonderful wedding of all time," Samantha said. "I just can't believe how beautiful you both are.

"So nice to see you, Mr. and Mrs. Whitfield," Will said, doubling as an usher for guests. "We're so delighted you could come."

"We wouldn't have missed it, Will. You know, this is what it's all about. These kids really do know the value of community."

Jim Connor walked in with baby Jimmy. Big sister Beth followed close by. Emma had shared with Will all about Beth's decision to enroll at Clemson instead of going to California, her original plan upon graduation in the spring. In the end, the panache—and wisdom—of the Juneberry women won her over.

Will sat them on the brides' side, finding a spot on the end of a back pew by Janette Kerr and her sister Claudia.

"It's nice to have you and your sister here today, Janette. Nice to see you both."

"Your day must already be off to a grand start, Will Madison."

"I have a lot to be thankful for."

"So do we all," she said. "Hope to see you later at the reception."

Will looked up to see a distinguished lady step inside the front doors of the church. She wore a beautiful winter coat and a matching hat from another era, but she wore it with such class and dignity that people turned to stare. Will knew her instantly, though it had been many years since he'd seen her. He walked to the front of the church to greet her.

"Hello, Annette," he said to the grand woman. Her eyes turned slowly to Will's and he knew that she recognized him. "We're so glad to have you with us today. May I show you to your seat?"

The woman moved her head in a measured sway. She wasn't strong enough to get around much on her own, and rarely left the assisted living center.

Will offered Annette his arm, she accepted it, and he escorted her to her seat next to Jim.

"It's been a long time, Annette. I hope you're feeling well."

She didn't answer. She just continued walking as if that activity took all of her concentration.

"Annette, Emma came back. After all these years," Will told her. He sensed that she was listening, even though she didn't respond.

"You were Hannah's favorite sister. You took care of all of us in such a special way. I have to believe what you did for us all so long ago has made today possible. I want to thank you for that."

Annette still didn't react but continued to walk with Will.

"Your seat's not far away, just a few more steps."

Will helped maneuver her around the end of the pew and helped her sit on the cushioned bench. Once in her seat, Annette turned her head and looked directly at Will.

"She … loved … Emma," Annette said, her eyes lined from the effects of a recent stroke. "She loved you."

Will felt a chill go through him as if his Hannah were speaking directly to him. Hannah did love Emma very much. He wished she could be there on this, the day of their only daughter's wedding. Will squeezed Annette's heavily veined hand, the past and the present inextricably tied in that touch. She had been there the day of his wedding, more than thirty years ago, helping Hannah in the bridal room with her beautiful wedding gown.

"Thank you, Annette," he said, wishing she could know even half the ways he meant it.

She turned her eyes back to the front, and Will walked away, wondering if somewhere in her mind she still thought of him and Hannah as "the kids."

Emma's cell phone buzzed on the vanity in the bridal room.

"Oh, who is calling me today!" she shrieked in mock frustration.

"No one's calling you," Christina told her. "That means you've got a text message. Don't you know anything cool?"

"I knew that," she said.

The women laughed and Emma flipped open the phone. She pressed all the buttons until the message appeared.

Marriage rocks! Congratulations!
Love, Lara

"Oh, well that's nice," Emma said.

"That reminds me, Emma," Samantha said. "Did you see the flowers from your firm? Someone named Robert Adler signed the card."

Thanks, Robert, Emma thought.

Samantha looked at the clock on the wall.

"You guys, it's almost time. They're going to start the music soon."

Christina and Emma stood and saw themselves for the first time in the full-length mirrors.

"Now, don't cry or you'll mess up your makeup," Samantha told them.

"Oh my gosh!" they both said of each other. "You look beautiful!"

Brian Collins knocked on the door.

"Ladies, are you ready? It's time."

Noel strummed his guitar and the music filled the sanctuary. The doors at the rear of the church opened, and the two most beautiful brides in Juneberry stood ready to be walked down the aisle.

Christina reached for her dad's arm and they began their unhurried promenade toward Bo. She concentrated on every step, wanting to always remember everything that happened that special day. She would never forget how they got there.

"Okay, honey. Are you ready?" Will said to Emma. He looked at her and found her eyes already staring at him, beginning to cry.

"I love you, Daddy. Thanks for waiting for me."

"You're the most beautiful daughter in all the world," Will said, smiling. Every prayer he'd ever prayed had been answered.

"Let's go," he said.

They strolled down the aisle together, Emma looking toward Michael in his cowboy hat. She loved him and was thrilled to spend the rest of her life with him. She couldn't imagine how she ever came to be so wonderfully loved.

When she reached the front, Emma whispered to Michael, "Knowing that you love me and that you waited for me fills my heart. Makes me want to be a wonderful wife to you."

Michael whispered back.

"You're in luck. We're getting married."

Pastor Brian Collins performed a magnificent ceremony; the couples exchanged their vows.

Michael thought about the other vow he took—to look after Emma. And he knew that Samantha was thinking about her vow, too. He wondered if a vow could ever be rescinded, if love could ever be taken back. Michael looked to Emma again, standing at his right, lost in her beauty and grace. He knew then, that this vow—the one they were making today—was forever.

"By the power vested in me by our Lord and Savior Jesus Christ, and the great state of South Carolina, I now pronounce you husband and wife, and husband and wife. Gentlemen, you may kiss your brides."

Michael took Emma in his arms and kissed her.

Bo kissed Christina and then she offered a whispered prayer of thanks to God.

The crowd stood and applauded, whistled, hooted, and howled.

Noel started playing the song "Blessed Be Your Name" and began to sing as the married couples made their way back down the aisle. Cameras flashed and the townspeople shook the couples' hands and wished them well.

Christina, Emma, Michael, and Bo poured out the front of the noisy church celebrating in the cold, crisp November air. All the leaves had fallen, and all the trees were bare.

"What a fall it's been," Christina said. "What a beautiful fall."

"Who can think of the fall at a time like this, Christina?" Emma said. "We just got married."

The brides held their husbands for warmth as they took in the gorgeous bright blue day.

"But it all happened in the fall. When it all started, we didn't know anything this glorious was about to happen."

"I know what you mean," Emma said. "It's like the seasons. When they start, you're one kind of person, and then when they end, you're somebody different."

"That's exactly what I mean."

"Would you say you're a different person, Emma?" Michael asked.

She thought of her last conversation with Noel, before the wedding was planned.

"I'm a completely different person," she said, looking at Christina, Bo, and Michael, seeing the tears in everyone's eyes. "A new creation, and I'll never be the same."

A week later, everyone came over to Will's house for a different kind of get-together: Thanksgiving dinner. Michael and Emma, Christina and Bo, Samantha and little Jimmy, Jim, Noel, Beth, Janette and her sister, Claudia, and Will sat around the long dinner table and ate, and talked, and laughed. They prayed, and they praised God, thanking Him for everything that He'd done in this season of their lives. They each had a lot to be thankful for.

Just before dessert, Emma excused herself for a moment. She climbed the stairs, stepped into the room she'd known so well as a child, sat down on the bed and looked over at the picture resting on a small white shelf. Traces of mud still coated the corners of the ornate gold frame. She had considered cleaning the frame, but in the end, decided to let it be. The photo had earned its dings and scars and she saw no reason to hide them. *After all*, she thought, *we all have them.* Emma kissed her fingers, then pressed them to the photo.

"I love you, Mom," she whispered. Emma listened to the sounds coming from downstairs and smiled. Everything was in its place. She turned an old engagement ring around her finger, next to the diamond ring from Michael, her true love found. Her husband, her father, and her best friends were down there, missing her. She stood and walked to the stairs. They wouldn't have to miss her any longer.

She was home.

... a little more ...

When a delightful concert comes to an end,
the orchestra might offer an encore.
When a fine meal comes to an end,
it's always nice to savor a bit of dessert.
When a great story comes to an end,
we think you may want to linger.
And so, we offer ...
AfterWords—just a little something more after you
have finished a David C. Cook novel.
We invite you to stay awhile in the story.
Thanks for reading!

Turn the page for ...

- **How to Write a Novel in Twelve Weeks**
- **Discussion Guide**
- **The Original Premise**
- **Deleted Scenes and Bonus Content**
- **Author Interview**
- **About the Author**

HOW TO WRITE A NOVEL IN TWELVE WEEKS

It was midsummer 2007. I stood on the convention floor at ICRS, the International Christian Retail Show in Atlanta, signing copies of my debut novel, *Providence: Once Upon a Second Chance*. I glanced down the queue of smiling faces waiting in line for a signed copy, wondering what they'd think of the new book by a first-time novelist.

I hoped they would like it. After all, I'd worked on *Providence* for over three years, all those late nights drinking coffee at my writing desk. By Intelligent Design (not mine), the manuscript found its way to Chip MacGregor of MacGregor Literary. He read the story and liked it, wanted to present it to David C. Cook publishing in Colorado Springs, and soon they expressed an interest too. A whirlwind. *Providence* was scheduled to be on store bookshelves by the first of August 2007.

More good news came along the way. Wholesale retailer Sam's Club decided to stock the novel in their stores. Eventually, they'd sell one-third of all printed copies of *Providence*. David C. Cook was interested in a second novel and asked to see what I had, but there was just one small problem: I'd never set out to become a novelist. The only idea I had was a title I thought might be interesting: *A Beautiful Fall*. I drew up a basic premise and sent it to Chip asking for his feedback. He liked the concept and sent a synopsis to Cook. In September, five weeks after *Providence* released, publishing contracts arrived for my second novel.

Cook was generous with the contract, suggesting a due date of January 2009 for the finished manuscript. The novel was slated to arrive in stores the following September, but two years just sounded like too long between a writer's first and second novels. I had the premise. I just needed to attach it to the bellows of creativity and let hard work inflate the story to full size. So I made an offer they could have refused. What if I turned in the new manuscript by, say, January 2008? Would it be possible to have *A Beautiful Fall* in stores by the following September?

Other writers had done it, written classics in less time. William Faulkner famously wrote *As I Lay Dying* in a mere forty-seven days. Contemporary author Ann Brashares wrote *The Sisterhood of the Traveling Pants*, her breakthrough best seller in just three weeks. And Charles Dickens gave the world the gift of *A Christmas Carol* after only two months with the quill and ink. How could there possibly be any pressure in having twelve weeks to write a follow-up to *Providence*? Well …

With *Providence*, I'd enjoyed the luxury of infinite time for redrafts, writing without the curfew of a deadline as I reworked the manuscript, learning the craft of novel writing through trial and error. With *A Beautiful Fall*, things would be different. I had a companion with me in the room as I wrote: the sound of sand pouring through an hourglass.

Once the project had been green-lighted, I established a three-creed rule to guide the process. I'd pray before every writing session, remain tuned into the Spirit enough to write down everything that moved me, and keep working, putting words down on paper.

I needed to know at all times I was on the right track, if that were possible. I had twelve weeks to scribe 90,000 words, flesh out characters who were barely stick-figure sketches, construct a believable small-town setting, and fill the in-betweens with emotional themes that could lift the story up, up, and away like a parasailer pulled by a speedboat.

The cursor blinked on the blank page. Like a downhill skier, I pushed through the starting gate and just let gravity take over. I didn't give myself time to get bogged down in literary navel gazing, or reshooting the scenes from different angles; there was only time to react to the story. It felt like I was making a movie, but the camera I was using held only ninety minutes of film. When filming stopped, I had to have a complete movie ready to hand over to my editor.

I caught a break. The characters and dialog developed quickly in the early days of writing, and story ideas came even while I was away from my Mac. I'd capture those thoughts on the fly, jotting down notes on a pad of yellow legal paper while driving through Nashville.

However, new challenges entered the scene. As soon as the writing on *A Beautiful Fall* was in full swing, so began the promotional travel I was scheduled to do for *Providence*. Trips were planned to key cities in Indiana, Pennsylvania, Georgia, Illinois, Michigan, and South Carolina. Calendar dates were shaded in October for radio interviews, TV appearances, sit-down talks with Web-based media, and phone interviews with magazines. Critical time was eaten up by travel days for bookstore appearances, fund-raising events for my Providence Cares foundation, and a college speaking tour. At the close of November, Thanksgiving brought a much-needed break, but my health still began to fray as I moved from one time commitment to another.

Christmas fell inside the hectic twelve-week writing window. My family urged me to take off a semester from my master's program at Rockbridge Seminary. I agreed, aware of the passing time, and trying to free up more of it. Meanwhile, my work as host of *Soul2Soul* radio continued. I'd work on *A Beautiful Fall* in the morning, then take a break to interview recording artists like Point of Grace, Selah, Jars of Clay, and Diamond Rio for the radio show.

Special opportunities arose that I didn't want to miss. I got the chance to host thirteen Penn State-Altoona college students on a mission trip to Mississippi. It was the start of thirty-three continual days of houseguests during the last month of book writing. And there were things I would have happily missed, like the ant infestation in my office ceiling vents during the final days of writing.

As new distractions and old obligations mounted, I still felt a sense of perfect peace. Somehow I knew the writing would get done if I kept working at it and believing. I leaned not unto my own understanding but trusted that everything, including rapidly disappearing hours, creeping ants, and the flu, could be overcome through Him.

The more time I spent writing *A Beautiful Fall*, the more I could see its possibilities. I'd mentally traveled to Juneberry as a visitor, but I was quickly becoming a resident. I liked walking into the small-town coffee shops and bakeries, sitting down with the faith community that met in the old church, and hearing about the picnics where Michael and Emma reminisced to each other on the South Carolina hills overlooking the lake. I discovered that people in Juneberry had stories to tell about the jewel those who live in small towns possess: their vital relationships with one another. Some characters in Juneberry wondered if there was something bigger and better outside the world where they lived, and I realized, so do we all.

The clock ticked, grains of sand swirled and fell through the hourglass, and time ripped pages from the wall calendar, but it happened: A completed first draft of the story was submitted to my editor at 11:59 p.m. on the scheduled due date.

I've been a published author for ten years now. It's interesting, because I never thought about becoming a writer, never thought about deadlines or choosing words to keep or toss away. It was just something I did—like following the three rules: "Pray before every writing session, write everything down, and keep words going onto the page."

This is how life makes sense to me, and how I spent twelve weeks one beautiful fall, 2007. A writer's pace may be hectic sometimes, but for readers, it's a whole different story. Welcome to Juneberry.

CC
April 2008

DISCUSSION GUIDE

Use these questions to discuss *A Beautiful Fall* in a reading group, or simply to explore the story from a new perspective.

1. Three love stories are shared in the pages of *A Beautiful Fall*: Emma and Michael's, Samantha and Jim's, and Christina and Bo's. Which story did you like best? Why?

2. What are Emma's personal strengths and weaknesses? Samantha's? Christina's?

3. The small town of Juneberry is a place of beauty and strong community. Have you ever known a place like Juneberry? What about the town did you identify with?

4. There are five strong male characters in *A Beautiful Fall*: Will, Bo, Michael, Noel, and Jim. What personal characteristics did they exhibit by their actions?

5. The theme of community, where neighbors help neighbors, runs throughout the story. Do you have a community that exhibits concern for others in your own life? What appeals to you about that sort of community?

6. Home is another major theme in *A Beautiful Fall*. Both Emma and Janette Kerr left home to search for a place where they belonged. In what ways can you relate this idea of leaving home in order to find it?

7. Michael and Samantha vowed to watch over Emma after her mother died. How did you react to two children making such an important pledge?

8. Parenthood is an important aspect of the story (e.g., Emma grows up without her mother, Will raises Emma as a single parent and endures twelve years of estrangement, Jim and Samantha help shape Noel into the faithful servant he becomes). Why do you think the author placed special emphasis on the role and experiences of parents in the story? How do your experiences compare to those of the characters?

9. Bo realized that Christina was an exceptional woman. Why do you think he hesitated before asking her to marry him? What caused him to change his mind?

What are other examples of this hesitancy in relationship?

10. Noel is an especially responsible and mature young man. Do you think it's realistic that a twenty-two-year-old could make such a positive impact in a community? What do you think contributed to Noel's maturity?

11. Christina Herry loves a man who for the longest time wouldn't commit to her. Was she right to hold on for so long? How did she find the patience to wait?

Five years ago, I jotted down the title *A Beautiful Fall* in a journal with a note that went something like this: "Woman falls from high career position into a better, simpler life. It happens during the fall." When David C. Cook asked if I had another novel, I found that journal entry and wrote the following premise to show them the direction I would take for a second novel. Much of the story stayed true to the premise, but you'll notice that some of the characters and plot points were merged together to speed up the storyline. Consider this a kind of behind-the-scenes look at story writing.

Synopsis:

Emma Madison is Boston's fastest-rising-star attorney. Her strong work ethic and personal ambition earned her a partnership at Adler, McCormick & Madison by age thirty. But when her father, Will Madison, suffers a stroke, Emma must return home to the small Southern town of Juneberry, South Carolina, to help arrange her father's affairs. What she thought would be a quick weekend trip is unexpectedly extended as Emma realizes the extent of his debilitated condition.

While caring for her father, Emma becomes reacquainted with the small town she broke ties with years ago to pursue big-city success. On a drive into Juneberry, she has a chance meeting with her old beau, Michael Evans, the love she walked away from fifteen years earlier. Michael was twenty-two then, Emma a college sophomore already invested in the education she knew was her ticket out. Theirs was an impassioned love affair that long, easy summer, and though it was difficult, when fall came, Emma returned to college to pursue her legal career. Michael remained in Juneberry, becoming the town's highly gifted carpenter, never ceasing in his love for Emma. She invites Michael to work on her father's house, which has fallen into disrepair.

Emma is telephoned by her best friend, Lara, still in Boston and eager to lure her back to the excitement of the law practice and a fast-paced single's world. Emma's boyfriend, attorney Colin Douglas, is also leaving frequent messages on her cell phone, since she's become increasing difficult to contact following her first encounter with Michael.

Emma is surprised by how much she has in common with the people of Juneberry. She values the counsel of her grandfather, Sam Turner, who shares his wisdom and stirs the faith she learned in child-hood but lost hold of in her twenties. Her cousin, Samantha Connor, becomes a new friend and trusted confidant as she teaches Emma the panache of the Juneberry women. Emma develops a mentoring friendship with Sara Prichett, the eighteen-year-old high school sen-ior who reminds Emma of herself, with the same burning desire to leave Juneberry after graduation. She also finds inspiration in Samantha's son, Noel Connor, the young college grad with an espe-cially strong faith and an expectation that the Lord has a calling on his life.

Emma's feelings confront her as she thinks over her life and her hard-fought identity as an independent woman. Her all-consuming career feels less important as she reconnects with the town of Juneberry and mends fences with her father. Her lifelong ambitions fall aside as she bonds with the small-town community. Emma treas-ures her single life, but feelings for Michael Evans are strong, rooted in vivid memories from the past, and kindled by an intense passion now.

Colin Douglas is worried about Emma. After conferring with

Lara, he travels to Juneberry to rescue Emma and bring her back to her senses. Emma must decide who she is. Is she Boston's star attorney with the platinum salary and a scorecard of courtroom victories? Or is she her father's daughter, bonded to generations of Juneberry women, and fulfilled by the discovery of the lost love of her life?

Autumn is bringing colorful and surprising changes. This season, attorney Emma Madison will leave a new home to find an old one, surrender a dream to take hold of the Dreamer, and cease living one life to be reborn in another. The corporate ladder climber is about to let go of the high rungs. Looks like it's going to be a beautiful fall.

DELETED SCENES AND BONUS CONTENT

Most DVDs include a special-features section, deleted scenes, and glimpses into the making of the movie. I wanted to share a couple of deleted sections and behind-the-scenes notes from *A Beautiful Fall*. This paragraph below was written in longhand in a yellow legal notebook I carry with me. It outlined my first thoughts on the character of 1960s movie starlet, Janette Kerr. After the premise was written, these were the first words I wrote for the novel:

Marjorie Kerr lived a simple life, or least she had for the past twenty years. Ever since she'd left Hollywood, California, in a powder blue Cadillac convertible in 1972 following a brief, tumultuous career as B-movie starlet. Marjorie had seen the studio system up close as a working contract actress to MGM, been cast in many B-movie player roles as night-club cigarette girls, passengers on trains, and chorus line dancers. She'd even played opposite Clark Gable in *Some Go East*, collecting his coins at an onstage newspaper stand and delivering her one line on cue: "Twenty-five cents." He'd replied: "Here you go, kid." But she left Hollywood. Left it and didn't ever care to go back …

This section below is an unedited swatch, a first-draft glimpse at *A Beautiful Fall* as it was being written. The barn-dance scene was written out of sequence with the rest of the novel. When this was written, none of the other scenes with Christina and Bo had been set to paper yet.

(Hayride Scene)

"Bo, thanks for coming on this hayride with me. Don't know why the others didn't want to come."

"Some people aren't as adventurous as you are."

Christina snuggled closer, tighter to Bo. The faces of the other couples were in shadows cast by the darkness of the orchard. There was no wind, but the night air was chilled.

"I'm glad you are."

The rumbling chug of Farmer Whitfield's tractor up ahead of them made all talk private. Just two people in a group sitting on a blanket on the trailer's floor, edged with bales of hay.

"You seem especially happy tonight. Having a good time?" Bo said.

"I'm having a wonderful time. I love being outdoors, even at night. I love being with all of our friends, and I love being here with you."

"Sounds like you've got everything you need."

"Yeah, Bo. I do. I just want the piece that's missing. Knowing it's always going to be this way."

Bo joked. "You want me to hold back the changing of time? Try and keep things just the way they are?"

"No," Christina let out in her soft voice of confidence and resolve. "I just want to wake up every morning with you sleeping next to me. That's all."

Christina lived by the confidence that if ideas could be put into words and expressed, then they could be understood. Bo was the kind of man who liked things he could put his hands on, not ideas that he couldn't wrap his mind around. Still, he felt guilty when he heard the words that sprang out from her heart. He knew where they came from. He knew Christina was honest and could only say what she felt on the inside. Sometimes he thought he would just ask her. Just surprise her one day with a ring and get the whole thing over with. Bo knew he would be marrying up. Christina was a jewel. His own dad had told him that at Thanksgiving the year before. She was smarter, she was better looking, and she had to be making more money than he. No, just give it another spring, another summer. They were having a great time. Why rush it?

"As long as I'm the last man you kiss before you go to bed, we're good. You aren't seeing someone else after I drop you off, are you?"

"Yes, Bo. I keep him in my laundry room."

Christina pinched Bo on his arm. The hayride turned the back loop of the dark trail and Christina watched the tractor's headlights pass over the apple-less trees. The clouds above them moved south, heading for warmer weather. The bark on the trees seemed to hold close for warmth. Could it be cooler than forty?

"Hey, after the ride why don't we invite everyone back to my house for hot chocolate or cider, or anything warm? Does that sound like a good idea?"

"Yeah, if everybody wants to. You're just cold now."

"Bo, I love these times when we're alone."

Christina sat in front of Bo on the blanket. She turned her head to face him.

"You know I love you, right?"

"Yeah, I think so."

"You know so. I couldn't make anything more clear."

Bo kept silent. Christina was in high spirits. This was everything she loved in one special night. He hoped she wasn't going to use this moment to scratch the marriage itch. He didn't think this was the time or place.

Christina reached her open hand up behind Bo's neck and pulled him down for a kiss. "Maybe just you should come to my place for cocoa."

Bo found the deep pool of Christina's eyes among the shadows of the night. She sat still as a statue before him, unblinking. He wondered just what went on inside her, and if he would possibly drown if he fell off the edge. He kissed her again, a long kiss, and knew how deep was her love. Just like the song that played on her stereo when he'd picked her up that night. Just like the question she was asking him. How deep?

The tractor rounded the last bend and pulled in under the bright naked exterior lights mounted high in the corners of the barn. They were again in the company of friends, greeters in the night happy to see the couples return to the party.

"Anyone in the mood for a late-night hangout session at my place? We can make it the first official lighting of the fireplace."

"Oh, it's so late, hon," Emma said, because she wanted to be alone with Michael.

"Yeah, it's getting kind of late," Samantha echoed Emma's thoughts, only for entirely different reasons. She was tired, tired enough to want to get home and go to sleep. It had been a wonderful night, but it was time to go to bed.

Jim fished the keys to the van out of his pocket and opened the driver door, turning on the dome light.

***

This last section is a deleted scene from chapter 1. Originally, I wanted to show a more complex relationship between Emma and Robert Adler. This became problematic fairly quickly, so I abandoned the idea. Here's a sketch of Robert Adler's thinking as he watched Emma in the courtroom in chapter 1.

Robert Adler, the firm's senior partner, sat in the fifth row of the courtroom watching the woman he'd hired eight years earlier. He'd then mentored, apprenticed, and groomed her to the full extent of legal and business maturity.

Had he been twenty years younger, maybe. Maybe he would have acted not as senior partner, or as senior anything, but as someone else in her life. Robert Adler observed Emma presenting a case before the judge and jury that was as solid as stainless steel, yet as warm as a woman's touch.

Hollywood calls that something extra the "it" that defines a person. Intelligence, humor, vulnerability, self-reliance—Adler saw those qualities in Emma the minute she'd taken her seat for the first of two interviews. When she'd told him the story of where she was from, down south, the Carolinas. And how far she'd come to Harvard law school, passing the Massachusetts state bar exam. Yet she'd retained so much of wherever it was she'd come from. That day he wondered if McCormick & Adler was a brilliant opportunity for Emma. Today in the courtroom he wondered if the firm was merely a stepping-stone on her inevitable journey into the stratosphere of practicing law.

AUTHOR INTERVIEW

Q: What's the story behind *A Beautiful Fall?*

A: *A Beautiful Fall* tells the story of Emma Madison, a woman who grew up in a small, idyllic Southern town called Juneberry, South Carolina. Her mother passes away when Emma is young, and when Emma turns eighteen, she leaves Juneberry. Sixteen years later she's a successful law partner in Boston. The day she wins her biggest court case, Emma gets a phone call that her father has suffered a heart attack. She goes back for the first time in years and the experience is life-changing.

Q: What do you like best about the stories and characters in *A Beautiful Fall?*

A: I like the three love stories about three couples in very different situations. I think readers will identify with at least one of the stories, but probably there are aspects of each love story that will resonate.

Q: *A Beautiful Fall* is set in the fictional town of Juneberry, South Carolina. Did you grow up in a small town?

A: Yes, I grew up in the small town of Leslie, Michigan, which has a population of about two thousand. I also live in a small town today, so things like going to a barn dance or walking at night through a historic Southern town are real experiences for me. I've always valued the experience of growing up in a small town because I think it gives a person a unique perspective on the world. You know just about everybody. My graduating class was just over a hundred people and many of them I'd gone to school with since kindergarten. Life in a small town also affords you the time and space to be alone, to carve out a place in the world for yourself, and to develop an individual identity.

Q: In *A Beautiful Fall*, your writing again centers on the issues of singleness. This is obviously something close to home for you. Would you like to elaborate?

A: My first two novels have dealt with the realities of living life as a single, i.e., missing someone you love, reaching for a partner who feels just out of grasp, and recovering from painful breakups that can stunt us from growing into what God may desire for us. In *A Beautiful Fall*, I wanted to show single life from several perspectives. Christina loves Bo, but she lives with the tension of not being able to have what she wants. Michael is committed to Emma, a woman who has moved on with her life. Emma has so invested herself in career and in running from the past that she doesn't really know what love in her life should look like. Bo's been shredded by his marriage and doesn't think he can go through anything that painful again. I think readers will identify with these situations because they're real-life experiences.

Q: What's your approach to writing a novel?

A: I start with a basic premise and let the story grow organically. I'm like a reader turning pages to find out what will happen in the story, so my first draft moves along quickly. I always pray before each writing session, and I like working without a predetermined direction or plot.

Q: What is it like being a man writing contemporary romantic fiction?

A: I like to think the stories I write are about people more than they're about falling in love. Just as love and partnership are important to people, likewise it's important to my characters. The greater number of layers there are in the story, the more it becomes something larger than just a love story. Readers are savvy, and I think they want to read a story that's original and involving for their emotions, mind, and spirit.

Q: *A Beautiful Fall* **is your second novel. What made you want to try writing a novel in just twelve weeks?**

A: Twelve weeks went by a lot faster than what I thought it would, but I think having such a tight deadline helped shape me as a novelist. I just had time to focus on the points that really mattered. However, I don't think I'll do it again. I'm writing my next novel right now, and knowing there are many months until it's due feels great.

Q: How can readers learn more about your work and ministry?

A: My Web site is chriscoppernoll.com. Readers will find my bio, info on my books, interviews, photos, speaking, and information on the Providence Cares Foundation. Or they can write me at chris@providencebook.com and get in touch with me that way.

ABOUT THE AUTHOR

Chris Coppernoll is the author of five books, including 2008's David C. Cook release, *A Beautiful Fall*, and his 2007 novel, *Providence*. He is the founder and host of the internationally syndicated radio program, *Soul2Soul*, a national speaker on issues of importance to singles, and an acclaimed interviewer of people of faith, including Amy Grant, Billy Ray Cyrus, Randy Travis, Frank Peretti, Max Lucado, Point of Grace, Ce Ce Winans, MercyMe, Sheila Walsh, Third Day, Casting Crowns, Natalie Grant, Brennan Manning, and Michael W. Smith. Chris holds a master's of ministry leadership degree from Rockbridge Seminary, and serves as a deacon at The People's Church outside Nashville, Tennessee.

Books by Chris Coppernoll:
A Beautiful Fall
Providence
God's Calling: Searching for Your Purpose in Life
Secrets of a Faith Well Lived
Soul2Soul

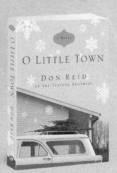

ANOTHER GOOD READ

FROM CHRIS COPPERNOLL

More than twenty years ago, a drunk driver ruined Jack Clayton's life. Now, living in a small Midwestern town just like the one he grew up in, Jack is haunted by the chilling memories of his past and an old love. Will he be able to defend his reputation and move on with his life, or will his history prove to be too much for the ministry he's spent all his life building?